SIR GAWAIN AND

SIR GAWAIN AND
THE GREEN KNIGHT

Middle English Text
with facing Translation

edited and translated by James Winny

broadview literary texts

Canadian Cataloguing in Publication Data

Gawain and the Grene Knight
    Sir Gawain and the Green Knight

Poems
ISBN 0-921149-94-8(bound) ISBN 0-921149-92-1 (pbk.)

1.Gawain (Legendary character) — Romances.
2. Arthurian romances. 3. Arthur, King — (Romances, etc.).
I. Winny, James. II. Title: Sir Gawain and the Green Knight

PR2065.G3 1992 821'.1 C92-094073-0

Broadview Press
Post Office Box 1243, Peterborough, Ontario, Canada K9J 7H5

in the United States of America:
3576 California Road, Orchard Park, NY 14127

in the United Kingdom:
B.R.A.D. Book Representation & Distribution Ltd.,
244A, London Road, Hadleigh, Essex. SS7 2DE

Broadview Press gratefully acknowledges the support of the Canada
Council, the Ontario Arts Council, and the Ministry of Canadian Heritage.

PRINTED IN CANADA

Contents

For Sean Kane
scholar, colleague, friend

Introduction

LITTLE IS KNOWN ABOUT *Sir Gawain and the Green Knight* apart from what the poem itself tells us. Its author is anonymous. The work is preserved in a single manuscript copy originally bound up with three other poems, of which *Pearl* is generally regarded as having the same author. The other two, *Patience* and *Cleanness*, are less certainly his, but like *Sir Gawain and the Green Knight* are written in alliterative verse though not divided into stanzas. The collection is known to have belonged to a private library in Yorkshire during the late sixteenth and early seventeenth centuries. It came to light in the nineteenth century, and *Sir Gawain and the Green Knight* was edited and printed for the first time in 1839. Two further editions followed in 1864 and 1869. In 1925 these were eclipsed by an edition produced by J.R.R. Tolkien and E.V. Gordon and published by the Oxford University Press. Their work was brought up to date in a second edition by Norman Davis in 1967. By that time the great interest and imaginative power of the poem had been generally acknowledged, and had attracted an increasing number of scholarly studies and commentaries. It now forms an established part of graduate and undergraduate courses in medieval literature at most universities, where the poet is recognised as an outstanding – though unfortunately nameless – literary figure of his age.

   The poem is written in a regional dialect characteristic of north-western England at the time of composition, which internal evidence suggests took place during the last quarter of the fourteenth century. That would mean that the Gawain poet was a contemporary of Chaucer, who died in 1400; but even a brief comparison of their work shows how widely they were separated linguistically and culturally. A reader familiar with Chaucer's English, which represents the language of London and the southeast, will find *Sir Gawain and the Green Knight* full of incomprehensible terms and surprises. That is not to say that the poem is everywhere obscure. Gawain's complimentary remarks to his host when he is shown the sides of meat cut from the wild boar present no great difficulty, even to a reader who has not encountered Middle English before:

That other knyght ful comly comended his dedez,
And praysed hit as gret prys that he proved hade,
For suche a brawne of a best, the bolde burne sayde,
Ne such sydes of a swyn segh he never are.

1629-32

The monosyllabic simplicity and directness of the passage is typical of
the poet's manner. On the other hand this sample of his vocabulary
does not suggest how many outlandish terms not found in Chaucer
are incorporated into the Gawain poet's work: *blonk, croked, gryndelston, harled, hendelayk, knokled, myd-over-under, myst-hakel, quethe,
ronkled, schunt, stel-bawe, traunt, thwarle, wlonk, wruxled*: words whose
abrasive quality evokes a world of gnarled and weatherworn shapes
into which Chaucer never ventured. In the northern country
reflected in the wintry landscapes of Sir Gawain and the Green
Knight, an older language seems to have persisted, its native bluntness
not tempered by French, a language which the poet associates with
the elaborately courtly manners displayed by Gawain and his charming hostess. When the lady declares that

of alle chevalry to chose, the chef thyng alosed
Is the lel layk of luf, the lettrure of armes,

1512-3

the sense of her remark is carried by six terms borrowed from Old
French – *chevalry, chef, alosed, lel, lettrure, armes*; and when Gawain as-
sures her that 'Soberly your servaunt, my soverayn I holde yow,' he
repays her lavish compliment both in his submission and in his elegant courtly terminology. The conscious accenting of French words
and expressions, some of them still unfamiliar to English audiences,
contrasts strongly with the poet's compact narrative style, which bases
itself upon terms as bare and rudimentary as the natural setting of the
story:

Thay were on a hille ful hyghe,
The quyte snaw lay bisyde;
The burne that rod hym by
Bede his mayster abide.

2087-90

From Chaucer a reader may gain the impression that the English and French components of his language have formed a comfortable liaison, so much so that he uses both indifferently and without reserving either for particular tasks. *Sir Gawain and the Green Knight* creates a different impression: that the two elements have not yet reached an accommodation, and that the poet and his audience are sufficiently alive to the nuances of words still novel and alien to their regional culture for French words to be used for distinctive purposes.

But the language of *Sir Gawain and the Green Knight* is not only a sometimes uneasy compound of Middle English and Old French. A small but significant part of the poet's vocabulary comes from sources hardly known to Chaucer. A number of Scandinavian languages, predominantly Old Norse, have contributed words to the poem in much the same way as the Viking settlements in the north of England have left their mark in such place-names as Scawdale, Skelwith, Ickornshaw, Keswick, and Grayrigg. Both the place-names and the Scandinavian element in the poem presumably date from the period of two centuries ending with the first millenium when northern England was held by the Danes. When *Sir Gawain and the Green Knight* was written, these once alien words had probably been part of the poet's dialect for between four hundred and six hundred years, and had been completely assimilated. Not all of them were unfamiliar to Chaucer or to modern readers – anger, skirt, ugly, window, for instance – but the Scandinavian element of the Gawain poet's vocabulary frequently makes itself felt in words characterised by their uncouth energy. So Gawain lies in bed while the snow 'snitered ful snart,' and later sets out for the valley where clouds seemed to graze the towering crags:

> The skwez of the scowtes skayned hym thoght.
>
> 2167

Although only a tenth of the poet's vocabulary is drawn from Scandinavian languages, these terms have an effect disproportionate to their numbers. The line that describes Gawain muttering uneasily in his sleep includes three alliterating words from Old Norse whose heavily dragging effect suggests his reluctance to meet the Green Knight again on the next day:

> In dregh droupyng of dreme draveled that noble.
>
> 1750

One of the problems facing a translator of the poem is that it is not possible to represent in modern English the diversity of the poet's language, or to show how he calls upon different aspects of his mixed vocabulary to vary the tone and the associations of his narrative.

The poem is composed in a unique stanza form, made up of a varying number of long alliterative lines followed by a bob and wheel: five short lines rhyming *ababa*, of which the first consists of only two syllables. The number of stressed alliterative words in each long line also varies. The norm is three, as in this passage:

> He chevez that chaunce at the chapel grene,
> Ther passes non bi that place so proude in his armes
> That he ne dyngez him to dethe with dynte of his honde.
>
> 2103-5.

But the line, 'Der drof in the dale, doted for drede,' has five such stresses, while 'For he watz breme, bor alther-grattest,' has only two; and 'This oritore is ugly, with erbez overgrowen' alliterates only weakly on vowels. The number of syllables in the long lines is not fixed, and can vary from seven – 'Thenne the knyght con calle ful hyghe' – to twice as many – "And sythen he keverez bi a cragge, and comez of a hole" – within the same stanza. In these respects the verse form allows the poet considerable freedom, but his control of the poem is evident in its length of a hundred and one stanzas, contrived as though to match the cycle of a year and a day which separates Gawain's encounters with the Green Knight. The same concern with circular form is suggested by the repetition of the opening line – 'Sithen the sege and the assaut watz sesed at Troye' – as the final long line of the poem, with a single change, and by the endlessness of the pentangle. The intricate literary design of *Pearl* is not repeated in the form and execution of *Sir Gawain and the Green Knight*, but the poem displays a strong feeling for elaborate symbolism and fine craftsmanship, and the story itself is a work of great ingenuity and – it seems right to suppose – originality.

To think so we must ignore the narrator's opening remarks about his own status and the traditional nature of the story he is about to begin. 'If ye wyl lysten this laye bot on litel quile,' he tells his audience,

I schal telle hit as-tyt, as I in toun herde,
    with tonge.

                                            31-32.

Listening implies an oral tale, as does the poet's remark that he has
heard the story told 'with tonge,' but his work has survived in a written form; 'with lel letteres loken,' as he goes on to say. Since a written
poem can be read aloud there is no confusion here, but evidently it
suits the poet's purposes to present himself as a simple popular entertainer whose occasional comments to his audience – 'I schal telle yow
how thay wroght' – and explanatory remarks about incidents in the
story – 'Wyt ye wel, hit watz worth wele ful hoge' – create an impression of the close relationship that a storyteller must maintain with
his listeners. In oral narration such remarks would arise spontane-
ously, but here they are contrived as part of a deliberate purpose. It is
not difficult to understand why the poet should have adopted the
manner of an oral tale in a written work. Alliterative poetry is addressed to the ear, not to the eye, and its effects are not fully realised
unless the 'rum-ram-ruf' of its pounding consonants is heard. Until
displaced by rhyming verse it was also the established form of English
poetry, and it seems evident from *Sir Gawain and the Green Knight* that
its author felt a strong attachment to native tradition and culture.
That may explain why he adopted the persona of a popular storyteller
in addressing his audience, when the tale itself – particularly the three
episodes in Gawain's bedchamber – prove him unusually cultivated
and well acquainted with the literature of courtly manners and ideals.
His playful attempt to present himself as a simple entertainer may
have been prompted by a feeling that such a character was appropriate to the 'outtrage awenture' he tells, which 'in londe so hatz ben
longe.' The remark is probably misleading. *Sir Gawain and the Green
Knight* represents the close fusion of two separate stories which may
have been individually familiar to the poet's audience, but which
have not survived in any similar combination that might have 'ben
longe' in England or any other country. The first is the legend of the
beheading-game, which provides the opening and closing episodes of
the poet's story. The other involves the sexual testing of Sir Gawain,
and takes up the central episodes of his adventure. Combining these
two tales into a single romance was not in itself a remarkable feat.
The poet's achievement lies in having amalgamated them in such a
way that while they appear unrelated, the outcome of one is deter-

mined by Gawain's behaviour in the quite separate circumstances of the other.

The earliest known example of the beheading-game legend appears in the Irish story *Fled Bricrend*, written down about the year 1100 but probably a good deal older (see Appendix A). It tells how a terrifying ogre enters the hall where the Ulaid heroes are gathered, carrying a huge club in one hand and an enormous axe in the other. He explains that he is searching for a man who will deal with him fairly, and that the reputation of the Ulaid has brought him there in the hope of finding one. The terms of fair play that he proposes are that he will cut off the head of one of the heroes, who on the following night will decapitate him. This arrangement is not accepted, and the ogre agrees to reverse the conditions by standing a blow forthwith and returning on the next day to give one in return. One of the heroes accepts the challenge and cuts off the ogre's head, filling the hall with blood; but the ogre rises, picks up his head and the axe, and leaves the hall, still bleeding profusely. When he returns on the following night his opponent shirks his undertaking to stand the return blow. Two further heroes take up the challenge with the same result, but when the ogre returns on the fourth night contemptuous of the false and cowardly Ulaid, Cu Chulaind (Cuchulainn) is present. He too decapitates the ogre and smashes the head for good measure. On the next night Cu Chulaind places his neck on the block to receive the return blow, and is mocked by the ogre because his neck does not cover the enormous block. Cu Chulaind rebukes the ogre for tormenting him, and insists on being despatched at once. The ogre raises the huge axe and brings it down on Cu Chulaind's neck with the blade uppermost. After praising Cu Chulaind's courage and fidelity the ogre vanishes. In a shorter version of the story he swings the axe at Cu Chulaind three times, each time with the blade reversed.

In *Sir Gawain and the Green Knight* the story takes substantially the same form but with many changes of detail. The ogre is no longer terrifyingly huge and ugly but physically attractive, splendidly dressed, and mounted on a horse which like himself is emerald green. He makes his challenge on New Year's Day and requires his opponent to stand the return blow a year and a day later at the Green Chapel, which must be found without directions. Gawain is chosen as the court's representative, promises to meet the Green Knight as stipulated, and decapitates him. The victim picks up his head, leaps into his saddle, and after reminding Gawain of his undertaking gallops away. At the Green Chapel a year later Gawain stands three swings from the Green Knight's axe. The first two are checked just short of his neck, and the third gashes the flesh as punishment for Gawain's dishonesty in a matter which has no evident connection with the beheading-game. In this and other respects *Sir Gawain and the Green Knight* is a much more elaborate and ingenious reworking of the legend, but its dependence upon that primitive story is obvious. There are reasons for supposing that the major changes in the Gawain poet's version of the tale – the challenger's colour, the midwinter setting, and the year's interval between blows, for instance – were of his own devising, for these are not inconsequential details but parts of the imaginative purpose that integrates the whole poem.

None of the analogues of the temptation theme used by the poet is very closely related to his story of Gawain's attempted seduction, and no source of the motif has been found in legend. In the Welsh *Mabinogion* Pwyll spends a year at the court of Arawn in his friend's likeness, sleeping with the queen but respecting her chastity; but while his self-restraint is tested no attempt is made to seduce him. The story is one of many legends which require the hero or heroine to undergo a trial of patience, forbearance or self-denial, usually in preparation for some task that demands special powers. The French romance of *Le Chevalier à l'Épée* is distantly related to this theme, and one of several works which seem to have contributed to the Gawain poet's version of the temptation story (see Appendix B). Here a knight called Sir Gawain is again the hero. Lost in a forest, he falls in with another knight who invites him to his house and then rides ahead to prepare for his arrival. Gawain is warned by a group of shepherds that this knight will not tolerate being disobeyed or opposed, and that he kills whoever resists his wishes. Nonetheless Gawain continues his journey, and at the house is introduced to his host's beautiful daughter, who is ordered not to oppose Gawain in anything. The girl falls in love with him and seeks to save his life by repeating the shepherds' warning. At bedtime her father orders her to sleep with Gawain, who realises with alarm that if he refuses his host's demand he will be killed, but that if he takes advantage of the girl he will deserve death for his ill-bred behaviour. Eventually, overcome by her beauty, Gawain risks an embrace. She warns him again, telling him how many knights have been killed for making the same base attempt upon her, and explaining that an enchanted sword in the bedroom will wound him if he persists. Gawain hesitates briefly, but when he renews his love-making the sword leaps out of its scabbard and wounds him slightly in the side. Still he is not willing to abandon the game, and it takes a more serious injury in the shoulder to persuade him to stop. When his host enters the bedroom in the morning he is astonished to find him alive, but after learning Gawain's name he realises that the sword has refused to kill the man it knows to be the best of all knights. As reward, the knight grants Gawain his daughter and his castle, and holds a great feast to celebrate the achievement of this perfect knight. Since Gawain does not willingly give up his would-be seduction but is forced to respect the girl by the threat of injury or death, his reputation seems undeserved, and the story does not illustrate the motif of moral or physical self-restraint in which it may have originated.

The Gawain poet reinstates this motif. When his hero's jovial host Bertilak insists that instead of joining the hunt Gawain shall lie in bed recovering from his winter journey, he secretly intends to send his wife to tempt Gawain during his absence from the castle. His proposal to Gawain, 'Ye schal lenge in your lofte,' is not an order, and there is no magic sword in the bedchamber to attack an adulterous guest; but the 'aghlych mayster' who waits for Gawain at the Green Chapel with an enormous axe seems ready to exact payment for any moral slip on Gawain's part, and does so before praising him as the most perfect of knights. Although the differences between the two stories are more striking than their similarities, the reliance of both tales upon the linked motifs of sexual restraint, wounding, and acclamation suggests a common source. However, the hero of *Sir Gawain and the Green Knight* is nicked by the axe-blade not for unchaste behaviour, but for not honouring the terms of an agreement with Bertilak, a separate element of the story for which no analogue is known. Bertilak invites Gawain to exchange the day's winnings with him when he returns from the chase, a swap likely to be to the knight's advantage. Gawain gives his word that he will observe the agreement faithfully, and does so on two successive days by giving Bertilak the kisses he has secretly received from his hostess; but on the third day he holds back a belt pressed upon him as a love-gift, believing it will protect him from the axe. When he keeps his tryst with the Green Knight, he discovers that the lady has revealed his dishonesty to Bertilak, now revealed as the Green Knight's counterpart. Although Gawain has withstood her trial of his sexual restraint, he has not been able to resist the instinct of self-preservation that made him withhold the belt. Like the beheading-game, this third element of the story follows a compact between the two players which must be faithfully observed, and involves a taking and a paying back on both sides. The Green Knight's rebuke after exposing Gawain's deceit, 'Trwe mon trwe restore,' sums up a principle which not only governs both games but applies to life generally. A true man must truly repay, whether by keeping his word or giving his creditor what is due, and must return to nature some of the profits and benefits taken from it. This simple axiom, expressed at a crucial moment in the story, helps to unite two of the three narrative elements of the tale. It also gives the poem a system of values which may represent the poet's personal outlook. The interlocking parts of his complex plot provide a reason for ignoring his opening remarks about an old and familiar oral tale, and his closing allusion to its place in 'the best boke of romaunce.' Considered as a whole, the poem is a work of striking originality, whose imaginative power is shown throughout in the force and vitality of its language and by an astonishing dénouement without equal in medieval fiction.

Translating poetry must always be a frustrating exercise, and the attempt to turn *Sir Gawain and the Green Knight* into modern English is no exception. While it is not always true that poetry consists of words, not ideas, there is enough truth in the remark to warn a translator that much of the original sense of this poem will be lost in the process. The description of the Green Knight's colourfully decorated horse provides a case in point:

> Dubbed wyth ful dere stonez, as the dok lasted,
> Sythen thrawen wyth a thwong a thwarle knot alofte.
>
> 193-4.

Translation can preserve the sense of the first line, which makes no special demands on language, but the second line is virtually untranslatable. Its literal meaning, 'Then tightly bound with a thong topped by an intricate knot,' is amplified by the sense of congestion created by the alliterated th- sounds in five of the words and intensified by 'thrawen', 'thwong,' and 'thwarle.' These three terms dominate the line, not by their literal sense but by their sound and form, which force the mouth to mimic the involved and tightly knotted decoration. When the line is rendered as 'And tied tight at the top with a triple knot' most of its sense leaks away, not only through the absence of 'thwong' and the substitution of 'triple' for 'thwarle,' but through the inability of modern English to match these expressive medieval terms. Again, not so much the meaning as the experience represented by the line,

> Mist muged on the mor, malt on the mountes,
> 2080

cannot be conveyed in translation, but for a different reason. The five alliterated words contribute an impression of impeded movement to the sense of the line, as though the hills had become adhesive, and the uneven stressing which falls on those words make it lurch clumsily, as if in sympathy with the uphill struggle. Translation cannot repeat these effects and preserve the literal meaning of the line. 'Muged,' meaning drizzled, has to be replaced, and when 'malt' is translated as melted the second half of the line goes flat. Rendered as 'Ugly mists / Merged damply with the moors and melted on the mountains,' a terse monosyllabic comment is so diluted and prolonged that almost nothing of its original character remains. Worse things can happen when the translator assumes a licence to edit the poem, either by omitting inconvenient phrases or by adding picturesque touches to the poet's work. Readers coming across this passage in a translation of the same stanza of Part 4,

> Brooks bubbled and broke over broken rocks,
> Flashing in freshets that waterfalls fed,

have nothing to warn them that the second line is a fanciful elaboration of the poet's line, 'Schyre schatterande on schorez, ther thay doun schowved,' which mentions neither freshets nor waterfalls. The same modern version of the poem softens the tone of the lady's complaint that she has yet to hear from Gawain any of the love-talk for which he is famous:

> 'Yet herde I never of your hed helde no wordez
> That ever longed to luf, lasse ne more'.
> 1523-4

The rebuke is direct and forceful, and although 'of your hed helde no wordez' is an oddly periphrastic way of referring to Gawain's conversation, it does not suggest that the lady has adopted a charmingly feminine form of address. But translation can ignore the poet's tone and put its own construction on her manner:

> 'Yet never has a fair phrase fallen from your lips
> Of the language of love, not one little word!'

The lady who boldly invades Gawain's bedroom and claims to have captured him is suddenly reduced to a plaintive and petulant figure, only distantly related to the challenging intruder who puts Gawain to the test. While the translation indicates the general form of her remark, which is not a pathetic appeal but a rebuke of Gawain's unresponsiveness to her presence, its adulteration of the original passage by calling upon sentiment – 'a fair phrase,' 'not one little word' – misrepresents the forthrightness of the lady's speech, whose aggressive tone is felt in her rousing conclusion, 'Why! ar ye lewed, that al the los weldez?... For schame!'

Inaccurate translation has several causes, of which the most insidious is illustrated by the two passages above: an assimilation of the poem as a private work which is unconsciously reshaped to reflect the translator's response to it. The reader then sees the original work not in a parallel as close as the second language and the exigencies of translation allow, but as if a sheet of coloured glass were interposed between the reader and it. A more persistent cause of inaccuracy and misrepresentation in translating *Sir Gawain and the Green Knight* lies in the attempt to render the alliterative measure, which cannot be reproduced without falsifying the original. Very few of the poet's lines can be transposed into modern English without altering either alliteration or meaning, and if the translator chooses to alliterate, the sense of the line must constantly be sacrificed. The process is almost palpable in the unremarkable line,

> Ther watz lokyng on lenthe the lude to beholde,
>
> 232

which does not mean, as one translator would have readers suppose, 'There were stares on all sides as the stranger spoke.' Because the poet's use of 'lude' for 'man' makes it impossible to follow him in alliterating on l-, the translator has substituted s-, which leads to more serious misrepresentation. The original line makes no reference to speaking and does not describe the Green Knight as a stranger. The need to alliterate has dictated the form of a new remark which takes away the wonder of the event, and all that remains of the poet's comment is 'stares' for 'lokyng.' A more striking example of the way accurate translation can fall victim to a search for alliterative terms occurs in the same translator's version of lines 307-8, which describe the Green Knight's mockery of the silence that follows his challenge:

> When the court kept its counsel he coughed aloud,
> And cleared his throat coolly, the clearer to speak.

But keeping counsel has the sense of preserving a secret, not of being struck dumb; the poet's 'coghed' means shouted, not coughed, and when the Green Knight 'rimed hym ful richely' he does not clear his throat but draws himself up disdainfully. As for 'coolly,' the word is an interpolation discredited by the raucous outburst that rounds off the Green Knight's speech, when he 'laghes so loude' that Arthur blushes with vexation. All these errors have their source in a determination to alliterate on c-, which has encouraged the translator to rewrite the passage in a form that no longer represents the incident described by the poet.

The rhyming section that completes each stanza presents a different problem to translation. The shift from long alliterative to short rhyming lines has the effect of a sudden gear-change from high to low, with a quickening of pace that rounds off one stanza and generates energy to begin the next. A typical example of the blunt and tightly compressed style of the bob and wheel occurs at the end of the boar-hunt, where the bob 'ful tyte' is followed by a vigorous quatrain:

> A hundreth houndez hym hent,
> That bremely con hym bite,
> Burnez hym broght to bent,
> And doggez to dethe endite.

> 1597-1600

The literal meaning of the passage is not in question: 'A hundred hounds seized him, who bite him fiercely. Men brought him to the bank, and the hounds kill him.' But so translated all the poet's rhymes must be replaced, with predictable consequences for the sense:

Hounds hasten by the score
To maul him, hide and head;
Men drag him in to shore
And dogs pronounce him dead.

Here the hounds do not seize but hasten – with a change of tense – 'by the score' to provide a rhyme with the third line, which apart from its faulty tense is well translated. The second line is not. It represents another free variation on the incident, to accommodate the alliteration on h- and to allow the final line to end on 'dead.' There the inept verb 'pronounce' credits the hounds with the kind of judgement that might be expected of a coroner rather than of frenzied animals, and although the translation keeps the energy of the original its attempt to reproduce the poet's rhyme-scheme ends in another misrepresentation of meaning. Distortion of tone is another consequence of maintaining rhyme at all costs:

'By Saint Giles,' the castellan quipped,
'You're the finest fellow I know:
Your wealth will have us whipped
If your trade continues so!'

We need not check the original text to know that this remark bears little relation to Bertilak's bantering comment, 'Ye ben ryche in a whyle,' or to the monosyllabic plainness of the whole passage. The incongruously mixed vocabulary, which combines the archaic 'castellan' – the constable of a castle, not its owner – with a schoolboy phrase 'finest fellow' in place of 'the beste' followed by an exaggerated idiom to make up a rhyme for 'quipped,' misrepresents the tone and the genial irony of Bertilak's remark. A respect for form over substance has resulted in a crude caricature of Bertilak's quietly sardonic remark.

With such examples of infidelity to the spirit and matter of the poem as warning, a translator must recognise that imitating its alliterative measure and its rhyming section will produce another version full of inaccuracies. He or she may then decide that since a modern version of the poem that misrepresents both its sense and its tone has very little value, alliteration and rhyme must take second place to fidelity to the text. There is, after all, little point in substituting for the original a line which alliterates on a different letter; in replacing, for instance

Heghe halowyng on hyghe with hathelez that myght,

1602

with a line that does not reproduce the strenuous effect of the poet's repeated aspirates, 'There was hallooing in high pride by all present,' and which throws in a banal committee-room phrase to make up the line. The present translation tries to represent as closely as possible the sense of the poem, without compromising that aim by insisting that the lines alliterate. It does not reproduce the exact literal sense of the original, which would be stilted and sometimes unintelligible, but tries to find a natural way of expressing the poet's ideas within lines of the same length, maintaining a metrical pulse that carries the narrative forward. For example, these two lines from the first episode of the boar-hunt,

For thre at the fyrst thrast he thryght to the erthe,
And sparred forth good sped boute spyt more,

1443-4

have been rendered less than literally as

For three men in one rush he threw on their backs,
And made away fast without doing more harm,

but without misrepresenting the incident described by the poet. The phrase 'on their backs' replaces 'to the erthe' as a more familiar expression, and 'in one rush' is substituted for 'at the fyrst thrast,' a phrase valuable chiefly for its alliterative final consonants. The changes favour the anapestic measure adopted for the whole translation, in part to compensate for the loss of alliteration – though that is preserved where it occurred naturally. Translating the bob and wheel proved impracticable if the sense of the passage was to be maintained. Even matching the poet's words with a modern equivalent of the same brevity is often a test of ingenuity, and the added difficulty of finding rhymes explains why translations of the bob and wheel are usually so faulty. Since the exciting effect of the abrupt change to short rhyming lines is a vital part of the poet's narrative presentation, the attempt has to be made. Here the problem was solved with one of the compromises that translation must adopt. The terseness of the original was retained, but the three alternate lines beginning with the bob were left unrhymed, and the other two were given rhymes or off-rhymes – evade, agreed; frost, quest; tooth, death. It is not a completely acceptable solution, but it gives a less misleading impression of the poet's lines than a translation that puts poetic form before substance. The present work does not leave the reader at the mercy of the translator's idiosyncrasies. Where the sense of the original is in doubt or the sequence of ideas has been changed, the Middle English text of the poem printed on the facing page provides a check upon the shortcomings of the translation.

The modernised text of *Sir Gawain and the Green Knight* printed here relies on the Oxford edition revised by Norman Davis, emended in a few instances listed in the notes. Every medievalist and student of Middle English who has used the Oxford edition must feel grateful to the original editors and their successor for their achievement. I am also indebted to Malcolm Andrew and Ronald Waldron, whose *Poems of the Pearl Manuscript* clarifies many obscurities of text and meaning. The modernised texts of the poem prepared by J.A. Burrow and R.A. Waldron respectively have also been helpful, as has the Everyman edition annotated by A.C. Crawley. My translation owes much to these workers in the field of fourteenth-century studies, and I am glad to acknowledge my indebtedness to them all. Equally sincere but more personal thanks are due to my friend and colleague Sean Kane, who has encouraged the project from the beginning and offered many suggestions which have helped to give this translation whatever merits it may possess.

James Winny
1992

References

Editions of the Poem referred to in the Introduction and Notes

Sir Gawain and the Green Knight, ed J.R.R. Tolkien and E.V. Gordon; Oxford 1925.
2nd edition of the above, ed. Norman Davis; Oxford 1967.
Pearl, Sir Gawain and the Green Knight, ed A.C. Cawley; London 1962.
Sir Gawain and the Green Knight, ed. R.A. Waldron; London 1970.
Sir Gawain and the Green Knight, ed. J.A. Burrow; London 1972.
The Poems of the Pearl Manuscript, ed. Malcolm Andrew and Ronald Waldron; London 1978.
'The Testin of Sir Gawayne,' ed Kenneth Sisam, in *Fourteenth Century Verse and Prose*; Oxford 1921.

Fitt 1

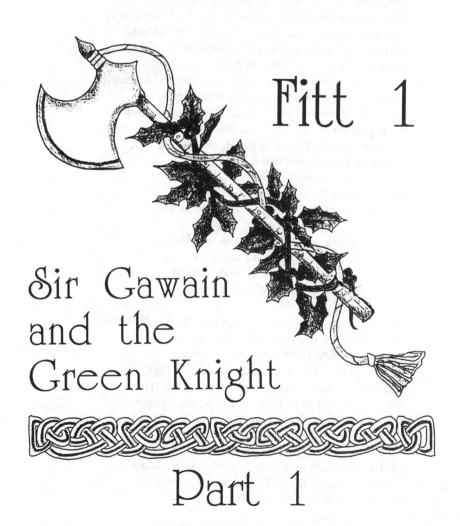

Sir Gawain and the Green Knight

Part 1

SIR GAWAYN AND THE GRENE KNYGHT

Sithen the sege and the assaut watz sesed at Troye,
The borgh brittened and brent to brondez and askez,
The tulk that the trammes of tresoun ther wroght
Watz tried for his tricherie, the trewest on erthe.
5   Hit watz Ennias the athel and his highe kynde
That sithen depreced provinces, and patrounes bicome
Welneghe of al the wele in the west iles.
Fro riche Romulus to Rome ricchis hym swythe,
With gret bobbaunce that burghe he biges upon fyrst,
10   And nevenes hit his aune nome, as hit now hat;
Tirius to Tuskan and teldes bigynnes,
Langaberde in Lumbardie lyftes up homes,
And fer over the French flod Felix Brutus
On mony bonkkes ful brode Bretayn he settez
15   with wynne;
        Where werre and wrake and wonder
        Bi sythez hatz wont therinne,
        And oft both blysse and blunder
        Ful skete hatz skyfted synne.

20   Ande quen this Bretayn watz bigged bi this burn rych,
Bolde bredden therinne, baret that lofden,
In mony turned tyme tene that wroghten.
Mo ferlyes on this folde han fallen here oft
Then in any other that I wot, syn that ilk tyme.
25   Bot of alle that here bult, of Bretaygne kynges,
Ay watz Arthur the hendest, as I haf herde telle.
Forthi an aunter in erde I attle to schawe,
That a selly in syght summe men hit holden,
And an outtrage awenture of Arthurez wonderez.
30   If ye wyl lysten this laye bot on little quile
I schal telle hit as-tit, as I in toun herde,

SIR GAWAIN AND THE GREEN KNIGHT

When the siege and the assault were ended at Troy,
The city laid waste and burnt into ashes,
The man who had plotted the treacherous scheme
Was tried for the wickedest trickery ever.
It was princely Aeneas and his noble kin   5
Who then subdued kingdoms, and came to be lords
Of almost all the riches of the western isles.
Afterwards noble Romulus hastened to Rome,
With great pride he gave that city its beginnings,
And calls it by his own name, which it still has.   10
Tirius goes to Tuscany and sets up houses,
Langobard in Lombardy establishes homes,
And far over the French sea Felix Brutus
On many broad hillsides settles Britain
            with delight;   15
       Where war and grief and wonder
       Have visited by turns,
       And often joy and turmoil
       Have alternated since.

And when Britain had been founded by this noble lord,   20
Valiant men bred there, who thrived on battle.
In many an age bygone they brought about trouble.
More wondrous events have occurred in this country
Than in any other I know of, since that same time.
But of all those who dwelt there, of the British kings   25
Arthur was always judged noblest, as I have heard tell.
And so an actual adventure I mean to relate
Which some men consider a marvellous event,
And a prodigious happening among tales about Arthur.
If you will listen to this story just a little while   30
I will tell it at once, as I heard it told

with tonge,
As hit is stad and stoken
In stori stif and stronge,

35   With lel letteres loken,

In londe so hatz ben longe.

This kyng lay at Camylot upon Krystmasse
With mony luflych lorde, ledez of the best,
Rekenly of the Rounde Table alle tho rich brether,

40   With rych revel oryght and rechles merthes.
Ther tournayed tulkes by tymez ful mony,
Justed ful jolilé thise gentyle knightes,
Sythen kayred to the court caroles to make.
For ther the fest watz ilyche ful fiften dayes,

45   With alle the mete and the mirthe that men couthe avyse;
Such glaume and gle glorious to here,
Dere dyn upon day, daunsyng on nyghtes,
Al watz hap upon heghe in hallez and chambrez
With lordez and ladies, as levest him thoght.

50   With all the wel of the worlde thay woned ther samen,
The most kyd knyghtez under Krystes selven,
And the lovelokkest ladies that ever lif haden,
And he the comlokest kyng that the court haldes;
For al watz this fayre folk in her first age,

55   on sille,

The hapnest under heven,
Kyng hyghest mon of wylle;
Hit were now gret nye to neven
So hardy a here on hille.

60   Wyle Nwe Yer watz so yep that hit watz nwe cummen,
That day doubble on the dece watz the douth served.
Fro the kyng watz cummen with knyghtes into the halle,
The chauntré of the chapel cheved to an ende,
Loude crye watz ther kest of clerkez and other,

65   Nowel nayted onewe, nevened ful ofte;
And sythen riche forth runnen to reche hondeselle,
Yeghed yeres-giftes on high, yelde hem bi hond,
Debated busyly aboute tho giftes;
Ladies laghed ful loude, thogh thay lost haden,

70   And he that wan watz not wrothe, that may ye wel trawe.

in court.
As it is written down
In story brave and strong,
Made fast in truthful words,   *35*
That has endured long.

The king spent that Christmas at Camelot
With many gracious lords, men of great worth,
Noble brothers-in-arms worthy of the Round Table,
With rich revelry and carefree amusement, as was right.   *40*
There knights fought in tournament again and again,
Jousting most gallantly, these valiant men,
Then rode to the court for dancing and song.
For there the festival lasted the whole fifteen days
With all the feasting and merry-making that could be devised: *45*
Such sounds of revelry splendid to hear,
Days full of uproar, dancing at night.
Everywhere joy resounded in chambers and halls
Among lords and ladies, whatever pleased them most.
With all of life's best they spent that time together,   *50*
The most famous warriors in Christendom,
And the loveliest ladies who ever drew breath,
And he the finest king who rules the court.
For these fair people were then in the flower of youth
                 in the hall.   *55*
          Luckiest under heaven,
          King of loftiest mind
          Hard it would be
          Bolder men to find

When New Year was so fresh that it had hardly begun,   *60*
Double helpings of food were served on the dais that day.
By the time the king with his knights entered the hall
When the service in the chapel came to an end,
Loud cries were uttered by the clergy and others,
'Nowel' repeated again, constantly spoken;   *65*
And then the nobles hurried to hand out New Year's gifts,
Cried their wares noisily, gave them by hand,
And argued excitedly over those gifts.
Ladies laughed out loud, even though they had lost,
And the winner was not angry, you may be sure.   *70*

Alle this mirthe thay maden to the mete tyme;
When thay had waschen worthyly thay wenten to sete,
The best burne ay abof, as hit best semed,
Whene Guenore, ful gay, graythed in the myddes,
75   Dressed on the dere des, dubbed al aboute,
Smal sendal bisides, a selure hir over
Of tryed tolouse, of tars tapites innoghe,
That were enbrawded and beten wyth the best gemmes
That myght be preved of prys wyth penyes to bye,
80   in daye.
      The comlokest to discrye
      Ther glent with yghen gray,
      A semloker that ever he syghe
      Soth moght no mon say.

85   Bot Arthure wolde not ete til al were served,
He watz so joly of his joyfnes, and sumquat childgered:
His lif liked hym lyght, he lovied the lasse
Auther to longe lye or to longe sitte,
So bisied him his yonge blod and his brayn wylde.
90   And also an other maner meved him eke
That he thurgh nobelay had nomen, he wolde never ete
Upon such a dere day er hym devised were
Of sum aventurus thyng an uncouthe tale,
Of sum mayn mervayle, that he myght trawe,
95   Of alderes, of armes, of other aventurus,
Other sum segg hym bisoght of sum siker knyght
To joyne wyth hym in justyng, in jopardé to lay
Lede, lif for lyf, leve uchon other,
As fortune wolde fulsun hom, the fayrer to have.
100   This watz the kynges countenaunce where he in court were,
At uch farande fest among his fre meny
           in halle.
      Therfore of face so fere
      He stightlez stif in stalle,
105   Ful yep in that Nw Yere
      Much mirthe he mas withalle.

Thus ther stondes in stale the stif kyng hisselven,
Talkkande bifore the hyghe table of trifles ful hende.
There gode Gawan watz graythed Gwenore bisyde,

All this merry-making went on until feasting time.
When they had washed as was fit they took their places,
The noblest knight in a higher seat, as seemed proper;
Queen Guenevere gaily dressed and placed in the middle,
Seated on the upper level, adorned all about;   75
Fine silk surrounding her, a canopy overhead
Of costly French fabric, silk carpets underfoot
That were embroidered and studded with the finest gems
That money could buy at the highest price
        anywhere.   80
    The loveliest to see
    Glanced round with eyes blue-grey;
    That he had seen a fairer one
    Truly could no man say.

But Arthur would not eat until everyone was served,   85
He was so lively in his youth, and a little boyish.
He hankered after an active life, and cared very little
To spend time either lying or sitting,
His young blood and restless mind stirred him so much.
And another habit influenced him too,   90
Which he had made a point of honour: he would never eat
On such a special day until he had been told
A curious tale about some perilous thing,
Of some great wonder that he could believe,
Of princes, of battles, or other marvels;   95
Or some knight begged him for a trustworthy foe
To oppose him in jousting, in hazard to set
His life against his opponent's, each letting the other,
As luck would assist him, gain the upper hand.
This was the king's custom when he was in court,   100
At each splendid feast with his noble company
        in hall.
    Therefore with proud face
    He stands there, masterful,
    Valiant in that New Year,   105
    Joking with them all.

So there the bold king himself keeps on his feet,
Chatting before the high table of charming trifles.
There good Gawain was seated beside Guenevere,

7

110　　And Agravayn à la dure mayn on that other syde sittes,
　　　　Bothe the kynges sistersunes and ful siker knightes;
　　　　Bischop Bawdewyn abof biginez the table,
　　　　And Ywan, Uryn son, ette with hymselven.
　　　　Thise were dight on the des and derworthly served,
115　　And sithen mony siker segge at the sidbordez.
　　　　Then the first cors come with crakkyng of trumpes,
　　　　Wyth mony baner ful bryght that therbi henged;
　　　　Nwe nakryn noyse with the noble pipes,
　　　　Wylde werbles and wyght wakned lote,
120　　That mony hert ful highe hef at her towches.
　　　　Dayntés dryven therwyth of ful dere metes,
　　　　Foysoun of the fresche, and on so fele disches
　　　　That pine to fynde the place the peple biforne
　　　　For to sette the sylveren that sere sewes halden
125　　　　　　on clothe.
　　　　　　　　Iche lede as he loved hymselve
　　　　　　　　Ther laght withouten lothe;
　　　　　　　　Ay two had disches twelve,
　　　　　　　　Good ber and bryght wyn bothe.

130　　Now wyl I of hor servise say yow no more,
　　　　For uch wyghe may wel wit no wont that ther were.
　　　　An other noyse ful newe neghed bilive
　　　　That the lude myght haf leve liflode to cach;
　　　　For unethe watz the noyce not a whyle sesed,
135　　And the fyrst cource in the court kyndely served,
　　　　Ther hales in at the halle dor an aghlich mayster,
　　　　On the most on the molde on mesure hyghe;
　　　　Fro the swyre to the swange so sware and so thik,
　　　　And his lyndes and his lymes so longe and so grete,
140　　Half etayn in erde I hope that he were,
　　　　Bot mon most I algate mynn hym to bene,
　　　　And that the myriest in his muckel that myght ride;
　　　　For of his bak and his brest al were his bodi sturne,
　　　　Both his wombe and his wast were worthily smale,
145　　And alle his fetures folyande, in forme that he hade,
　　　　　　ful clene;
　　　　　　　　For wonder of his hwe men hade,
　　　　　　　　Set in his semblaunt sene;
　　　　　　　　He ferde as freke were fade,

And Agravain à la Dure Main on the other side;   110
Both the king's nephews and outstanding knights.
Bishop Baldwin heads the table in the highest seat,
And Ywain, son of Urien, dined as his partner.
These knights were set on the dais and sumptuously served,
And after them many a true man at the side tables.   115
Then the first course was brought in with trumpets blaring,
Many colourful banners hanging from them.
The novel sound of kettledrums with the splendid pipes
Waked echoes with shrill and tremulous notes,
That many hearts leapt at the outburst of music.   120
At the same time servings of such exquisite food,
Abundance of fresh meat, in so many dishes
That space could hardly be found in front of the guests
To set down the silverware holding various stews
                      on the board.   125
            Each man who loved himself
            Took ungrudged, pair by pair,
            From a dozen tasty dishes,
            And drank good wine or beer.

Now I will say nothing more about how they were served,   130
For everyone can guess that no shortage was there.
Another noise, quite different, quickly drew near,
So that the king might have leave to swallow some food.
For hardly had the music stopped for a moment,
And the first course been properly served to the court,   135
When there bursts in at the hall door a terrible figure,
In his stature the very tallest on earth.
From the waist to the neck so thick-set and square,
And his loins and his limbs so massive and long,
In truth half a giant I believe he was,   140
But anyway of all men I judge him the largest,
And the most attractive of his size who could sit on a horse.
For while in back and chest his body was forbidding,
Both his belly and waist were becomingly trim,
And every part of his body equally elegant   145
                      in shape.
            His hue astounded them,
            Set in his looks so keen;
            For boldly he rode in,

150   And overal enker-grene.

And al grathed in grene this gome and his wedes:
A strayte cote ful streght, that stek on his sides,
A meré mantile abof, mensked withinne
With pelure pured apert, the pane ful clene
155   With blythe blaunner ful bryght, and his hode bothe,
That watz laght fro his lokkez and layde on his schulderes;
Heme wel-haled hose of that same,
That spenet on his sparlyr, and clene spures under
Of bryght golde, upon silk bordes barred ful ryche,
160   And scholes under schankes there the schalk rides;
And all his vesture verayly watz clene verdure,
Bothe the barres of his belt and other blythe stones,
That were richely rayled in his aray clene
Aboutte hymself and his sadel, upon silk werkez.
165   That were to tor for to telle of tryfles the halve
That were enbrauded abof, wyth bryddes and flyghes,
With gay gaudi of grene, the gold ay inmyddes.
The pendauntes of his payttrure, the proude cropure,
His molaynes, and alle the metail anamayld was thenne,
170   The steropes that he stod on stayned of the same,
And his arsounz al after and his athel skyrtes,
That ever glemered and glent al of grene stones;
The fole that he ferkkes on fyn of that ilke,
                    sertayn.
175   A grene hors gret and thikke,
             A stede ful stif to strayne,
             In brawden brydel quik;
             To the gome he watz ful gayn.

Wel gay watz this gome gered in grene,
180   And the here of his hed of his hors swete.
Fayre fannand fax umbefoldes his schulderes;
A much berd as a busk over his brest henges,
That wyth his highlich here that of his hed reches
Watz evesed al umbetorne abof his elbowes,
185   That half his armes ther-under were halched in the wyse
Of a kyngez capados that closes his swyre;
The mane of that mayn hors much to hit lyke,
Wel cresped and cemmed, wyth knottes ful mony

Completely emerald green.   *150*

And all arrayed in green this man and his clothes:
A straight close-fitting coat that clung to his body,
A pleasant mantle over that, adorned within
With plain trimmed fur, the facing made bright
With gay shining ermine, and his hood of the same   *155*
Thrown back from his hair and laid over his shoulders.
Neat tightly-drawn stockings coloured to match
Clinging to his calf, and shining spurs below
Of bright gold, over embroidered and richly striped silk;
And without shoes on his feet there the man rides.   *160*
And truly all his clothing was brilliant green,
Both the bars on his belt and other gay gems
That were lavishly set in his shining array
Round himself and his saddle, on embroidered silk.
It would be hard to describe even half the fine work   *165*
That was embroidered upon it, the butterflies and birds,
With lovely beadwork of green, always centred upon gold.
The pendants on the breast-trappings, the splendid crupper,
The bosses on the bit, and all the metal enamelled.
The stirrups he stood in were coloured the same,   *170*
And his saddlebow behind him and his splendid skirts
That constantly glittered and shone, all of green gems;
The horse that he rides entirely of that colour,
              in truth.
        A green horse huge and strong,   *175*
        A proud steed to restrain,
        Spirited under bridle,
        But obedient to the man.

Most attractive was this man attired in green,
With the hair of his head matching his horse.   *180*
Fine outspreading locks cover his shoulders;
A great beard hangs down over his chest like a bush,
That like the splendid hair that falls from his head
Was clipped all around above his elbows,
So that his upper arms were hidden, in the fashion   *185*
Of a royal capados that covers the neck.
That great horse's mane was treated much the same,
Well curled and combed, with numerous knots

Folden in with a fildore aboute the fayre grene,
190 Ay a herle of the here, an other of golde;
The tayl and his toppyng twynnen of a sute,
And bounden bothe wyth a bande of a bryght grene,
Dubbed wyth ful dere stonez, as the dok lasted,
Sythen thrawen wyth a thwong a thwarle knot alofte,
195 Ther mony bellez ful bryght of brende golde rungen.
Such a fole upon folde, ne freke that hym rydes,
Watz never sene in that sale wyth syght er that tyme,
with yghe.
He loked as layt so lyght,
200 So sayd al that hym syghe;
Hit semed as no mon myght
Under his dynttez dryghe.

Whether hade he no helme ne no hawbergh nauther,
Ne no pysan ne no plate that pented to armes,
205 Ne no schafte ne no schelde to schwve ne to smyte,
Bot in his on honde he hade a holyn bobbe,
That is grattest in grene when grevez ar bare,
And an ax in his other, a hoge and unmete,
A spetos sparthe to expoun in spelle, quoso myght.
210 The lenkthe of an elnyerde the large hede hade,
The grayn al of grene stele and of golde hewen,
The bit burnyst bryght, with a brod egge
As wel schapen to schere as scharp rasores,
The stele of a stif staf the sturne hit bi grypte,
215 That watz wounden wyth yrn to the wandez ende,
And al bigraven with grene in gracios werkes;
A lace lapped aboute, that louked at the hede,
And so after the halme halched ful ofte,
Wyth tryed tasselez therto tacched innoghe
220 On botounz of the bryght grene brayden ful ryche.
This hathel heldez hym in and the halle entres,
Drivande to the heghe dece, dut he no wothe,
Haylsed he never one, bot heghe he over loked.
The fyrst word that he warp, 'Where is,' he sayd,
225 'The governour of this gyng? Gladly I wolde
Se that segg in syght, and with hymself speke
raysoun.'
To knyghtez he kest his yghe,

Plaited with gold thread around the fine green,
Always a strand of his hair with another of gold.   *190*
His tail and his forelock were braided to match,
Both tied with a ribbon of brilliant green,
Studded with costly gems to the end of the tail,
Then tightly bound with a thong to an intricate knot
Where many bright bells of burnished gold rang.   *195*
No such horse upon earth, nor such a rider indeed,
Had any man in that hall before thought to see
        with his eyes.
    His glance was lightning swift,
    All said who saw him there;   *200*
    It seemed that no one could
    His massive blows endure.

Yet he had no helmet nor hauberk either,
No neck-armour or plate belonging to arms,
No spear and no shield to push or to strike;   *205*
But in one hand he carried a holly-branch
That is brilliantly green when forests are bare,
And an axe in the other, monstrously huge;
A cruel battle-axe to tell of in words, if one could.
The great head was as broad as a measuring-rod,   *210*
The spike made entirely of green and gold steel,
Its blade brightly burnished, with a long cutting-edge
As well fashioned to shear as the keenest razor.
The grim man gripped the handle, a powerful staff,
That was wound with iron to the end of the haft   *215*
And all engraved in green with craftsmanly work.
It had a thong wrapped about it, fastened to the head,
And then looped round the handle several times,
With many splendid tassels attached to it
With buttons of bright green, richly embroidered.   *220*
This giant bursts in and rides through the hall,
Approaching the high dais, disdainful of peril,
Greeting none, but haughtily looking over their heads.
The first words he spoke, 'Where is,' he demanded,
'The governor of this crowd? Glad should I be   *225*
To clap eyes on the man, and exchange with him
        a few words.'
    He looked down at the knights,

And reled hym up and doun;
230 He stemmed, and con studie
Quo walt ther most renoun.

Ther watz lokyng on lenthe the lude to beholde,
For uch mon had mervayle quat hit mene myght
That a hathel and a horse myght such a hwe lach
235 As growe gren as the gres and grener hit semed,
Then grene aumayl on golde glowande bryghter.
Al studied that ther stod, and stalked hym nerre
With al the wonder of the worlde what he worche schulde.
For fele sellyez had thay sen, bot such never are;
240 Forthi for fantoun and fayryye the folk there hit demed.
Therfore to answare watz arghe mony athel freke,
And al stouned at his steven and stonstil seten
In a swogh sylence thurgh the sale riche;
As al were slypped upon slepe so slaked hor lotez
245 in hyghe;
I deme hit not al for doute,
Bot sum for cortaysye,
Bot let hym that al schulde loute
Cast unto that wyghe.

250 Thenne Arthour bifore the high dece that aventure byholdez,
And rekenly hym reverenced, for rad was he never,
And sayde, 'Wyghe, welcum iwys to this place,
The hede of this ostel Arthour I hat;
Lyght luflych adoun and lenge, I the praye,
255 And quat-so thy wylle is we schal wyt after.'
'Nay, as help me,' quoth the hathel, 'he that on hygh syttes,
To wone any quyle in this won hit watz not myn ernde;
Bot for the los of the, lede, is lyft up so hyghe,
And thy burgh and thy burnes best ar holden,
260 Stifest under stel-gere on stedes to ryde,
The wyghtest and the worthyest of the worldes kynde,
Preve for to playe wyth in other pure laykez,
And here is kydde cortaysye, as I haf herd carp,
And that hatz wayned me hider, iwyis, at this tyme.
265 Ye may be seker bi this braunch that I bere here
That I passe as in pes, and no plyght seche;
For had I founded in fere in feghtyng wyse,

As he rode up and down,
Then paused, waiting to see   *230*
Who had the most renown.

For long there was only staring at the man,
For everyone marvelled what it could mean
That a knight and a horse might take such a colour
And become green as grass, and greener it seemed   *235*
Than green enamel shining brightly on gold.
All those standing there gazed, and warily crept closer,
Bursting with wonder to see what he would do;
For many marvels they had known, but such a one never;
So the folk there judged it phantasm or magic.   *240*
For this reason many noble knights feared to answer:
And stunned by his words they sat there stock-still,
While dead silence spread throughout the rich hall
As though everyone fell asleep, so was their talk stilled
        at a word.   *245*
    Not just for fear, I think,
    But some for courtesy;
    Letting him whom all revere
    To that man reply.

Then Arthur confronts that wonder before the high table,   *250*
And saluted him politely, for afraid was he never,
And said, 'Sir, welcome indeed to this place;
I am master of this house, my name is Arthur.
Be pleased to dismount and spend some time here, I beg,
And what you have come for we shall learn later.'   *255*
'No, by heaven,' said the knight, 'and him who sits there,
To spend time in this house was not the cause of my coming.
But because your name, sir, is so highly regarded,
And your city and your warriors reputed the best,
Dauntless in armour and on horseback afield,   *260*
The most valiant and excellent of all living men,
Courageous as players in other noble sports,
And here courtesy is displayed, as I have heard tell,
And that has brought me here, truly, on this day.
You may be assured by this branch that I carry   *265*
That I approach you in peace, seeking no battle.
For had I travelled in fighting dress, in warlike manner,

15

I have a hauberghe at home and a helme bothe,
A schelde and a scharp spere, schinande bryghte,
270 Ande other weppenes to welde, I wene wel, als;
Bot for I wolde no were, my wedez ar softer.
Bot if thou be so bold as alle burnez tellen,
Thou wyl grant me godly the gomen that I ask
bi ryght.'
275 Arthour con onsware,
And sayd, 'Sir cortays knyght,
If thou crave batayl bare,
Here faylez thou not to fyght.'

'Nay, frayst I no fyght, in fayth I the telle,
280 Hit arn aboute on this bench bot berdlez chylder.
If I were hasped in armes on a heghe stede,
Here is no mon me to mach, for myghtez so wayke.
Forthy I crave in this court a Crystemas gomen,
For hit is Yol and Nwe Yer, and here ar yep mony.
285 If any so hardy in this hous holdez hymselven,
Be so bolde in his blod, brayn in hys hede,
That dar stifly strike a strok for an other,
I schal gif hym of my gyft thys giserne ryche,
This ax, that is hevé innogh, to hondele as hym lykes,
290 And I schal bide the fyrst bur as bare as I sitte.
If any freke be so felle to fonde that I telle,
Lepe lyghtly me to, and lach this weppen,
I quit-clayme hit for ever, kepe hit as his awen,
And I schal stonde hym a strok, stif on this flet,
295 Ellez thou wyl dight me the dom to dele hym an other
barlay;
And yet gif hym respite
A twelmonyth and a day;
Now hyghe, and let se tite
300 Dar any herinne oght say.'

If he hem stouned upon fyrst, stiller were thanne
Alle the heredmen in halle, the hyghe and the lowe.
The renk on his rouncé hym ruched in his sadel,
And runischly his red yghen he reled aboute,
305 Bende his bresed browez, blycande grene,
Wayved his berde for to wayte quo-so wolde ryse.

I have a hauberk at home and a helmet too,
A shield and a keen spear, shining bright,
And other weapons to brandish, I assure you, as well;   *270*
But since I look for no combat I am not dressed for battle.
But if you are as courageous as everyone says,
You will graciously grant me the game that I ask for
        by right.'
      In answer Arthur said,   *275*
      'If you seek, courteous knight,
      A combat without armour,
      You will not lack a fight.'

'No, I seek no battle, I assure you truly,
Those about me in this hall are but beardless children.   *280*
If I were locked in my armour on a great horse,
No one here could match me with their feeble powers.
Therefore I ask of the court a Christmas game,
For it is Yule and New Year, and here are brave men in plenty.
If anyone in this hall thinks himself bold enough,   *285*
So doughty in body and reckless in mind
As to strike a blow fearlessly and take one in return,
I shall give him this marvellous battle-axe as a gift,
This ponderous axe, to use as he pleases;
And I shall stand the first blow, unarmed as I am.   *290*
If anyone is fierce enough to take up my challenge,
Run to me quickly and seize this weapon,
I renounce all claim to it, let him keep it as his own,
And I shall stand his blow unflinching on this floor,
Provided you assign me the right to deal such a one   *295*
        in return.
      And yet grant him respite
      A twelvemonth and a day.
      Now hurry, and let's see
      What any here dare say.'   *300*

If he petrified them at first, even stiller were then
All the courtiers in that place, the great and the small.
The man on the horse turned himself in his saddle,
Ferociously rolling his red eyes about,
Bunched up his eyebrows, bristling with green,   *305*
Swung his beard this way and that to see whoever would rise.

When non wolde kepe hym with carp he coghed ful hyghe,
Ande rimed hym ful richely, and ryght hym to speke:
'What, is this Arthures hous?' quoth the hathel thenne,
310   'That al the rous rennes of thurgh ryalmes so mony?
Where is now your sourquydrye and your conquestes,
Your gryndellayk and your greme, and your grete wordes?
Now is the revel and the renoun of the Rounde Table
Overwalt wyth a worde of on wyghes speche,
315   For al dares for drede withoute dynt schewed!'
Wyth this he laghes so loude that the lorde greved;
The blod schot for scham into his schyre face
                and lere;
            He wex as wroth as wynde,
320   So did alle that ther were.
            The kyng as kene bi kynde
            Then stod that stif mon nere,

And sayde, 'Hathel, by heven, thy askyng is nys,
And as thou foly hatz frayst, fynde the behoves.
325   I know no gome that is gast of thy grete wordes,
Gif me now thy geserne, upon Godez halve,
And I schal baythen thy bone that thou boden habbes.'
Lyghtly lepez he him to, and laght at his honde,
Then feersly that other freke upon fote lyghtis.
330   Now hatz Arthure his axe, and the halme grypez,
And sturnely sturez hit aboute, that stryke wyth hit thoght.
The stif mon hym bifore stod upon hyght,
Herre then ani in the hous by the hede and more.
With sturne schere ther he stod he stroked his berde,
335   And wyth a countenaunce dryghe he drogh doun his cote,
No more mate ne dismayd for his mayn dintez
Then any burne upon bench hade broght hym to drynk
                of wyne.
            Gawan, that sate bi the quene,
340   To the kyng he can enclyne:
            'I beseche now with sayez sene
            This melly mot be myne.

'Wolde ye, worthilych lorde,' quoth Wawan to the kyng,
'Bid me bowe fro this benche, and stonde by yow there,
345   That I wythoute vylanye myght voyde this table,

When no one would answer he cried out aloud,
Drew himself up grandly and started to speak.
'What, is this Arthur's house?' said the man then,
'That everyone talks of in so many kingdoms?   *310*
Where are now your arrogance and your victories,
Your fierceness and wrath and your great speeches?
Now the revelry and repute of the Round Table
Are overthrown with a word from one man's mouth,
For you all cower in fear before a blow has been struck!'   *315*
Then he laughs so uproariously that the king took offence;
The blood rushed into his fair face and cheek
      for shame.
      Arthur grew red with rage,
      As all the others did.   *320*
      The king, by nature bold,
      Approached that man and said,

'Sir, by heaven, what you demand is absurd,
And since you have asked for folly, that you deserve.
No man known to me fears your boastful words;   *325*
Hand over your battle-axe, in God's name,
And I shall grant the wish that you have requested.'
He quickly goes to him and took the axe from his hand.
Then proudly the other dismounts and stands there.
Now Arthur has the axe, grips it by the shaft,   *330*
And grimly swings it about, as preparing to strike.
Towering before him stood the bold man,
Taller than anyone in the court by more than a head.
Standing there grim-faced he stroked his beard,
And with an unmoved expression then pulled down his coat,   *335*
No more daunted or dismayed by those powerful strokes
Than if any knight in the hall had brought him a measure
      of wine.
      Seated by Guenevere
      Then bowed the good Gawain: *340*
      'I beg you in plain words
      To let this task be mine.'

Said Gawain to the king, 'If you would, noble lord,
Bid me rise from my seat and stand at your side,
If without discourtesy I might leave the table,   *345*

19

And that my legge lady lyked not ille,
I wolde com to your counseyl bifore your cort riche.
For me think hit not semly, as hit is soth knawen,
Ther such an askyng is hevened so hyghe in your sale,

350 Thagh ye yourself be talenttyf, to take hit to yourselven,
Whil mony so bolde yow aboute upon bench sytten
That under heven I hope non hagherer of wylle,
Ne better bodyes on bent ther baret is rered.
I am the wakkest, I wot, and of wyt feblest,

355 And lest lur of my lyf, quo laytes the sothe:
Bot for as much as ye are myn em I am only to prayse,
No bounté bot your blod I in my bodé knowe;
And sythen this note is so nys that noght hit yow falles,
And I have frayned hit at yow fyrst, foldez hit to me;

360 And if I carp not comlyly, let alle this cort rych
bout blame.'
Ryche togeder con roun,
And sythen thay redden alle same,
To ryd the kyng wyth croun

365 And gif Gawan the game.

Then comaunded the kyng the knyght for to ryse;
And he ful radly upros, and ruchched hym fayre,
Kneled doun bifore the kyng, and cachez that weppen;
And he luflyly hit hym laft, and lyfte up his honde

370 And gef hym Goddez blessyng, and gladly hym biddes
That his hert and his honde schulde hardi be bothe.
'Kepe the, cosyn,' quoth the kyng, 'that thou on kyrf sette,
And if thou redez hym ryght, redly I trowe
That thou schal byden the bur that he schal bede after.'

375 Gawan gotz to the gome with giserne in honde,
And he baldly hym bydez, he bayst never the helder.
Then carppez to Sir Gawan the knyght in the grene,
'Refourme we oure forwardes, er we fyrre passe.
Fyrst I ethe the, hathel, how that thou hattes

380 That thou me telle truly, as I tryst may.'
'In god fayth,' quoth the goode knyght, 'Gawan I hatte,
That bede the this buffet, quat-so bifallez after,
And at this tyme twelmonyth take at the an other
Wyth what weppen so thou wylt, and wyth no wygh ellez

385 on lyve.'

And that my liege lady were not displeased,
I would offer you counsel before your royal court.
For it seems to me unfitting, if the truth be admitted,
When so arrogant a request is put forward in hall,
Even if you are desirous, to undertake it yourself   *350*
While so many brave men sit about you in their places
Who, I think, are unrivalled in temper of mind,
And without equal as warriors on field of battle.
I am the weakest of them, I know, and the dullest-minded,
So my death would be least loss, if truth should be told;   *355*
Only because you are my uncle am I to be praised,
No virtue I know in myself but your blood;
And since this affair is so foolish and unfitting for you,
And I have asked you for it first, it should fall to me.
And if my request is improper, let not this royal court   *360*
      bear the blame.'
      Nobles whispered together
      And agreed on their advice,
      That Arthur should withdraw
      And Gawain take his place.   *365*

Then the king commanded Gawain to stand up,
And he did so promptly, and moved forward with grace,
Kneeled down before the king and laid hold of the weapon;
And Arthur gave it up graciously, and lifting his hand
Gave Gawain God's blessing, and cheerfully bids   *370*
That he bring a strong heart and firm hand to the task.
'Take care, nephew,' said the king, 'that you strike one blow,
And if you deal it aright, truly I believe
You will wait a long time for his stroke in return.'
Gawain approaches the man with battle-axe in hand,   *375*
And he waits for him boldly, with no sign of alarm.
Then the knight in the green addresses Gawain,
'Let us repeat our agreement before going further.
First I entreat you, sir, that what is your name
You shall tell me truly, that I may believe you.'   *380*
'In good faith,' said that virtuous knight, 'I am called Gawain,
Who deals you this blow, whatever happens after,
On this day next year to accept another from you
With what weapon you choose, and from no other person
      on earth.'   *385*

That other onswarez agayn,
'Sir Gawan, so mot I thryve,
As I am ferly fayn
This dint that thou schal dryve.

390 Bigog,' quoth the grene knyght, 'Sir Gawan, me lykes
That I schal fange at thy fust that I haf frayst here.
And thou hatz redily rehersed, bi resoun ful trwe,
Clanly al the covenaunt that I the kynge asked,
Saf that thou schal siker me, segge, bi thi trawthe,
395 That thou schal seche me thiself, where-so thou hopes
I may be funde upon folde, and foch the such wages
As thou deles me to-day bifore this douthe ryche.'
'Where schulde I wale the?' quoth Gawan, 'Where is thy place?
I wot never where thou wonyes, bi hym that me wroght,
400 Ne I know not the, knyght, thy cort ne thi name.
Bot teche me truly therto, and telle me how thou hattes,
And I schal ware alle my wyt to wynne me theder,
And that I swere the for sothe, and by my seker traweth.'
'That is innogh in Nwe Yer, hit nedes no more,'
405 Quoth the gome in the grene to Gawan the hende;
'Yif I the telle trwly quen I the tape have,
And thou me smothely hatz smyten, smartly I the teche
Of my hous and my home and myn owene nome,
Then may thou frayst my fare and forwardez holde;
410 And if I spende no speche, thenne spedez thou the better,
For thou may leng in thy londe and layt no fyrre —
bot slokes!
Ta now thy grymme tole to the,
And lat se how thou cnokez.'
415 'Gladly, sir, for sothe,'
Quoth Gawan: his ax he strokes.

The grene knyght upon grounde graythely hym dresses,
A littel lut with the hed, the lere he discoverez,
His longe lovelych lokkez he layd over his croun,
420 Let the naked nec to the note schewe.
Gawan gripped to his ax and gederes hit on hyght,
The kay fot on the folde he before sette,
Let hit doun lyghtly lyght on the naked,
That the scharp of the schalk schyndered the bones,

The other man replied,
'Sir Gawain, as I live,
I am extremely glad
This blow is yours to give.

By God,' said the Green Knight, 'Sir Gawain, I am pleased   390
That I shall get from your hands what I have asked for here.
And you have fully repeated, in exact terms,
Without omission the whole covenant I put to the king;
Except that you shall assure me, sir, on your word,
That you will seek me yourself, wherever you think   395
I may be found upon earth, to accept such payment
As you deal me today before this noble gathering.'
'Where shall I find you?' said Gawain, 'Where is your dwelling?
I have no idea where you live, by him who made me;
Nor do I know you, sir, your court nor your name.   400
Just tell me truly these things, and what you are called,
And I shall use all my wits to get myself there,
And that I swear to you honestly, by my pledged word.'
'That is enough for the moment, it needs nothing more,'
Said the man in green to the courteous Gawain,   405
'If I answer you truly after taking the blow,
And you have dextrously struck me, I will tell you at once
Of my house and my home and my proper name,
Then you can pay me a visit and keep your pledged word;
And if I say nothing, then you will fare better,   410
For you may stay in your country and seek no further —
          but enough!
     Take up your fearsome weapon
     And let's see how you smite.'
     Said Gawain, 'Gladly, indeed,'   415
     Whetting the metal bit.

The Green Knight readily takes up his position,
Bowed his head a little, uncovering the flesh,
His long lovely hair he swept over his head,
In readiness letting the naked neck show.   420
Gawain grasped the axe and lifts it up high,
Setting his left foot before him on the ground,
Brought it down swiftly on the bare flesh
So that the bright blade slashed through the man's spine

425   And schrank thurgh the schyire grece, and schade hit in twynne,
That the bit of the broun stel bot on the grounde.
The fayre hede fro the halce hit to the erthe,
That fele hit foyned wyth hir fete, there hit forth roled;
The blod brayed from the body, that blykked on the grene;
430   And nawther faltered ne fel the freke never the helder,
Bot stythly he start forth upon styf schonkes,
And runyschly he raght out, there as renkkez stoden,
Laght to his lufly hed, and lyft hit up sone;
And sythen bowez to his blonk, the brydel he cachchez,
435   Steppez into stelbawe and strydez alofte,
And his hede by the here in his honde haldez.
And as sadly the segge hym in his sadel sette
As non unhap had hym ayled, thagh hedlez he were
               in stedde.
440   He brayde his bulk aboute,
        That ugly bodi that bledde;
        Moni on of hym had doute
        Bi that his resounz were redde.

For the hede in his honde he haldez up even,
445   Toward the derrest on the dece he dressez the face,
And hit lyfte up the yghe-lyddez and loked ful brode,
And meled thus much with his muthe, as ye may now here:
'Loke, Gawan, thou be graythe to go as thou hettez,
And layte as lelly til thou me, lude, fynde,
450   As thou hatz hette in this halle, herande thise knyghtes;
To the grene chapel thou chose, I charge the, to fotte
Such a dunt as thou hatz dalt, disserved thou habbez
To be yederly yolden on Nw Yeres morn.
The knyght of the grene chapel men knowen me mony,
455   Forthi me for to fynde if thou fraystez, faylez thou never.
Therfore com, other recreaunt be calde thou behoves.'
With a runisch rout the raynez he tornez,
Halled out at the hal dor, his hed in his hande,
That the fyr of the flynt flaghe fro fole hoves.
460   To quat kyth he becom knwe non there,
Never more then thay wyste from quethen he watz wonnen.
              What thenne?
        The kyng and Gawan thare
        At that grene thay laghe and grenne;

And cut through the white flesh, severing it in two,   425
So that the shining steel blade bit into the floor.
The handsome head flew from the neck to the ground,
And many courtiers kicked at it as it rolled past.
Blood spurted from the trunk, gleamed on the green dress,
Yet the man neither staggered nor fell a whit for all that,   430
But sprang forward vigorously on powerful legs,
And fiercely reached out where knights were standing,
Grabbed at his fine head and snatched it up quickly,
And then strides to his horse, seizes the bridle,
Puts foot into stirrup and swings into his seat,   435
His other hand clutching his head by the hair;
And the man seated himself on horseback as firmly
As if he had suffered no injury, though headless he sat
      in his place.
     He turned his body round,   440
     That gruesome trunk that bled;
     Many were struck by fear
     When all his words were said.

For he holds up the head in his hand, truly,
Turns its face towards the noblest on the dais,   445
And it lifted its eyelids and glared with wide eyes,
And the mouth uttered these words, which you shall now hear:
'See, Gawain, that you carry out your promise exactly,
And search for me truly, sir, until I am found,
As you have sworn in this hall in the hearing of these knights.   450
Make your way to the Green Chapel, I charge you, to get
Such a blow as you have dealt, rightfully given,
To be readily returned on New Year's Day.
As the Knight of the Green Chapel I am widely known,
So if you make search to find me you cannot possibly fail.   455
Therefore come, or merit the name of craven coward.'
With a fierce jerk of the reins he turns his horse
And hurtled out of the hall door, his head in his hand,
So fast that flint-fire sparked from the hoofs.
What land he returned to no one there knew,   460
Any more than they guessed where he had come from.
      What then?
     Seeing that green man go,
     The king and Gawain grin;

465   Yet breved watz hit ful bare
      A mervayl among tho menne.

    Thagh Arther the hende kyng at hert hade wonder,
    He let no semblaunt be sene, bot sayde ful hyghe
    To the comlych quene wyth cortays speche,
470   'Dere dame, to-day demay yow never;
    Wel bycommes such craft upon Cristmasse,
    Laykyng of enterludez, to laghe and to syng,
    Among thise kynde caroles of knyghtez and ladyez.
    Never the lece to my mete I may me wel dres,
475   For I haf sen a selly, I may not forsake.'
    He glent upon Sir Gawen, and gaynly he sayde,
    'Now sir, heng up thyn ax, that hatz innogh hewen.'
    And hit watz don abof the dece on doser to henge,
    Ther alle men for mervayl myght on hit loke,
480   And bi trwe tytel therof to telle the wonder.
    Thenne thay bowed to a borde thise burnes togeder,
    The kyng and the gode knyght, and kene men hem served
    Of alle dayntyez double, as derrest myght falle;
    Wyth alle maner of mete and mynstralcie bothe,
485   Wyth wele walt thay that day, til worthed an ende
       in londe.
     Now thenk wel, Sir Gawan,
     For wothe that thou ne wonde
     This aventure for to frayn
490   That thou hatz tan on honde.

Yet they both agreed   465
They had a wonder seen.

Although inwardly Arthur was deeply astonished,
He let no sign of this appear, but loudly remarked
To the beautiful queen with courteous speech,
'Dear lady, let nothing distress you today.   470
Such strange goings-on are fitting at Christmas,
Putting on interludes, laughing and singing,
Mixed with courtly dances of ladies and knights.
None the less, I can certainly go to my food,
For I have seen something wondrous, I cannot deny.'   475
He glanced at Sir Gawain, and aptly he said,
'Now sir, hang your axe up, for it has severed enough.'
And it was hung above the dais, on a piece of tapestry,
Where everyone might gaze on it as a wonder,
And the living proof of this marvellous tale.   480
Then these two men together walked to a table,
The king and the good knight, and were dutifully served
With delicious double helpings befitting their rank.
With every kind of food and minstrelsy
They spent that day joyfully, until daylight ended   485
            on earth.
        Now take good care, Gawain,
        Lest fear hold you back
        From leaving on the quest
        You have sworn to undertake.   490

Part 2

Fitt 2

This hanselle hatz Arthur of aventurus on fyrst
In yonge yer, for he yerned yelpyng to here.
Thagh hym wordez were wane when thay to sete wenten,
Now ar thay stoken of sturne werk, stafful her hond.
495   Gawan watz glad to begynne those gomnez in halle,
Bot thagh the ende be hevy haf ye no wonder;
For thagh men ben mery quen thay han mayn drynk,
A yere yernes ful yerne, and yeldez never lyke,
The forme to the fynisment foldez ful selden.
500   Forthi this Yol overyede, and the yere after,
And uche sesoun serlepes sued after other:
After Crystenmasse com the crabbed lentoun
That fraystez flesch wyth the fysche and fode more symple;
Bot thenne the weder of the worlde wyth wynter hit threpez,
505   Colde clengez adoun, cloudez upliften,
Schyre schedez the rayn in schowrez ful warme,
Fallez upon fayre flat, flowrez there schewen,
Bothe groundez and the grevez grene ar her wedez,
Bryddez busken to bylde, and bremlych syngen
510   For solace of the softe somer that sues therafter
            bi bonk;
        And blossumez bolne to blowe
        Bi rawez rych and ronk,
        Then notez noble innoghe
515   Ar herde in wod so wlonk.

After the sesoun of somer wyth the soft wyndez,
Quen Zeferus syflez hymself on sedez and erbez,
Wela wynne is the wort that waxes theroute,
When the donkande dewe dropez of the levez,
520   To bide a blysful blusch of the bryght sunne.
Bot then hyghes hervest, and hardenes hym sone,
Warnez hym for the wynter to wax ful rype.
He dryves wyth droght the dust for to ryse
Fro the face of the folde to flyghe ful hyghe;

This wonder has Arthur as his first New Year's gift
When the year was newborn, for he loved hearing challenges.
Though words were wanting when they sat down at table,
Now a grim task confronts them, their hands are cram-full.
Gawain was glad enough to begin those games in the hall,   *495*
But if the outcome prove troublesome don't be surprised;
For though men are light-hearted when they have strong drink,
A year passes swiftly, never bringing the same;
Beginning and ending seldom take the same form.
And so that Yule went by, and the year ensuing,   *500*
Each season in turn following the other.
After Christmas came mean-spirited Lent,
That tries the body with fish and plainer nourishment;
But then the weather on earth battles with winter,
The cold shrinks downwards, clouds rise higher,   *505*
And shed sparkling rain in warming showers,
Falling on smiling plains where flowers unfold.
Both open fields and woodlands put on green dress;
Birds hasten to build, and rapturously sing
For joy of gentle summer that follows next   *510*
          on the slopes.
     And flowers bud and blossom
     In hedgerows rich with growth,
     And many splendid songs
     From woodlands echo forth.   *515*

Then comes the summer season with gentle winds,
When Zephirus blows softly on seeding grasses and plants,
Beautiful is the growth that springs from the seed,
When the moistening dew drips from the leaves
To await a joyful gleam of the bright sun.   *520*
But then autumn comes quickly and urges it on,
Warns it to ripen before winter's approach.
Dry winds of autumn force the dust to fly
From the face of the earth high into the air;

525 Wrothe wynde of the welkyn wrastelez with the sunne,
  The levez lancen fro the lynde and lyghten on the grounde,
  And al grayes the gres that grene watz ere.
  Thenne al rypez and rotez that ros upon fyrst,
  And thus yirnez the yere in yisterdayez mony,
530 And wynter wyndez agayn, as the worlde askez,
     no fage;
    Til Meghelmas mone
    Watz cumen wyth wynter wage;
    Then thenkkez Gawan ful sone
535   Of his anious vyage.

  Yet quyl Al-hal-day with Arther he lenges;
  And he made a fare on that fest for the frekez sake,
  With much revel and ryche of the Rounde Table.
  Knyghtez ful cortays and comlych ladies
540 Al for luf of that lede in longynge thay were,
  Bot never the lece ne the later thay nevened bot merthe;
  Mony joylez for that jentyle japez ther maden.
  And aftter mete with mournyng he melez to his eme,
  And spekez of his passage, and pertly he sayde,
545 'Now, lege lorde of my lyf, leve I yow ask;
  Ye knowe the cost of this case, kepe I no more
  To telle yow tenez therof, never bot trifel;
  Bot I am boun to the bur barely to-morne
  To sech the gome of the grene, as God wyl me wysse.'
550 Then the best of the burgh bowed togeder,
  Aywan and Errik, and other ful mony,
  Sir Doddinaval de Savage, the duc of Clarence,
  Launcelot and Lyonel, and Lucan the gode,
  Sir Boos and Sir Bydver, big men bothe,
555 And mony other menskful, with Mador de la Port.
  Alle this compayny of court com the kyng nerre
  For to counseyl the knyght, with care at her hert.
  There watz much derve doel driven in the sale
  That so worthé as Wawan schulde wende on that ernde,
560 To dryve a delful dynt, and dele no more
     wyth bronde.
    The knyght mad ay god chere,
    And sayde, 'Quat schuld I wonde?
    Of destinés derf and dere

Fierce winds of heaven wrestle with the sun,   525
Leaves are torn from the trees and fall to the ground,
And all withered is the grass that was green before.
Then all ripens and rots that had sprung up at first,
And in so many yesterdays the year wears away,
And winter comes round again, as custom requires,   530
        in truth;
      Until the Michaelmas moon
      Brought hint of winter's frost;
      And into Gawain's mind
      Come thoughts of his grim quest.   535

Yet until All Saints' Day he lingers in court,
And Arthur made a feast on that day to honour the knight,
With much splendid revelry at the Round Table.
The most courteous of knights and beautiful ladies
Grieved out of love for that noble man,   540
But no less readily for that spoke as if unconcerned.
Many troubled for that nobleman made joking remarks.
And after the feast sorrowfully he addressed his uncle,
Raised the matter of his quest, and openly said,
'Liege lord of my being, I must ask for your leave;   545
You know the terms of this matter, and I have no wish
To bother you with them, saving one small point;
But tomorrow without fail I set out for the blow,
To seek this man in green, as God will direct me.'
Then the noblest in the court gathered together,   550
Ywain and Eric, and many others,
Sir Dodinal le Sauvage, the duke of Clarence,
Lancelot and Lionel, and Lucan the good,
Sir Bors and Sir Bedevere, both powerful men,
And several other worthy knights, including Mador de la Port.   555
This group of courtiers approached the king,
To give advice to Gawain with troubled hearts.
Much deep sorrowing was heard in the hall
That one as noble as Gawain should go on that quest,
To stand a terrible blow, and never more brandish   560
        his sword.
      Keeping an unchanged face
      'What should I fear?' he said;
      For whether kind or harsh

565   What may mon do bot fonde?'

He dowellez ther al that day, and dressez on the morn,
Askez erly hys armez, and alle were thay broght.
Fyrst a tulé tapit tyght over the flet,
And miche watz the gild gere that glent theralofte.
570   The stif mon steppez theron, and the stel hondelez,
Dubbed in a dublet of a dere tars,
And sythen a crafty capados, closed aloft,
That wyth a bryght blaunner was bounden withinne.
Thenne set thay the sabatounz upon the segge fotez,
575   His legez lapped in stel with luflych greves,
With polaynez piched therto, policed ful clene,
Aboute his knez knaged wyth knotez of golde;
Queme quyssewes then, that coyntlych closed
His thik thrawen thyghez, with thwonges to tachched;
580   And sythen the brawden bryné of bryght stel ryngez
Umbeweved that wygh upon wlonk stuffe,
And wel bornyst brace upon his bothe armes,
With gode cowters and gay, and glovez of plate,
And alle the godlych gere that hym gayn schulde
585   that tyde;
         Wyth ryche cote-armure
         His gold sporez spend with pryde,
         Gurde wyth a bront ful sure
         With silk sayn umbe his syde.

590   When he watz hasped in armes, his harnays watz ryche:
The lest lachet other loupe lemed of golde.
So harnayst as he watz he herknez his masse,
Offred and honoured at the heghe auter.
Sythen he come to the kyng and to his cort-ferez,
595   Lachez lufly his leve at lordez and ladyez;
And thay him kyst and conveyed, bikende hym to Kryst.
Bi that watz Gryngolet grayth, and gurde with a sadel
That glemed ful gayly with mony golde frenges,
Ayquere naylet ful nwe, for that note ryched;
600   The brydel barred aboute, with bryght golde bounden,
The apparayl of the payttrure and of the proude skyrtez,
The cropore and the covertor, acorded wyth the arsounez;
And al watz rayled on red ryche golde naylez,

A man's fate must be tried.'   *565*

He stays there all that day, and makes ready the next,
Calls early for his accoutrement, and all was brought in.
First a crimson carpet was stretched over the floor,
A heap of gilded armour gleaming brightly piled there.
The brave knight steps on it and examines his armour,   *570*
Dressed in a costly doublet of silk
Under a well-made capados, fastened at the top
And trimmed with white ermine on the inside.
Then they fitted metal shoes upon the knight's feet,
Clasped his legs in steel with elegant greaves   *575*
With knee-pieces attached to them, highly polished
And fastened to his knees with knots of gold.
Next fine cuisses that neatly enclosed
His thick muscular thighs, with thongs attached,
And then the linked mail-shirt made of bright steel rings   *580*
Covered that man and his beautiful clothes:
Well burnished braces on both his arms,
With fine elbow-pieces and gloves of steel plate,
And all the splendid equipment that would benefit him
          at that time;   *585*
          With costly coat-armour,
          His gold spurs worn with pride,
          Girt with a trusty sword,
          A silk belt round him tied.

All locked in his armour his gear looked noble: *590*
The smallest fastening or loop was gleaming with gold.
In armour as he was, he went to hear mass
Offered and celebrated for him at the high altar.
Then he comes to the king and his fellows at court,
Graciously takes his leave of lords and ladies;   *595*
And they kissed and escorted him, commending him to Christ.
By then Gringolet was ready, fitted with a saddle
That splendidly shone with many gold fringes,
Newly studded all over for that special purpose;
The bridle striped all along, and trimmed with bright gold;   *600*
The adornment of the trapping and the fine saddle-skirts,
The crupper and the horse-cloth matched the saddle-bows,
All covered with gold studs on a background of red,

That al glytered and glent as glem of the sunne.
605 Thenne hentes he the helme, and hastily hit kysses,
That watz stapled stifly, and stoffed wythinne.
Hit watz hyghe on his hede, hasped bihynde,
Wyth a lyghtly urysoun over the aventayle,
Enbrawden and bounden wyth the best gemmez
610 On brode sylkyn borde, and bryddez on semez,
As papjayez paynted pervyng bitwene,
Tortors and trulofez entayled so thyk
As mony burde theraboute had ben seven wynter
        in toune.
615 　　The cercle watz more o prys
　　That umbeclypped hys croun,
　　Of diamauntez a devys
　　That bothe were bryght and broun.

Then thay schewed hym the schelde, that was of schyr goulez,
620 Wyth the pentangel depaynt of pure gold hwez.
He braydez hit by the bauderyk, aboute the hals kestes,
That bisemed the segge semlyly fayre.
And quy the pentangel apendez to that prynce noble
I am in tent yow to telle, thof tary hyt me schulde:
625 Hit is a syngne that Salomon set sumquyle
In bytoknyng of trawthe, bi tytle that hit habbez,
For hit is a figure that haldez fyve poyntez,
And uche lyne umbelappez and loukez in other,
And ayquere hit is endelez; and Englych hit callen
630 Overal, as I here, the endeles knot.
Forthy hit acordez to this knyght and to his cler armez,
For ay faythful in fyve and sere fyve sythez
Gawan watz for gode knawen, and as golde pured,
Voyded of uche vylany, wyth vertuez ennourned
635 　　　　in mote;
　　Forthy the pentangel nwe
　　He ber in schelde and cote,
　　As tulk of tale most trwe
　　And gentylest knyght of lote.

640 Fyrst he watz funden fautlez in his fyve wyttez,
And eft fayled never the freke in his fyve fyngres,
And alle his afyaunce upon folde watz in the fyve woundez

So that the whole glittered and shone like the sun.
Then Gawain seizes his helmet and kisses it quickly,   605
That was strongly stapled and padded inside.
It stood high on his head, fastened at the back
With a shining silk band over the mailed neck-guard,
Embroidered and studded with the finest gems
On a broad border of silk with birds covering the seams -   610
Popinjays depicted between periwinkles,
Turtledoves and true-love flowers embroidered so thick
As if many women had worked on it seven years
       in town.
    A circlet still more precious   615
    Was ringed about his head,
    Made with perfect diamonds
    Of every brilliant shade.

Then they brought out the shield of shining gules,
With the pentangle painted on it in pure gold.   620
He swings it over his baldric, throws it round his neck,
Where it suited the knight extremely well.
And why the pentangle should befit that noble prince
I intend to explain, even should that delay me.
It is a symbol that Solomon designed long ago   625
As an emblem of fidelity, and justly so;
For it is a figure consisting of five points,
Where each line overlaps and locks into another,
And the whole design is continuous, and in England is called
Everywhere, I am told, the endless knot.   630
Therefore it suits this knight and his shining arms,
For always faithful in five ways, and five times in each case,
Gawain was reputed as virtuous, like refined gold,
Devoid of all vice, and with all courtly virtues
       adorned.
    So this new-painted sign   635
    He bore on shield and coat,
    As man most true of speech
    And fairest-spoken knight.

First he was judged perfect in his five senses,   640
And next his five fingers never lost their dexterity;
And all his earthly faith was in the five wounds

That Cryst caght on the croys, as the crede tellez;
And quere-so-ever thys mon in melly watz stad,
His thro thoght watz in that, thurgh alle other thyngez,
That alle his forsnes he feng at the fyve joyez
That the hende heven-quene had of hir chylde;
At this cause the knyght comlyche hade
In the inore half of his schelde hir image depaynted,
That quen he blusched therto his belde never payred.
The fyft fyve that I fynde that the frek used
Watz fraunchyse and felaghschyp forbe al thyng,
His clannes and his cortaysye croked were never,
And pité, that passez alle poyntez: thyse pure fyve
Were harder happed on that hathel then on any other.
Now alle these fyve sythez, for sothe, were fetled on this knyght,
And uchone halched in other, that non ende hade,
And fyched upon fyve poyntez, that fayld never,
Ne samned never in no syde, ne sundred nouther,
Withouten ende at any noke I oquere fynde,
Whereever the gomen bygan, or glod to an ende.
Therfore on his schene schelde schapen watz the knot
Ryally wyth red golde upon rede gowlez,
That is the pure pentaungel wyth the peple called
      with lore.
    Now graythed is Gawan gay,
    And laght his launce ryght thore,
    And gef them alle goud day,
    He wende for evermore.

He sperres the sted with the spurez and sprong on his way,
So stif that the ston-fyr stroke out therafter.
Al that sey that semly syked in hert,
And sayde softly al same segges til other,
Carande for that comly, 'Bi Kryst, hit is scathe
That thou leude, schal be lost, that art of lyf noble!
To fynde hys fere upon folde, in fayth, is not ethe.
Warloker to haf wroght had more wyt bene,
And haf dyght yonder dere a duk to have worthed;
A lowande leder of ledez in londe hym wel semez,
And so had better haf ben then britned to noght,
Hadet wyth an alvisch mon, for angardez pryde.
Who knew ever any kyng such counsel to take

That Christ suffered on the cross, as the creed declares.
And wherever this man found himself in battle
His fixed thought was that, above all other things,   *645*
All his fortitude should come from the five joys
That the mild Queen of Heaven found in her child.
For this reason the gracious knight had
Her image depicted on the inside of his shield,
So that when he glanced at it his heart never quailed.   *650*
The fifth group of five the man respected, I hear,
Was generosity and love of fellow-men above all;
His purity and courtesy were never lacking,
And surpassing the others, compassion: these noble five
Were more deepy implanted in that man than any other.   *655*
Now truly, all these five groups were embodied in that knight,
Each one linked to the others in an endless design,
Based upon five points that was never unfinished,
Not uniting in one line nor separating either;
Without ending anywhere at any point that I find,   *660*
No matter where the line began or ran to an end.
Therefore the knot was fashioned on his bright shield
Royally with red gold upon red gules,
That is called the true pentangle by learned people
        who know.   *665*
     Now Gawain, lance in hand,
     Is ready to depart;
     He bade them all farewell,
     Not to return, he thought.

He set spurs to his horse and sprang on his way   *670*
So vigorously that sparks flew up from the stones.
All who watched that fair knight leave sighed from the heart,
And together whispered one to another,
Distressed for that handsome one, 'What a pity indeed
That your life must be squandered, noble as you are!   *675*
To find his equal on earth is not easy, in faith.
To have acted more cautiously would have been much wiser,
And have appointed that dear man to become a duke:
To be a brilliant leader of men, as he is well suited,
And would better have been so than battered to nothing,   *680*
Beheaded by an ogrish man out of excessive pride.
Whoever knew a king to take such foolish advice

As knyghtez in cavelaciounz on Crystmasse gomnez!'
Wel much watz the warme water that waltered of yghen,
685 When that semly syre soght fro tho wonez
thad daye.
He made non abode,
Bot wyghtly went hys way;
Mony wylsum way he rode,
690 The bok as I herde say.

Now ridez this renk thurgh the ryalme of Logres,
Sir Gawan, on Godez halve, thagh hym no gomen thoght.
Oft leudlez and alone he lengez on nyghtez
Ther he fonde noght hym byfore the fare that he lyked.
695 Hade he no fere bot his fole by frythez and dounez,
Ne no gome bot God bi gate wyth to carp,
Til that he neghed ful neghe into the Northe Walez.
Alle the iles of Anglesay on lyft half he haldez,
And farez over the fordez by the forlondez,
700 Over at the Holy Hede, til he hade eft bonk
In the wyldrenesse of Wyrale; wonde ther bot lyte
That auther God other gome wyth goud hert lovied.
And ay he frayned as he ferde, at frekez that he met,
If thay hade herde any karp of a knyght grene,
705 In any grounde theraboute, of the grene chapel;
And al nykked hym wyth nay, that never in her lyve
Thay seye never no segge that watz of suche hwez
of grene.
The knyght tok gates straunge
710 In mony a bonk unbene,
His cher ful oft con chaunge
That chapel er he myght sene.

Mony klyf he overclambe in contrayez straunge,
Fer floten fro his frendez fremedly he rydez.
715 At uche warthe other water ther the wyghe passed
He fonde a foo hym byfore, bot ferly hit were,
And that so foule and so felle that feght hym byhode.
So mony mervayl bi mount ther the mon fyndez,
Hit were to tore for to telle of the tenthe dole.
720 Sumwhyle wyth wormez he werrez, and with wolves als,
Sumwhyle wyth wodwos that woned in the knarrez,

As knights offer in arguments about Christmas games?'
A great deal of warm water trickled from eyes
When that elegant lord set out from the city   *685*
       that day.
     He did not linger there,
     But swiftly went his way;
     Taking perplexing roads
     As I have heard books say.   *690*

Now rides this knight through the realm of England,
Sir Gawain, in God's name, though he found it no pleasure.
Often friendless and alone he passes his nights,
Finding before him no food that he liked.
He had no fellow but his horse by forest and hill,   *695*
And no one but God to talk to on the way,
Until he came very close to the north part of Wales.
All the islands of Anglesey he keeps on his left,
And crosses over the fords at the headlands,
There at the Holyhead, and came ashore again   *700*
In the wilderness of Wirral. There few people lived
Whom either God or good-hearted men could love.
And always as he rode he asked those whom he met
If they had heard anyone speak of a green knight
Or of a green chapel in any place round about;   *705*
And they all answered him no, that never in their lives
Had they ever seen a man who had such colour
       of green.
     Strange roads the knight pursued
     Through many a dreary space,   *710*
     Turning from side to side
     To find the meeting-place.

Many fells he climbed over in territory strange,
Far distant from his friends like an alien he rides.
At every ford or river where the knight crossed   *715*
He found an enemy facing him, unless he was in luck,
And so ugly and fierce that he was forced to give fight.
So many wonders befell him in the hills,
It would be tedious to recount the least part of them.
Sometimes he fights dragons, and wolves as well,   *720*
Sometimes with wild men who dwelt among the crags;

Bothe wyth bullez and berez, and borez otherquyle,
And etaynez that hym anelede of the heghe felle;
Nade he ben dughty and dryghe, and Dryghtyn had served,
725 Douteles he hade ben ded and dreped ful ofte.
For werre wrathed hym not so much that wynter nas wors,
When the colde cler water fro the cloudez schadde,
And fres er hit falle myght to the fale erthe.
Ner slayn wyth the slete he sleped in his yrnes
730 Mo nyghtez then innoghe in naked rokkez,
Ther as claterande fro the crest the colde borne rennez,
And henged heghe over his hede in hard iisse-ikkles.
Thus in peryl and payne and plytes ful harde
Bi contray caryez this knyght, tyl Krystmasse even,
735 al one;
The knyght wel that tyde
To Mary made his mone,
That ho hym red to ryde
And wysse hym to sum wone.

740 Bi a mounte on the morne meryly he rydes
Into a forest ful dep, that ferly watz wylde;
Highe hillez on uche a halve, and holtwodez under
Of hore okez ful hoge a hundreth togeder;
The hasel and the haghthorne were harled al samen,
745 With roghe raged mosse rayled aywhere,
With mony bryddez unblythe upon bare twyges,
That pitosly ther piped for pyne of the colde.
The gome upon Gryngolet glydez hem under,
Thurgh mony misy and myre, mon al hym one,
750 Carande for his costes, lest he ne kever schulde
To se the servyse of that syre, that on that self nyght
Of a burde watz borne, our baret to quelle;
And therfore sykyng he sayde, 'I beseche the, lorde,
And Mary, that is myldest moder so dere,
755 Of sum herber ther heghly I myght here masse,
And thy matynez to-morne, mekely I ask,
And therto prestly I pray my pater and ave
and crede.'
He rode in his prayere,
760 And cryed for his mysdede,
He sayned hym in sythes sere,

Both with bulls and with bears, and at other times boars,
And ogres who chased him across the high fells.
Had he not been valiant and resolute, trusting in God,
He would surely have died or been killed many times.   725
For fighting troubled him less than the rigorous winter,
When cold clear water fell from the clouds
And froze before it could reach the faded earth.
Half dead with the cold Gawain slept in his armour
More nights than enough among the bare rocks,   730
Where splashing from the hilltops the freezing stream runs,
And hung over his head in hard icicles.
Thus in danger, hardship and continual pain
This knight rides across the land until Christmas Eve
        alone.   735
      Earnestly Gawain then
      Prayed Mary that she send
      Him guidance to some place
      Where he might lodging find.

Over a hill in the morning in splendour he rides   740
Into a dense forest, wondrously wild;
High slopes on each side and woods at their base
Of massive grey oaks, hundreds growing together;
Hazel and hawthorn were densely entangled,
Thickly festooned with coarse shaggy moss,   745
Where many miserable birds on the bare branches
Wretchedly piped for torment of the cold.
The knight on Gringolet hurries under the trees,
Through many a morass and swamp, a solitary figure,
Troubled about his plight, lest he should be unable   750
To attend mass for that lord who on that same night
Was born of a maiden, our suffering to end;
And therefore sighing he prayed, 'I beg of you, Lord,
And Mary, who is gentlest mother so dear,
For some lodging where I might devoutly hear mass   755
And your matins tomorrow, humbly I ask;
And to this end promptly repeat my pater and ave
        and creed.'
      Bewailing his misdeeds,
      And praying as he rode,   760
      He often crossed himself

And sayde, 'Cros Kryst me spede!'

Nade he sayned hymself, segge, bot thrye,
Er he watz war in the wod of a wone in a mote,
765 Abof a launde, on a lawe, loken under boghez
Of mony borelych bole aboute bi the diches:
A castle the comlokest that ever knyght aghte,
Pyched on a prayere, a park al aboute,
With a pyked palays pyned ful thik,
770 That umbeteye mony tre mo then two myle.
That holde on that on syde the hathel avysed
As hit schemered and schon thurgh the schyre okez;
Thenne hatz he hendly of his helme, and heghly he thonkez
Jesus and sayn Gilyan, that gentyle ar bothe,
775 That cortaysly had hym kydde, and his cry herkened.
'Now bone hostel,' cothe the burne, 'I beseche yow yette!'
Thenne gerdez he to Gryngolet with the gilt helez,
And he ful chauncely hatz chosen to the chef gate,
That broght bremly the burne to the bryge ende
780   in haste.
    The bryge watz breme upbrayde,
    The gatez were stoken faste,
    The wallez were wel arayed
    Hit dut no wyndez blaste.

785 The burne bode on blonk, that on bonk hoved
Of the depe double dich that drof to the place;
The walle wod in the water wonderly depe,
And eft a ful huge heght hit haled upon lofte
Of harde hewen ston up to the tablez,
790 Enbaned under the abataylment in the best lawe;
And sythen garytez ful gaye gered bitwene,
Wyth mony luflych loupe that louked ful clene:
A better barbican that burne blusched upon never.
And innermore he behelde that halle ful hyghe,
795 Towres telded bytwene, trochet ful thik,
Fayre fylyolez that fyghed, and ferlyly long,
With corvon coprounez craftyly sleghe.
Chalkwhyt chymnees ther ches he innoghe
Upon bastel rovez, that blenked ful quyte;
800 So mony pynakle paynted watz poudred ayquere,

44

Crying, 'Prosper me, Christ's blood!'

Hardly had he crossed himself, that man, three times,
Before he caught sight through the trees of a moated building
Standing over a field, on a mound, surrounded by boughs   765
Of many a massive tree-trunk enclosing the moat:
The most splendid castle ever owned by a knight,
Set on a meadow, a park all around,
Closely guarded by a spiked palisade
That encircled many trees for more than two miles.   770
That side of the castle Sir Gawain surveyed
As it shimmered and shone through the fine oaks;
Then graciously takes off his helmet, and devoutly thanks
Jesus and St Julian, who kindly are both,
Who had treated him courteously, and listened to his prayer.   775
'Now good lodging,' said the man, 'I beg you to grant!'
Then he urged Gringolet forward with his gilt spurs,
And by good chance happened upon the main path
That led the knight directly to the end of the drawbridge
      with speed.   780
    The bridge was drawn up tight,
    The gates were bolted fast.
    The walls were strongly built,
    They feared no tempest's blast.

The knight sat on his horse, pausing on the slope   785
Of the deep double ditch that surrounded the place.
The wall stood in the water incredibly deep,
And then soared up above an astonishing height,
Made of squared stone up to the cornice,
With coursings under battlements in the latest style.   790
At intervals splendid watch-towers were placed,
With many neat loop-holes that could be tightly shut:
Better outworks of a castle the knight had never seen.
Further inside he noticed a lofty hall
With towers set at intervals, richly ornate,   795
Splendid pinnacles fitted into them, wonderfully tall,
Topped by carved crocketing, skilfully worked.
Chalk-white chimneys he saw there without number
On the roofs of the towers, that brilliantly shone.
So many painted pinnacles were scattered everywhere,   800

Among the castel carnelez clambred so thik
That pared out of papure purely hit semed.
The fre freke on the fole hit fayre innoghe thoght,
If he myght kever to com the cloyster wythinne,
805   To herber in that hostel whyl halyday lested,
        avinant.
      He calde, and son ther com
      A porter pure plesaunt,
      On the wal his ernde he nome,
810   And haylsed the knyght erraunt.

'Gode sir,' quoth Gawan, 'woldez thou go myn ernde,
To the hegh lorde of this hous, herber to crave?'
'Ye, Peter,' quoth the porter, 'and purely I trowee
That ye be, wyghe, welcum to wone quyle yow lykez.'
815   Then yede the wyghe yerne and com agayn swythe,
And folke frely hym wyth, to fonge the knyght.
Thay let doun the grete draght and derely out yeden,
And kneled doun on her knes upon the colde erthe
To welcum this ilk wygh as worthy hom thoght;
820   Thay yolden hym the brode gate, yarked up wyde,
And he hem raysed rekenly, and rod over the brygge.
Sere segges hym sesed by sadel, quel he lyght,
And sythen stabled his stede stif men innoghe.
Knyghtez and swyerez comen doun thenne
825   For to bryng this buurne wyth blys into halle;
Quen he hef up his helme, ther hyghed innoghe
For to hent it at his honde, the hende to serven;
His bronde and his blasoun both thay token.
Then haylsed he ful hendly tho hathelez uchone,
830   And mony proud mon ther presed that prynce to honour.
Alle hasped in his hegh wede to halle thay hym wonnen,
Ther fayre fyre upon flet fersly brenned.
Thenne the lorde of the lede loutez fro his chambre
For to mete wyth menske the mon on the flor;
835   He sayde, 'Ye ar welcum to welde as yow lykez
That here is: al is yowre awen, to have at yowre wylle
        and welde.'
      'Graunt mercy,' quoth Gawayn,
      'Ther Kryst hit yow foryelde.'
840   As frekez that semed fayn

Thickly clustered among the castle's embrasures,
That, truly, the building seemed cut out of paper.
To the noble on the horse it was an attractive thought
That he might gain entrance into the castle,
To lodge in that building during the festival days   *805*
        at his ease.
    A cheerful porter came
    In answer to his shout,
    Who stationed on the wall
    Greeted the questing knight.   *810*

'Good sir,' said Gawain, 'will you carry my message
To the master of this house, to ask for lodging?'
'Yes, by St Peter,' said the porter, 'and I truly believe
That you are welcome, sir, to stay as long as you please.'
Then the man went speedily and quickly returned,   *815*
Bringing others with him, to welcome the knight.
They lowered the great drawbridge and graciously came out,
Kneeling down on their knees upon the cold ground
To welcome this knight in the way they thought fit.
They gave him passage through the broad gate, set open wide,   *820*
And he courteously bade them rise, and rode over the bridge.
Several men held his saddle while he dismounted,
And then strong men in plenty stabled his horse.
Knights and squires came down then
To escort this man joyfully into the hall.   *825*
When Gawain took off his helmet, several jumped forward
To receive it from his hand, serving that prince.
His sword and his shield they took from him both.
Then he greeted politely every one of these knights,
And many proud men pressed forward to honour that noble.   *830*
Still dressed in his armour they brought him into hall,
Where a blazing fire was fiercely burning.
Then the lord of that company comes down from his chamber,
To show his respect by meeting Gawain there.
He said, 'You are welcome to do as you please   *835*
With everything here: all is yours, to have and command
        as you wish.'
    Said Gawain, 'Thanks indeed,
    Christ repay your noblesse.'
    Like men overjoyed   *840*

Ayther other in armez con felde.

Gawan glynte on the gome that godly hym gret,
And thught hit a bolde burne that the burgh aghte;
A hoge hathel for the nonez, and of hyghe eldee;
845 Brode, bryght, watz his berde, and al bever-hwed,
Sturne, stif on the stryththe on stalworth schonkez,
Felle face as the fyre, and fre of hys speche,
And wel hym semed, for sothe, as the segge thught,
To lede a lortschyp in lee of leudez ful gode.
850 The lorde hym charred to a chambre, and chefly cumaundez
To delyver hym a leude, hym lowly to serve;
And there were boun at his bode burnez innoghe,
That broght hym to a bryght boure, ther beddyng was noble,
Of cortynes of clere sylk wyth cler golde hemmez,
855 And covertorez ful curious with comlych panez
Of bryght blaunner above, enbrawded bisydez,
Rudelez rennande on ropez, red golde ryngez,
Tapitez tyght to the wowe of tuly and tars,
And under fete, on the flet, of folyande sute.
860 Ther he watz dispoyled, wyth speches of myerthe,
The burne of his bruny and of his bryght wedez.
Ryche robes ful rad renkkez hym broghten,
For to charge and to chaunge, and chose of the best.
Sone as he on hent, and happed therinne,
865 That sete on hym semly wyth saylande skyrtez,
The ver by his visage verayly hit semed
Welnegh to uche hathel, alle on hwes
Lowande and lufly alle his lymmez under,
That a comloker knyght never Kryst made,
870   hem thoght.
        Whethen in worlde he were,
        Hit semed as he moght
        Be prynce withouten pere
        In felde ther felle men foght.

875 A cheyer byfore the chemné, ther charcole brenned,
Watz grathed for Sir Gawan graythely with clothez,
Whyssynes upon queldepoyntes that koynt wer bothe;
And thenne a meré mantyle watz on that mon cast
Of a broun bleeaunt, enbrauded ful ryche

Each hugged the other close.

Gawain studied the man who greeted him courteously,
And thought him a bold one who governed the castle ,
A great-sized knight indeed, in the prime of life;
Broad and glossy was his beard, all reddish-brown,   845
Stern-faced, standing firmly on powerful legs;
With a face fierce as fire, and noble in speech,
Who truly seemed capable, it appeared to Gawain,
Of being master of a castle with outstanding knights.
The lord led him to a chamber and quickly orders   850
A man to be assigned to him, humbly to serve;
And several attendants stood ready at his command
Who took him to a fine bedroom with marvellous bedding;
Curtains of pure silk with shining gold borders,
And elaborate coverlets with splendid facing   855
Of bright ermine on top, embroidered all around;
Curtains on golden rings, running on cords.
Walls covered with hangings from Tharsia and Toulouse
And underfoot on the floor of a matching kind.
There he was stripped, with joking remarks,   860
That knight, of his mail-shirt and his fine clothes.
Men hurried to bring him costly robes
To choose from the best of them, change and put on.
As soon as he took one and dressed himself in it,
Which suited him well with its flowing skirts,   865
Almost everyone truly supposed from his looks
That spring had arrived in all its colours;
His limbs so shining and attractive under his clothes
That a handsomer knight God never made,
                    it seemed.   870
          Wherever he came from,
          He must be, so they thought,
          A prince unparalleled
          In field where warriors fought.

A chair before the fireplace where charcoal glowed   875
Was made ready with coverings for Gawain at once:
Cushions set on quilted spreads, both skilfully made,
And then a handsome robe was thrown over the man
Made of rich brown material, with embroidery rich,

880 And fayre furred wythinne with fellez of the best,
Alle of ermyn in erde, his hode of the same;
And he sette in that settel semlych ryche,
And achaufed hym chefly, and thenne his cher mended.
Sone watz telded up a tabil on trestez ful fayre,
885 Clad wyth a clene clothe that cler quyt schewed,
Sanap, and salure, and sylverin sponez.
The wyghe wesche at his wylle and went to his mete:
Seggez hym served semly innoghe,
Wyth sere sewes and sete, sesounde of the best,
890 Double-felde, as hit fallez, and fele kyn fischez,
Summe baken in bred, summe brad on the gledez,
Summe sothen, summe in sewe savered with spyces,
And ay sawes so sleghe that the segge lyked.
The freke calde hit a fest ful frely and ofte
895 Ful hendely, quen alle the hatheles rehayted hym at onez,
        as hende,
    'This penaunce now ye take,
    And eft hit schal amende.'
    That mon much merthe con make,
900   For wyn in his hed that wende.

Thenne watz spyed and spured upon spare wyse
Bi prevé poyntez of that prynce, put to hymselven,
That he biknew cortaysly of the court that he were
That athel Arthure the hende haldez hym one,
905 That is the ryche ryal kyng of the Rounde Table,
And hit watz Wawen hymself that in that won syttez,
Comen to that Krystmasse, as case hym then lymped.
When the lorde hade lerned that he the leude hade,
Loude laghed he therat, so lef hit hym thoght,
910 And alle the men in that mote maden much joye
To apere in his presense prestly that tyme,
That alle prys and prowes and pured thewes
Apendes to hys persoun, and praysed is ever;
Byfore alle men upon molde his mensk is the most.
915 Uch segge ful softly sayde to his fere:
'Now schal we semlych se sleghtez of thewez
And the teccheles termes of talkyng noble,
Wich spede is in speche unspurd may we lerne,
Syn we haf fonged that fyne fader of nurture.

And well fur-lined inside with the very best pelts,   880
All of ermine in fact, with a matching hood.
Becomingly rich in attire he sat in that chair,
Quickly warmed himself, and then his expression softened.
Soon a table was deftly set up on trestles,
Spread with a fine tablecloth, brilliantly white,   885
With overcloth and salt-cellar, and silver spoons.
When he was ready Gawain washed and sat down to his meal.
Men served him with every mark of respect,
With many excellent dishes, wonderfully seasoned,
In double portions, as is fitting, and all kinds of fish: 890
Some baked in pastry, some grilled over coals,
Some boiled, some in stews flavoured with spices,
Always with subtle sauces that the knight found tasty.
Many times he graciously called it a feast,
Courteously when the knights all urged him together,   895
             as polite,
    'Accept this penance now,
    Soon you'll be better fed.'
    Gawain grew full of mirth
    As wine went to his head.   900

Then he was tactfully questioned and asked
By discreet enquiry addressed to that prince,
So that he must politely admit he belonged to the court
Which noble Arthur, that gracious man, rules alone,
Who is the great and royal king of the Round Table;   905
And that it was Gawain himself who was sitting there,
Having arrived there at Christmas, as his fortune chanced.
When the lord of the castle heard who was his guest,
He laughed loudly at the news, so deeply was he pleased;
And all the men in the castle were overjoyed   910
To make the acquaintance quickly then
Of the man to whom all excellence and valour belongs,
Whose refined manners are everywhere praised,
And whose fame exceeds any other person's on earth.
Each knight whispered to his companion,   915
'Now we shall enjoy seeing displays of good manners,
And the irreproachable terms of noble speech;
The art of conversation we can learn unasked,
Since we have taken in the source of good breeding.

920   God hatz geven us his grace godly for sothe,
        That such a gest as Gawan grauntez us to have,
        When burnez blythe of his burthe schal sitte
            and synge.
        In menyng of manerez mere
925   This burne now schal us bryng,
        I hope that may hym here
        Schal lerne of luf-talkyng.'

        Bi that the diner watz done and the dere up
        Hit watz negh at the niyght neghed the tyme.
930   Chaplaynez to the chapeles chosen the gate,
        Rungen ful rychely, ryght as thay schulden,
        To the hersum evensong of the hyghe tyde.
        The lorde loutes therto, and the lady als,
        Into a cumly closet coyntly ho entrez.
935   Gawan glydez ful gay and gos theder sone;
        The lorde laches hym by the lappe and ledez hym to sytte,
        And couthly hym knowez and callez hym his nome,
        And sayde he watz the welcomest wyghe of the worlde;
        And he hym thonkked throly, and ayther halched other,
940   And seten soberly samen the servise quyle.
        Thenne lyst the lady to loke on the knyght,
        Thenne com ho of hir closet with mony cler burdez.
        Ho watz the fayrest in felle, of flesche and of lyre,
        And of compas and colour and costes, of all other,
945   And wener then Wenore, as the wyght thoght.
        Ho ches thurgh the chaunsel to cheryche that hende:
        An other lady hir lad bi the lyft honde,
        That watz alder then ho, an auncian hit semed,
        And heghly honowred with hathelez aboute.
950   Bot unlyke on to loke tho ladyes were,
        For if the yonge watz yep, yolwe watz that other;
        Riche red on that on rayled ayquere,
        Rugh ronkled chekez that other on rolled;
        Kerchofes of that on, wyth mony cler perlez,
955   Hir brest and hir bryght throte bare displayed,
        Schon schyrer then snawe that schedez on hillez;
        That other wyth a gorger watz gered over the swyre,
        Chymbled over hir blake chyn with chalkquyte vayles,
        Hir frount folden in sylk, enfoubled ayquere,

Truly, God has been gracious to us indeed,   920
In allowing us to receive such a guest as Gawain,
Whose birth men will happily sit down and celebrate
       in song.
    In knowledge of fine manners
    This man has expertise;   925
    I think that those who hear him,
    Will learn what love-talk is.'

When dinner was finished and Gawain had risen,
The time had drawn on almost to night:
Chaplains made their way to the castle chapels,   930
Rang their bells loudly, just as they should,
For devout evensong on that holy occasion.
The lord makes his way there, and his lady too,
Who gracefully enters a finely carved pew.
Gawain hastens there, smartly dressed, and quickly arrives;   935
The lord takes him by the sleeve and leads him to a seat,
And greets him familiarly, calling him by his name,
And said he was the welcomest guest in the world.
Gawain thanked him heartily, and the two men embraced,
And sat gravely together while the service lasted.   940
Then the lady wished to set eyes on the knight
And left her pew with many fair women.
She was the loveliest on earth in complexion and features,
In figure, in colouring and behaviour above all others,
And more beautiful than Guenevere, it seemed to the knight.   945
She came through the chancel to greet him courteously,
Another lady leading her by the left hand,
Who was older than she, an aged one it seemed,
And respectfully treated by the assembled knights.
But very different in looks were those two ladies,   950
For where the young one was fresh, the other was withered;
Every part of that one was rosily aglow:
On that other, rough wrinkled cheeks hung in folds.
Many bright pearls adorned the kerchiefs of one,
Whose breast and white throat, uncovered and bare,   955
Shone more dazzling than snow new-fallen on hills;
The other wore a gorget over her neck,
Her swarthy chin wrapped in chalkwhite veils,
Her forehead enfolded in silk, muffled up everywhere,

960   Toreted and treleted with tryfles aboute,
That noght watz bare of that burde bot the blake browes,
The tweyne yghen and the nase, the naked lyppez,
And those were soure to se and sellyly blered;
A mensk lady on molde mon may hire calle,
965   for Gode!
      Hir body watz schort and thik,
      Hir buttokez balgh and brode,
      More lykkerwys on to lyk
      Watz that scho hade on lode.

970   When Gawayn glent on that gay, that graciously loked,
Wyth leve laght of the lorde he lent hem agaynes;
The alder he haylses, heldande ful lowe,
The loveloker he lappez a lyttel in armez,
He kysses hir comlyly, and knyghtly he melez.
975   Thay kallen hym of aquoyntaunce, and he hit quyk askez
To be hir servaunt sothly, if hemself lyked.
Thay tan hym bytwene hem, wyth talkyng hym leden
To chambre, to chemné, and chefly thay asken
Spycez, that unsparely men speded hom to bryng,
980   And the wynnelych wyne therwith uche tyme.
The lorde luflych aloft lepez ful ofte,
Mynned merthe to be made upon mony sythez,
Hent heghly of his hode, and on a spere henged,
And wayned hom to wynne the worchip therof,
985   That most myrthe myght meve that Crystenmasse whyle:
'And I schal fonde, bi my fayth, to fylter wyth the best
Er me wont the wede, with help of my frendez.'
Thus wyth laghande lotez the lorde hit tayt makez,
For to glade Sir Gawayn with gomnez in halle
990   that nyght,
      Til that hit watz tyme
      The lord comaundet lyght;
      Sir Gawen his leve con nyme
      And to his bed hym dight.

995   On the morne, as uch mon mynez that tyme
That Dryghtyn for oure destyné to deye watz borne,
Wele waxez in uche a won in world for his sake;
So did hit there on that day thurgh dayntés mony.

With embroidered hems and lattice-work of tiny stitching,   960
So that nothing was exposed of her but her black brows,
Her two eyes and her nose, her naked lips,
Which were repulsive to see and shockingly bleared.
A noble lady indeed you might call her,
        by God!   965
      With body squat and thick,
      And buttocks bulging broad,
      More delectable in looks
      Was the lady whom she led.

Gawain glanced at that beauty, who favoured him with a look,   970
And taking leave of the lord he walked towards them.
The older one he salutes with a deep bow,
And takes the lovelier one briefly into his arms,
Kisses her respectfully and courteously speaks.
They ask to make his acquaintance, and he quickly begs   975
Truly to be their servant, if that would please them.
They place him between them and lead him, still chatting,
To a private room, to the fireplace, and immediately call
For spiced cakes, which men hurried to bring them unstinted,
Together with marvellous wine each time they asked.   980
The lord jumps up politely on several occasions,
Repeatedly urging his guests to make merry;
Graciously pulled off his hood and hung it on a spear,
And encouraged them to gain honour by winning it,
So that the Christmas season would abound with mirth.   985
'And I shall try, on my word, to compete with the best,
Before I lose my hood, with the help of my friends.'
Thus with laughing words the lord makes merry,
To keep Sir Gawain amused with games in hall
        that night,   990
      Until it was so late
      That lights were ordered in;
      Then taking courteous leave
      To chamber went Gawain.

On the next day, when everyone remembers the time   995
When God who died for our salvation was born,
Joy spreads through every dwelling on earth for his sake.
So did it there on that day, through numerous pleasures;

Bothe at mes and at mele messes ful quaynt
1000 Derf men upon dece drest of the best.
The olde auncian wyf heghest ho syttez,
The lorde lufly her by lent, as I trowe;
Gawan and the gay burde togeder thay seten,
Even inmyddez, as the messe metely come,
1005 And sythen thurgh al the sale as hem best semed.
Bi uche grome at his degré graythely watz served,
Ther watz mete, ther watz myrthe, ther watz much joye,
That for to telle therof hit me tene were,
And to poynte hit yet I pyned me paraventure.
1010 Bot yet I wot that Wawen and the wale burde
Such comfort of her compaynye caghten togeder
Thurgh her dere dalyaunce of her derne wordez,
Wyth clene cortays carp closed fro fylthe,
That hor play watz passande uche prynce gomen,
1015   in vayres.
Trumpes and nakerys,
Much pypyng ther repayres;
Uche mon tented hys,
And thay two tented thayres.

1020 Much dut watz ther dryven that day and that other,
And the thryd as thro thronge in therafter;
The joye of sayn Jonez day watz gentyle to here,
And watz the last of the layk, leudez ther thoghten.
Ther wer gestes to go upon the gray morne,
1025 Forthy wonderly thay woke, and the wyn dronken,
Daunsed ful dreghly wyth dere carolez.
At the last, when hit watz late, thay lachen her leve,
Uchon to wende on his way that watz wyghe straunge.
Gawan gef hym god day, the godmon hym lachchez,
1030 Ledes hym to his awen chambre, the chemné bysyde,
And there he drawez hym on dryghe, and derely hym thonkkez
Of the wynne worschip that he hym wayved hade,
As to honour his hous on that hygh tyde,
And enbelyse his burgh with his bele chere.
1035 'Iwysse, sir, quyl I leve, me worthez the better
That Gawayn hatz ben my gest at Goddez awen fest.'
'Grant merci, sir,' quoth Gawayn, 'in god fayth hit is yowrez,
Al the honour is your awen — the heghe kyng yow yelde!

Both light meals and great dishes cunningly prepared
And of exquisite quality bold men served on the dais.   1000
The ancient lady sits in the place of honour,
The lord politely taking his place by her, I believe.
Gawain and the lovely lady were seated together,
Right in the middle of the table, where food duly came,
And was then served throughout the hall in proper sequence.   1005
By the time each man had been served according to rank,
Such food and such merriment, so much enjoyment were there
That to tell you about it would give me much trouble,
Especially if I tried to describe it in detail.
Yet I know that Gawain and his beautiful partner   1010
Found such enjoyment in each other's company,
Through a playful exchange of private remarks,
And well-mannered small-talk, unsullied by sin,
That their pleasure surpassed every princely amusement,
            for sure.   1015
        Trumpets, kettledrums
        And piping roused all ears.
        Each man fulfilled his wishes,
        And those two followed theirs.

Great joy filled that day and the one following,   1020
And a third as delightful came pressing after;
The revelry on St John's Day was glorious to hear,
And was the end of the festivities, the people supposed.
The guests were to leave early next morning,
And so they revelled all night, drinking the wine   1025
And ceaselessly dancing and carolling songs.
At last, when it was late, they take their leave,
Each one who was a guest there to go on his way.
Gawain bids goodbye to his host, who takes hold of him,
Leads him to his own room, beside the fire,   1030
And there he detains him, thanks him profusely
For the wonderful kindness that Gawain had shown
By honouring his house at that festive time,
And by gracing the castle with his charming presence.
'Indeed, sir, as long as I live I shall be the better   1035
Because Gawain was my guest at God's own feast.'
'All my thanks, sir,' said Gawain, 'in truth it is yours,
All the honour falls to you, and may the high king repay you!

And I am wyghe at your wylle to worch youre hest,
1040 As I am halden therto, in hyghe and in lowe,
bi right.'
The lorde fast can hym payne
To holde lenger the knyght;
To hym answarez Gawayn
1045 Bi non way that he myght.

Then frayned the freke ful fayre at himselven
Quat derve dede had hym dryven at that dere tyme
So kenly fro the kyngez kourt to kayre al his one,
Er the halidayez holly were halet out of toun.
1050 'For sothe, sir,' quoth the segge, 'ye sayn bot the trawthe,
A heghe ernde and a hasty me hade fro tho wonez,
For I am sumned myselfe to sech to a place,
I ne wot in the worlde whederwarde to wende hit to fynde.
I nolde bot if I hit negh myght on Nw Yeres morne
1055 For alle the londe inwyth Logres, so me oure lorde help!
Forthy, sir, this enquest I require yow here,
That ye telle me with trawthe if ever ye tale herde
Of the grene chapel, quere hit on grounde stondez,
And of the knyght that hit kepes, of colour of grene.
1060 Ther watz stabled bi statut a steven us bitwene
To mete that mon at that mere, yif I myght last;
And of that ilk Nw Yere bot neked now wontez,
And I wolde loke on that lede, if God me let wolde,
Gladloker, bi Goddez sun, then any god welde!
1065 Forthi, iwysse, bi yowre wylle, wende me bihoves,
Naf I now to busy bot bare thre dayez,
And me als fayn to falle feye as fayly of myyn ernde.'
Thenne laghande quoth the lorde, 'Now leng the byhoves,
For I schal teche yow to that terme bi the tymes ende,
1070 The grene chapayle upon grounde greve yow no more;
Bot ye schal be in yowre bed, burne, at thyn ese,
Quyle forth dayez, and ferk on the fyrst of the yere,
And cum to that merk at mydmorn, to make quat yow likez
in spenne.
1075 Dowellez whyle New Yeres daye,
And rys, and raykez thenne,
Mon schal yow sette in waye,
Hit is not two myle henne.'

And I am at your commandment to act on your bidding,
As I am duty bound to in everything, large or small,   1040
      by right.'
   The lord tried strenuously
   To lengthen Gawain's stay,
   But Gawain answered him
   That he could not delay.   1045

Then the lord politely enquired of the knight
What pressing need had forced him at that festive time
So urgently from the royal court to travel all alone,
Before the holy days there had completely passed.
'Indeed, sir,' said the knight, 'you are right to wonder;   1050
A task important and pressing drove me into the wild,
For I am summoned in person to seek out a place
With no idea whatever where it might be found.
I would not fail to reach it on New Year's morning
For all the land in England, so help me our Lord!   1055
Therefore, sir, this request I make of you now,
That you truthfully tell me if you ever heard talk
Of a Green Chapel, wherever it stands upon earth,
And of a knight who maintains it, who is coloured green.
A verbal agreement was settled between us   1060
To meet that man at that place, should I be alive,
And before that New Year little time now remains;
And I would face that man, if God would allow me,
More gladly, by God's son, than come by great wealth!
With your permission, therefore, I must indeed leave: 1065
I have now for my business only three short days,
And would rather be struck dead than fail in my quest.'
Then the lord said, laughing, 'Now you must stay,
For I shall direct you to your meeting at the year's end.
Let the whereabouts of the Green Chapel worry you no more;   1070
For you shall lie in your bed, sir, taking your ease
Until late in the day, and leave on the first of the year,
And reach that place at midday, to do whatever pleases you
      there.
    Stay till the year's end,   1075
    And leave on New Year's Day;
    We'll put you on the path,
    It's not two miles away.'

Thenne watz Gawan ful glad, and gomenly he laghed:
1080 'Now I thonk yow thryvandely thurgh alle other thynge,
Now acheved is my chaunce, I schal at your wylle
Dowelle, and ellez do quat ye demen.'
Thenne sesed hym the syre and set hym bysyde,
Let the ladiez be fette to lyke hem the better.
1085 Ther watz seme solace by hemself stille;
The lorde let for luf lotez so myry
As wygh that wolde of his wyte, ne wyst quat he myght.
Thenne he carped to the knyght, criande loude,
'Ye han demed to do the dede that I bidde;
1090 Wyl ye halde this hes here at thys onez?'
'Ye, sir, for sothe,' sayd the segge trwe,
'Whyl I byde in yowre borghe, be bayn to yowre hest.'
'For ye haf travayled,' quoth the tulk, 'towen fro ferre,
And sythen waked me wyth, ye arn not wel waryst
1095 Nauther of sostnaunce ne of slepe, sothly I knowe;
Ye schal lenge in your lofte, and lyghe in your ese
To-morn quyle the messequyle, and to mete wende
When ye wyl, wyth my wyf, that wyth yow schal sitte
And comfort yow with compayny, til I to cort torne;
1100   ye lende,
    And I schal erly ryse,
    On huntyng wyl I wende.'
    Gavayn grantez alle thyse,
    Hym heldande, as the hende.

1105 'Yet firre,' quoth the freke, 'a forwarde we make:
Quat-so-ever I wynne in the wod hit worthez to yourez,
And quat chek so ye acheve chaunge me therforne.
Swete, swap we so, sware with trawthe,
Quether, leude, so lymp, lere other better.'
1110 'Bi God,' quoth Gawayn the gode, 'I grant thertylle,
And that yow lyst for to layke, lef hit me thynkes.'
'Who bryngez uus this beverage, this bargayn is maked':
So sayde the lorde of that lede; thay laghed uchone,
Thay dronken and dalyeden and dalten untyghtel,
1115 Thise lordez and ladyez, quyle that hem lyked;
And sythen with Frenkysch fare and fele fayre lotez
Thay stoden and stemed and stylly speken,

Then Gawain was overjoyed, and merrily laughed:
'Now I thank you heartily for this, above everything else,   *1080*
Now my quest is accomplished, I shall at your wish
Remain here, and do whatever else you think fit.'
Then the host seized him, set Gawain by his side,
And bid the ladies be fetched to increase their delight.
They had great pleasure by themselves in private;   *1085*
In his excitement the lord uttered such merry words
Like a man out of his mind, not knowing what he did.
Then he said to the knight exuberantly,
'You have agreed to carry out whatever deed I ask,
Will you keep this promise now, at this very instant?'   *1090*
'Yes, sir, assuredly,' said the true knight,
'While I am under your roof, I obey your bidding.'
'You have wearied yourself,' said the man, 'travelling from far,
And then revelled all night with me: you have not recovered
Either your lost sleep or your nourishment, I am sure.   *1095*
You shall stay in your bed and lie at your ease
Tomorrow until mass-time, and then go to dine
When you like, with my wife, who will sit at your side
And be your charming companion until I come home.
     You stay;   *1100*
  And I shall rise at dawn
  And hunting will I go.'
  All this Gawain grants,
  With a well-mannered bow.

'Yet further,' said the man, 'let us make an agreement: *1105*
Whatever I catch in the wood shall become yours,
And whatever mishap comes your way give me in exchange.
Dear sir, let us swap so, swear me that truly,
Whatever falls to our lot, worthless or better.'
'By God,' said the good Gawain, 'I agree to that,   *1110*
And your love of amusement pleases me much.'
'If someone brings us drink, it will be an agreement,'
Said the lord of that company: everyone laughed.
They drank wine and joked and frivolously chatted
For as long as it pleased them, these lords and ladies;   *1115*
And then with exquisite manners and many gracious words
They stood at a pause, conversing quietly,

Kysten ful comlyly and kaghten her leve.
With mony leude ful lyght and lemande torches
1120 Uche burne to his bed watz broght at the laste,
    ful softe.
      To bed yet er thay yede,
      Recorded covenauntez ofte;
      The olde lorde of that leude
1125   Cowthe wel halde layk alofte.

Kissed each other affectionately and then took their leave.
With many brisk servingmen and gleaming torches
Each man was at last escorted to a bed   *1120*
       downy soft.
    Yet first, and many times
    Again the terms were sworn;
    The master of those folk
    Knew how to foster fun.   *1125*

Fitt 3

Part 3

Ful erly bifore the day the folk uprysen,
Gestes that go wolde hor gromez thay calden,
And thay busken up bilyve blonkkez to sadel,
Tyffen her takles, trussen her males,
1130   Richen hem the rychest, to ryde alle arayde,
Lepen up lightly, lachen her brydeles,
Uche wyghe on his way ther hym wel lyked.
The leve lorde of the londe watz not the last
Arayed for the rydyng, with renkkes ful mony;
1135   Ete a sop hastyly, when he hade herde masse,
With bugle to bent-felde he buskez bylyve.
By that any daylyght lemed upon erthe
He with his hatheles on hyghe horsses weren.
Thenne thise cacheres that couthe cowpled hor houndez,
1140   Unclosed the kenel dore and calde hem theroute,
Blwe bygly in buglez thre bare mote;
Braches bayed therfore and breme noyse maked;
And thay chastysed and charred on chasyng that went,
A hundreth of hunteres, as I haf herde telle,
1145   of the best.
              To trystors vewters yod,
              Couples huntes of kest;
              Ther ros for blastez gode
              Gret rurd in that forest.

1150   At the fyrst quethe of the quest quaked the wylde;
Der drof in the dale, doted for drede,
Highed to the hyghe, bot heterly thay were
Restayed with the stablye, that stoutly ascryed.
Thay let the herttez haf the gate, with the hyghe hedes,
1155   The breme bukkez also with hor brode paumez;
For the fre lorde hade defende in fermysoun tyme
That ther schulde no mon meve to the male dere.
The hindez were halden in with hay! and war!
The does dryven with gret dyn to the depe sladez.

Early before daybreak the household arose;
Guests who were leaving called for their grooms,
And they hurried quickly to saddle horses,
Make equipment ready and pack their bags.
The noblest prepare themselves to ride finely dressed,   1130
Leap nimbly into saddle, seize their bridles,
Each man taking the path that attracted him most.
The well-loved lord of the region was not the last
Prepared for riding, with a great many knights;
Snatched a hasty breakfast after hearing mass,   1135
And makes ready for the hunting-field with bugles blowing.
By the time the first glimmers of daylight appeared
He and his knights were mounted on horse.
Then experienced huntsmen coupled the hounds,
Unlocked the kennel door and ordered them out,   1140
Loudly blowing three long notes on their horns.
Hounds bayed at the sound and made a fierce noise;
And those who went straying were whipped in and turned back,
A hundred hunters, as I have been told,
        of the best.   1145
      With keepers at their posts
      Huntsmen uncoupled hounds;
      Great clamour in the woods
      From mighty horn-blasts sounds.

At the first sound of the hunt the wild creatures trembled;   1150
Deer fled from the valley, frantic with fear,
And rushed to the high ground, but were fiercely turned back
By the line of beaters, who yelled at them savagely.
They let the stags with their tall antlers pass,
And the wonderful bucks with their broad horns;   1155
For the noble lord had forbidden that in the close season
Anyone should interfere with the male deer.
The hinds were held back with shouts of hay! and war!
The does driven with great noise into the deep valleys.

1160 Ther myght mon se, as thay slypte, slenting of arwes —
At uche wende under wande wapped a flone —
That bigly bote on the broun with ful brode hedez.
What! thay brayen and bleden, bi bonkkez thay deyen,
And ay rachches in a res radly hem folwes,
1165 Hunterez wyth hyghe horne hasted hem after
Wyth such a crakkande kry as klyffes haden brusten.
What wylde so atwaped wyghes that schotten
Watz al toraced and rent at the resayt,
Bi thay were tened at the hyghe and taysed to the wattres;
1170 The ledez were so lerned at the lowe trysteres,
And the grehoundez so grete, that geten hem bylyve
And hem tofylched, as fast as frekez myght loke,
                    ther-ryght.
            The lorde for blys abloy
1175   Ful ofte con launce and lyght,
            And drof that day wyth joy
            Thus to the derk nyght.

Thus laykez this lorde by lynde-wodez evez,
And Gawayn the god mon in gay bed lygez,
1180 Lurkkez quyl the daylyght lemed on the wowes,
Under covertour ful clere, cortyned aboute;
And as in slomeryng he slode, sleghly he herde
A littel dyn at his dor, and dernly upon;
And he hevez up his hed out of the clothes,
1185 A corner of the cortyn he caght up a lyttel,
And waytez warly thiderwarde quat hit be myght.
Hit watz the ladi, loflyest to beholde,
That drow the dor after hir ful dernly and stylle,
And bowed towarde the bed; and the burne schamed,
1190 And layde hym doun lystyly and let as he slepte;
And ho stepped stilly and stel to his bedde,
Kest up the cortyn and creped withinne,
And set hir ful softly on the bed-syde,
And lenged there selly longe to loke quen he wakened.
1195 The lede lay lurked a ful longe quyle,
Compast in his concience to quat that cace myght
Meve other mount — to mervayle hym thoght,
Bot yet he sayde in hymself, 'More semly hit were
To aspye wyth my spelle in space quat ho wolde.'

There you might see, as they ran, arrows flying —   1160
At each turn in the wood a shaft shot through the air —
Deeply piercing the hide with their wide heads.
What! they cry out and bleed, on the slopes they are slaughtered,
And always swiftly pursued by the rushing hounds;
Hunters with screaming horns gallop behind   1165
With such an ear-splitting noise as if cliffs had collapsed.
Those beasts that escaped the men shooting at them
Were all pulled down and killed at the receiving points,
As they were driven from the high ground down to the streams.
The men at the lower stations were so skilful,   1170
And the greyhounds so large, that they seized them quickly
And tore them down as fast as men could number,
        right there.
    On horseback and on foot
    The lord, filled with delight,   1175
    Spent all that day in bliss
    Until the fall of night.

Thus this nobleman sports along the edges of woods,
And the good man Gawain lies in his fine bed,
Lying snug while the daylight gleamed on the walls,   1180
Under a splendid coverlet, shut in by curtains.
And as he lazily dozed, he heard slily made
A little noise at his door and it stealthily open;
And he raised up his head from the bedclothes,
Lifted a corner of the curtain a little,   1185
And takes a glimpse warily to see what it could be.
It was the lady, looking her loveliest,
Who shut the door after her carefully, not making a sound,
And came towards the bed. The knight felt confused,
And lay down again cautiously, pretending to sleep;   1190
And she approached silently, stealing to his bed,
Lifted the bed-curtain and crept within,
And seating herself softly on the bedside,
Waited there strangely long to see when he would wake.
The knight shammed sleep for a very long while,   1195
Wondering what the matter could be leading to
Or portend. It seemed an astonishing thing,
Yet he told himself, 'It would be more fitting
To discover straightway by talking just what she wants.'

1200   Then he wakenede, and wroth, and to hir warde torned,
       And unlouked his yghe-lyddez, and let as hym wondered,
       And sayned hym, as bi his saghe the saver to worthe,
           with hande.
           Wyth chynne and cheke ful swete,
1205   Both quit and red in blande,
           Ful lufly con ho lete
           Wyth lyppez smal laghande.

       'God moroun, Sir Gawayn,' sayde that gay lady,
       Ye ar a sleper unslyghe, that mon may slyde hider;
1210   Now ar ye tan as-tyt! Bot true uus may schape,
       I schal bynde yow in your bedde, that be ye trayst.'
       Al laghande the lady lanced tho bourdez.
       'Goud moroun, gay,' quoth Gawayn the blythe,
       'Me schal worthe at your wille, and that me wel lykez,
1215   For I yelde me yederly, and yeghe after grace,
       And that is the best, be my dome, for me byhovez nede':
       And thus he bourded agayn with mony a blythe laghter.
       'Bot wolde ye, lady lovely, then leve me grante,
       And deprece your prysoun, and pray hym to ryse,
1220   I wolde bowe of this bed, and busk me better;
       I schulde kever the more comfort to karp yow wyth.'
       'Nay, for sothe, beau sire,' sayde that swete,
       'Ye schal not rise of your bedde, I rych yow better.
       I schal happe yow here that other half als,
1225   And sythen karp wyth my knyght that I kaght have;
       For I wene wel, iwysse, Sir Wowen ye are,
       That alle the worlde worchipez quere-so ye ride;
       Your honour, your hendelayk is hendely praysed
       With lordez, wyth ladyes, with alle that lyf bere.
1230   And now ye are here, iwysse, and we bot oure one;
       My lorde and his ledez ar on lenthe faren,
       Other burnez in her bedde, and my burdez als,
       The dor drawen and dit with a derf haspe;
       And sythen I have in this hous hym that al lykez,
1235   I schal ware my whyle wel, quyl hit lastez,
           with tale.
           Ye ar welcum to my cors,
           Yowre awen won to wale,
           Me behovez of fyne force

Then he wakened and stretched and turned towards her,   1200
Opened his eyes and pretended surprise,
And crossed himself as if protecting himself by prayer
        and this sign.
    With lovely chin and cheek
    Of blended colour both,   1205
    Charmingly she spoke
    From her small laughing mouth.

'Good morning, Sir Gawain,' said that fair lady,
'You are an unwary sleeper, that one can steal in here:
Now you are caught in a moment! Unless we agree on a truce,   1210
I shall imprison you in your bed, be certain of that!'
Laughing merrily the lady uttered this jest.
'Good morning, dear lady,' said Gawain gaily,
'You shall do with me as you wish, and that pleases me much,
For I surrender at once, and beg for your mercy,   1215
And that is best, in my judgement, for I simply must.'
Thus he joked in return with a burst of laughter.
'But if, lovely lady, you would grant me leave
And release your captive, and ask him to rise,
I would get out of this bed and put on proper dress,   1220
And then take more pleasure in talking with you.'
'No, indeed not, good sir,' said that sweet one,
'You shall not leave your bed, I intend something better.
I shall tuck you in here on both sides of the bed,
And then chat with my knight whom I have caught.   1225
For I know well, in truth, that you are Sir Gawain,
Whom everyone reveres wherever you go;
Your good name and courtesy are honourably praised
By lords and by ladies and all folk alive.
And now indeed you are here, and we two quite alone,   1230
My husband and his men have gone far away,
Other servants are in bed, and my women too,
The door shut and locked with a powerful hasp;
And since I have under my roof the man everyone loves,
I shall spend my time well, while it lasts,   1235
        with talk.
    You are welcome to me indeed,
    Take whatever you want;
    Circumstances force me

1240   Your servaunt be, and schale.'

    'In god fayth,' quoth Gawayn, 'gayn hit me thynkkez,
    Thagh I be not now he that ye of speken;
    To reche to such reverence as ye reherce here
    I am wyghe unworthy, I wot wel myselven.
1245 Bi God, I were glad, and yow god thoght,
    At saghe other at servyce that I sette myght
    To the plesaunce of your prys — hit were a pure joye.'
    'In god fayth, Sir Gawayn,' quoth the gay lady,
    The prys and the prowes that plesez al other,
1250 If I hit lakked other set at lyght, hit were little daynté;
    Bot hit ar ladyes innoghe that lever were nowthe
    Haf the, hende, in hor holde, as I the habbe here,
    To daly with derely your daynté wordez,
    Kever hem comfort and colen her carez,
1255 Then much of the garysoun other gold that thay haven.
    Bot I louve that ilk lorde that the lyfte haldez
    I have hit holly in my honde that al desyres,
        thurghe grace.'
      Scho made hym so gret chere,
1260   That watz so fayr of face,
      The knyght with speches skere
      Answered to uche a case.

    'Madame,' quoth the myry mon, 'Mary yow yelde,
    For I haf founden, in god fayth, yowre fraunchis nobele,
1265 And other ful much of other folk fongen bi hor dedez,
    Bot the daynté that thay delen, for my disert nys even,
    Hit is the worchyp of yourself, that noght bot wel connez.'
    'Bi Mary,' quod the menskful, 'me thynk hit an other;
    For were I worth al the wone of wymmen alyve,
1270 And al the wele of the worlde were in my honde,
    And I schulde chepen and chose to cheve me a lorde,
    For the costes that I haf knowen upon the, knyght, here,
    Of bewté and debonerté and blythe semblaunt,
    And that I haf er herkkened and halde hit here trwee,
1275 Ther schulde no freke upon folde bifore yow be chosen.'
    'Iwysse, worthy,' quoth the wyghe, 'ye haf waled wel better,
    Bot I am proude of the prys that ye put on me,
    And soberly your servaunt, my soverayn I holde yow,

To be your true servant.'   *1240*

'Truly,' replied Gawain, 'I am greatly honoured,
Though I am not in fact such a man as you speak of.
To deserve such respect as you have just described
I am completely unworthy, I know very well.
I should be happy indeed, if you thought it proper,   *1245*
That I might devote myself by words or by deed
To giving you pleasure: it would be a great joy.'
'In all truth, Sir Gawain,' replied the beautiful lady,
'If the excellence and gallantry everyone admires
Were I to slight or disparage, that would hardly be courteous;   *1250*
But a great many ladies would much rather now
Hold you, sir, in their power as I have you here,
To spend time amusingly with your charming talk,
Delighting themselves and forgetting their cares,
Than much of the treasure or wealth they possess.   *1255*
But I praise that same lord who holds up the heavens,
I have completely in my grasp the man everyone longs for,
            through God's grace.'
        Radiant with loveliness
        Great favour she conferred;   *1260*
        The knight with virtuous speech
        Answered her every word.

'Lady,' said the man pleasantly, 'may Mary repay you,
For I have truly made proof of your great generosity,
And many other folk win credit for their deeds;   *1265*
But the respect shown to me is not at all my deserving:
That honour is due to yourself, who know nothing but good.'
'By Mary,' said the noble lady, 'to me it seems very different;
For if I were the worthiest of all women alive,
And held all the riches of the earth in my hand,   *1270*
And could bargain and pick a lord for myself,
For the virtues I have seen in you, sir knight, here,
Of good looks and courtesy and charming manner —
All that I have previously heard and now know to be true —
No man on earth would be picked before you.'   *1275*
'Indeed, noble lady,' said the man, 'you have chosen much better,
But I am proud of the esteem that you hold me in,
And in all gravity your servant, my sovereign I consider you,

And yowre knyght I becom, and Kryst yow foryelde.'
1280 Thus thay meled of muchquat til mydmorn paste,
And ay the lady let lyk as hym loved mych.
The freke ferde with defence, and feted ful fayre;
Thagh ho were burde bryghtest the burne in mynde hade,
The lasse luf in his lode for lur that he soght
1285   bout hone —
The dunte that schulde hym deve,
And nedez hit most be done.
The lady thenn spek of leve,
He granted hir ful sone.

1290 Thenne ho gef hym god day, and wyth a glent laghed,
And as ho stod, ho stonyed hym wyth ful stor wordez:
'Now he that spedez uche spech this disport yelde yow!
Bot that ye be Gawan, hit gotz in mynde.'
'Querfore?' quoth the freke, and freschly he askez,
1295 Ferde lest he hade fayled in fourme of his castes;
Bot the burde hym blessed, and 'Bi this skyl' sayde:
'So god as Gawayn gaynly is halden,
And cortaysye is closed so clene in hymselven,
Couth not lightly haf lenged so long wyth a lady,
1300 Bot he had craved a cosse, bi his courtayse,
Bi sum towch of summe tryfle at sum talez ende.'
Then quoth Wowen, 'Iwysse, worthe as yow lykez;
I schal kysse at your comaundement, as a knyght fallez,
And fire, lest he displese yow, so plede hit no more.'
1305 Ho comes nerre with that and cachez hym in armez,
Loutez luflych adoun and the leude kysses.
Thay comly bykennen to Kryst ayther other;
Ho dos hir forth at the dore withouten dyn more;
And he ryches hym to ryse and rapes hym sone,
1310 Clepes to his chamberlayn, choses his wede,
Bowez forth, quen he watz boun, blythely to masse;
And thenne he meved to his mete that menskly hym keped,
And made myry al day, til the mone rysed,
          with game.
1315   Watz never freke fayrer fonge
Bitwene two so dyngne dame,
The alder and the yonge;
Much solace set thay same.

And declare myself your knight, and may Christ reward you.'
So they chatted of this and that until late morning,   1280
And always the lady behaved as if loving him much.
The knight reacted cautiously, in the most courteous of ways,
Though she was the loveliest woman he could remember:
He felt small interest in love because of the ordeal he must face
    very soon —   1285
  To stand a crushing blow,
  In helpless sufferance.
  Of leaving then she spoke,
  The knight agreed at once.

Then she bade him goodbye, glanced at him and laughed,   1290
And as she stood astonished him with a forceful rebuke:
'May he who prospers each speech repay you this pleasure!
But that you should be Gawain I very much doubt.'
'But why?' said the knight, quick with his question,
Fearing he had committed some breach of good manners;   1295
But the lady said 'bless you' and replied, 'For this cause;
So good a knight as Gawain is rightly reputed,
In whom courtesy is so completely embodied,
Could not easily have spent so much time with a lady
Without begging a kiss, to comply with politeness,   1300
By some hint or suggestion at the end of a remark.'
Then Gawain said, 'Indeed, let it be as you wish;
I will kiss at your bidding, as befits a knight,
And do more, rather than displease you, so urge it no further.'
With that she approaches him and takes him in her arms,   1305
Stoops graciously over him and kisses the knight.
They politely commend each other to Christ's keeping:
She goes out of the room without one word more.
And he prepares to get up as quickly as he can,
Calls for his chamberlain, selects his clothes,   1310
Makes his way, when he was ready, contentedly to mass;
And then went to his meal that worthily awaited him,
And made merry all day until the moon rose
    with games.
  Never knight was entertained   1315
  By such a worthy pair,
  One old, the other young;
  Much pleasure did they share.

And ay the lorde of the londe is lent on his gamnez,
1320   To hunt in holtez and hethe at hyndez barayne;
Such a sowme he ther slowe bi that the sunne heldet,
Of dos and of other dere, to deme were wonder.
Thenne fersly thay flokked in folk at the laste,
And quykly of the quelled dere a querré thay maked.
1325   The best bowed therto with burnez innoghe,
Gedered the grattest of gres that ther were,
And didden hem derely undo as the dede askez;
Serched hem at the asay summe that ther were,
Two fyngeres thay fonde of the fowlest of alle.
1330   Sythen thay slyt the slot, sesed the erber,
Schaved wyth a scharp knyf, and the schyre knitten;
Sythen rytte thay the four lymmes, and rent of the hyde,
Then brek thay the balé, the bowelez out token
Lystily for laucyng the lere of the knot;
1335   Thay gryped to the gargulun, and graythely departed
The wesaunt fro the wynt-hole, and walt out the guttez;
Then scher thay out the schulderez with her scharp knyvez,
Haled hem by a lyttel hole to have hole sydes.
Sithen britned thay the brest and brayden hit in twynne,
1340   And eft at the gargulun bigynez on thenne,
Ryvez hit up radly ryght to the byght,
Voydez out the avanters, and verayly therafter
Alle the rymez by the rybbez radly thay lance;
So ryde thay of by resoun bi the rygge bonez,
1345   Evenden to the haunche, that henged al samen,
And heven it up al hole, and hwen hit of there,
And that thay neme for the noumbles bi nome, as I trowe,
        bi kynde;
    Bi the byght al of the thyghes
1350   The lappez thay lance bihynde;
    To hewe hit in two thay hyghes,
    Bi the bakbon to unbynde.

Bothe the hede and the hals thay hwen of thenne,
And sythen sunder thay the sydez swyft fro the chyne,
1355   And the corbeles fee thay kest in a greve;
Thenn thurled they ayther thik side thurgh bi the rybbe,
And henged thenne ayther bi hoghes of the fourchez,

And still the lord of that land is absorbed in his sport,
Chasing through woodland and heath after barren hinds.   1320
What a number he killed by the time the day ended
Of does and other deer would be hard to imagine.
Then proudly the hunters flocked together at the end,
And quickly made a quarry of the slaughtered deer.
The noblest pressed forward with many attendants,   1325
Gathered together the fattest of the deer,
And neatly dismembered them as ritual requires.
Some of those who examined them at the assay
Found two inches of flesh in the leanest of them.
Then they slit the base of the throat, took hold of the gullet,   1330
Scraped it with a sharp knife and knotted it shut;
Next they cut off the four legs and ripped off the hide,
Then broke open the belly and took out the entrails
Carefully to avoid loosening the ligature of the knot.
They took hold of the throat, and quickly separated   1335
The gullet from the windpipe, and threw out the guts.
Then they cut round the shoulders with their keen knives,
Drawing them through an aperture to keep the sides whole.
Next they cut open the breast and split it in two,
And then one of them turns again to the throat   1340
And swiftly lays open the body right to the fork,
Throws out the neck-offal, and expertly then
Quickly severs all the membranes on the ribs.
So correctly they cut off all the offal on the spine
Right down to the haunches, in one unbroken piece,   1345
And lifted it up whole, and cut it off there;
And to that they give the name of numbles, I believe,
              as is right.
          Then where the hind legs fork
          At the back they cut the skin,
          Then hacked the carcass in two,   1350
          Swiftly along the spine.

Both the head and the neck they cut off next,
And then rapidly separate the sides from the chine;
And the raven's fee in a thicket they threw.
Then they pierced both thick sides through the ribs,   1355
Hanging each of them by the hocks of their legs,

Uche freke for his fee, as fallez for to have.
Upon a felle of the fayre best fede thay thayr houndes
1360 Wyth the lyver and the lyghtez, the lether of the paunchez,
And bred bathed in blod blende theramongez.
Baldely thay blw prys, bayed thayr rachchez,
Sythen fonge thay her flesche, folden to home,
Strakande ful stoutly mony stif motez.
1365 Bi that the daylyght watz done the douthe watz al wonen
Into the comly castel, ther the knyght bidez
ful stille,
Wyth blys and bryght fyr bette.
The lorde is comen thertylle;
1370 When Gawayn wyth hym mette
Ther watz bot wele at wylle.

Thenne comaunded the lorde in that sale to samen alle the meny,
Bothe the ladyes on lowe to lyght with her burdes
Bifore alle the folk on the flette, frekez he beddez
1375 Verayly his venysoun to fech hym byforne,
And al godly in gomen Gawayn he called,
Techez hym to the tayles of ful tayt bestes,
Schewez hym the schyree grece schorne upon rybbes.
'How payez yow this play? haf I prys wonnen?
1380 Have I thryvandely thonk thurgh my craft served?'
'Ye, iwysse,' quoth that other wyghe, 'here is wayth fayrest
That I sey this seven yere in sesoun of wynter.'
'And al I gif yow, Gawayn,' quoth the gome thenne,
'For by acorde of covenaunt ye crave hit as your awen.'
1385 'This is soth,' quoth the segge, 'I say yow that ilke:
That I haf worthyly wonnen this wonez wythinne,
Iwysse with as god wylle hit worthez to yourez.'
He hasppez his fayre hals his armez wythinne,
And kysses hym as comlyly as he couthe awyse:
1390 'Tas yow there my chevicaunce, I cheved no more;
I wowche hit saf fynly, thagh feler hit were.'
'Hit is god,' quoth the godmon, 'grant mercy therfore.
Hit may be such hit is the better, and ye me breve wolde
Where ye wan this ilk wele bi wytte of yorselven.'
1395 'That watz not forward,' quoth he, 'frayst me no more.
For ye haf tan that yow tydez, trawe non other
ye mowe.'

For each man's payment, as his proper reward.
They put food for their hounds on a fine beast's skin —
The liver and lights, the lining of the stomach,   1360
And bread soaked in blood, mixed up together.
Noisily they blew capture, their hounds barking,
Then shouldering their venison they started for home,
Vigorously sounding many loud single notes.
By the time daylight failed they had ridden back   1365
To the splendid castle, where the knight waits
                    undisturbed,
              With joy and bright fire warm.
              Then into hall the lord
              Came, and the two men met   1370
              In joyfullest accord.

Then the lord commanded the household to assemble in hall,
And both ladies to come downstairs with their maids.
In front of the gathering he orders his men
To lay out his venison truly before him;   1375
And with playful courtesy he called Gawain to him,
Reckons up the tally of well-grown beasts,
Points out the splendid flesh cut from the ribs.
'Does this game please you? have I won your praise?
Do I deserve hearty thanks for my hunting skill?'   1380
'Yes indeed,' said the other, 'This is the finest venison
That I have seen for many years in the winter season.'
'And I give it all to you, Gawain,' said the man then,
'For by the terms of our compact you may claim it as yours.'
'That is true,' said the knight, 'and I say the same to you: 1385
What I have honourably won inside this castle,
With as much good will truly shall be yours.'
He takes the other's strong neck in his arms,
And kisses him as pleasantly as he could devise.
'Take here my winnings, I obtained nothing else;   1390
I bestow it on you freely, and would do so were it more.'
'It is excellent,' said the lord, 'Many thanks indeed.
It could be even better if you would inform me
Where you won this same prize by your cleverness.'
'That was not in our agreement,' said he, 'ask nothing else;   1395
For you have had what is due to you, expect to receive
                    nothing more.'

Thay laghed, and made hem blythe
Wyth lotez that were to lowe;
1400   To soper thay yede as-swythe,
Wyth dayntés nwe innowe.

And sythen by the chymné in chamber thay seten,
Wyghez the walle wyn weghed to hem oft,
And efte in her bourdyng thay baythen in the morn
1405   To fylle the same forwardez that thay byfore maden:
Wat chaunce so bytydez hor chevysaunce to chaunge,
What nwez so thay nome, at naght quen thay metten.
Thay acorded of the covenauntez byfore the court alle;
The beverage watz broght forth in bourde at that tyme,
1410   Thenne thay lovelych leghten leve at the last,
Uche burne to his bedde busked bylyve.
Bi that the coke hade crowen and cakled bot thryse
The lorde watz lopen of his bedde, the leudez uchone;
So that the mete and the masse watz metely delyvered,
1415   The douthe dressed to the wod er any day sprenged,
           to chace;
        Hegh with hunte and hornez
        Thurgh playnez thay passe in space,
        Uncoupled among tho thornez
1420   Rachez that ran on race.

Sone thay calle of a quest in a ker syde,
The hunt rehayted the houndez that hit fyrst mynged,
Wylde wordez hym warp wyth a wrast noyce;
The howndez that hit herde hastid thider swythe,
1425   And fellen as fast to the fuyt, fourty at ones;
Thenne such a glaver ande glam of gedered rachchez
Ros that the rocherez rungen aboute;
Hunterez hem hardened with horne and wyth muthe.
Then al in a semblé sweyed togeder
1430   Bitwene a flosche in that fryth and a foo cragge;
In a knot bi a clyffe, at the kerre syde,
Ther as the rogh rocher unrydely was fallen,
Thay ferden to the fyndyng, and frekez hem after;
Thay umbekesten the knarre and the knot bothe,
1435   Wyghez, whyl thay wysten wel wythinne hem it were,
The best that ther breved watz wyth the blodhoundez.

They laughed and joked awhile
In speech deserving praise;
Then quickly went to sup   1400
On new delicacies.

Afterwards they sat by the fire in the lord's chamber,
And servants many times brought in marvellous wine;
And once again in their jesting they agreed the next day
To observe the same covenant as they had made before: 1405
Whatever fortune befell them, to exchange what they won,
Whatever new things they were, at night when they met.
They renewed the agreement before the whole court —
The pledge-drink was brought in with jokes at that time —
Then they graciously took leave of each other at last,   1410
Every man hastening quickly to bed.
By the time cock-crow had sounded three times
The lord had leapt out of bed and each of his men,
So that breakfast and mass were duly done,
And long before daybreak they were all on their way   1415
                to the chase.
        Through fields they canter soon,
        Loud with hunting-horns;
        Headlong the hounds run   1420
        Uncoupled among the thorns.

Soon they give tongue at the edge of a marsh;
The huntsman urged on the hounds that found the scent first,
Shouting at them wildly in a loud voice.
The hounds who heard him raced there in haste
And rushed towards the trail, forty of them together.   1425
Then such a deafening babel from gathered hounds rose
That the rocky bank echoed from end to end.
Huntsmen encouraged them with horn-blasts and shouts;
And then all in a throng they rushed together
Between a pool in that thicket and a towering crag.   1430
On a wooded knoll near a cliff at the edge of the marsh
Where fallen rocks were untidily scattered,
They ran to the dislodging, with men at their heels.
The hunters surrounded both the crag and the knoll
Until they were certain that inside their circle   1435
Was the beast which had made the bloodhounds give tongue.

Thenne thay beten on the buskez, and bede hym upryse,
And he unsoundyly out soght seggez overthwert;
On the sellokest swyn swenged out there,
1440   Long sythen fro the sounder that sighed for olde,
For he watz borelych and brode, bor alther-grattest,
Ful grymme quen he gronyed; thenne greved mony,
For thre at the fyrst thrast he thryght to the erthe,
And sparred forth good sped boute spyt more.
1445   Thise other halowed hyghe! ful hyghe, and hay! hay! cryed,
Haden hornez to mouthe, heterly rechated;
Mony watz the myry mouthe of men and of houndez
That buskkez after this bor with bost and wyth noyse
         to quelle.
1450   Ful ofte he bydez the baye,
      And maymez the mute inn melle;
      He hurtez of the houndez, and thay
      Ful yomerly yaule and yelle.

Schalkez to shote at hym schowen to thenne,
1455   Haled to hym of her arewez, hitten hym oft;
Bot the poyntez payred at the pyth that pyght in his scheldez,
And the barbez of his browe bite non wolde;
Thagh the schaven schafte schyndered in pieces,
The hede hypped agayn were-so-ever hit hitte.
1460   Bot quen the dyntez hym dered of her dryghe strokez,
Then, braynwod for bate, on burnez he rasez,
Hurtz hem ful heterly ther he forth hyghez,
And mony arghed therat, and on lyte droghen.
Bot the lorde on a lyght horce launces hym after,
1465   As burne bolde upon bent his bugle he blowez,
He rechated, and rode thurgh ronez ful thyk,
Suande this wylde swyn til the sunne schafted.
This day wyth this ilk dede thay dryven on this wyse,
Whyle oure luflych lede lys in his bedde,
1470   Gawayn graythely at home, in gerez ful ryche
        of hewe.
      The lady noght forgate
      Com to hym to salue;
      Ful erly ho watz hym ate
1475   His mode for to remwe.

Then they beat on the bushes and called him to come out;
And he broke cover ferociously through a line of men.
An incredible wild boar charged out there,
Which long since had left the herd through his age,   1440
For he was massive and broad, greatest of all boars,
Terrible when he snorted. Then many were dismayed,
For three men in one rush he threw on their backs,
And made away fast without doing more harm.
The others shouted 'hi!' and 'hay, hay!' at the tops of their voices,   1445
Put horns to mouth and loudly sounded recall.
Many hunters and hounds joyfully gave tongue,
Hurrying after this boar with outcry and clamour
       to kill.
      Often he stands at bay,   1450
      And maims the circling pack,
      Wounding many hounds
      That piteously yelp and bark.

Men press forward to shoot at him then,
Loosed their arrows at him, hit him many times;   1455
But those that struck his shoulders were foiled by their toughness,
And none of them could pierce through the bristles on his brow.
Although the polished shaft shivered into pieces,
The head rebounded away wherever it struck.
But when the hits hurt him with their constant blows,   1460
Frenzied with fighting he turns headlong on the men,
And injures them savagely when he charges out,
So that many grew fearful and drew back further.
But the lord on a lively horse races after him,
Like a valiant hunter, blowing his horn.   1465
He urged the hounds on, and through dense thickets rode
Following this wild boar until the sun went down.
So they spent the day in this manner, in this wild chase,
While our gracious knight lies in his bed:
Gawain, happily at home amid bright-coloured bedding   1470
       so rich.
      Nor did the lady fail
      To wish her guest good day;
      Early she was there
      His mood to mollify.   1475

Ho commes to the cortyn, and at the knyght totes.
Sir Wawen her welcumed worthy on fyrst,
And ho hym yeldez agayn ful yerne of hir wordez,
Settez hir softly by his syde, and swythely ho laghez,
1480 And wyth a luflych loke ho layde hym thyse wordez:
'Sir, yif ye be Wawen, wonder me thynkkez,
Wyghe that is so wel wrast alway to god,
And connez not of compaynye the costez undertake;
And if mon kennes yow hom to knowe, ye kest hom of your mynde;
1485 Thou hatz foryeten yederly that yisterday I taght te
Bi alder-trest token of talk that I cowthe.'
'What is that?' quoth the wyghe, 'Iwysse I wot never;
If hit be sothe that ye breve, the blame is myn awen.'
'Yet I kende yow of kyssyng,' quoth the clere thenne,
1490 'Quere-so countenaunce is couthe quikly to clayme;
That bicumes uche a knyght that cortaysy uses.'
'Do way,' quoth that derf mon, 'my dere, that speche;
For that durst I not do, lest I devayed were.
If I were werned, I were wrang, iwysse, yif I profered.'
1495 'Ma fay,' quoth the meré wyf, 'ye may not be werned,
Ye ar stif innoghe to constrayne wyth strenkthe, yif yow lykez,
Yif any were so vilanous that yow devaye wolde.'
'Ye, be God,' quoth Gawayn, 'good is your speche;
Bot threte is unthryvande in thede ther I lende,
1500 And uche gift that is geven not with goud wylle.
I am at your comaundement, to kysse quen yow lykez,
Ye may lach quen yow lyst, and leve quen yow thynkkez,
            in space.'
        The lady loutez adoun
1505   And comlyly kysses his face;
        Much speche thay ther expoun
        Of druryes greme and grace.

'I woled wyt at yow, wyghe,' that worthy then sayde,
'And yow wrathed not therwyth, what were the skylle
1510 That so yong and so yepe as ye at this tyme,
So cortayse, so knyghtly, as ye ar knowen oute —
And of alle chevalry to chose, the chef thyng alosed
Is the lel layk of luf, the lettrure of armes;
For to telle of this tevelyng of this trwe knyghtez,
1515 Hit is the tytelet token and tyxt of her werkkez;

She comes to the curtain and peeps in at the knight.
Sir Gawain welcomes her politely at once,
And she returns his greeting with eager speech,
Seats herself gently at his side and quickly laughs,
And with a charming glance at him uttered these words: 1480
'Sir, if you are Gawain, it astonishes me
That a man always so strongly inclined to good,
Cannot grasp the rules of polite behaviour,
And if someone instructs him, lets them drop out of mind.
You have quickly forgotten what I taught you yesterday,   1485
By the very truest lesson I could put into words.'
'What was that?' said the knight, 'Indeed, I don't know at all.
If what you say is true, the blame is all mine.'
'Yet I told you about kissing,' the fair lady replied,
'To act quickly wherever a glance of favour is seen;   1490
That befits every knight who practises courtesy.'
'Dear lady, enough of such talk,' said that brave man,
'For I dare not do that, lest I were refused.
If repulsed, I should be at fault for having presumed.'
'Ma foi,' said the gay lady, 'you could not be refused;   1495
You are strong enough to force your will if you wish,
If any woman were so ill-mannered as to reject you.'
'Yes, indeed,' said Gawain, 'what you say is quite true;
But in my country force is considered ignoble,
And so is each gift that is not freely given.   1500
I am at your disposal, to kiss when it pleases you,
You may take one when you like, and stop as seems good,
        in a while.'
        She bends down over him
        And gives the knight a kiss;   1505
        For long they then discuss
        Love's misery and bliss.

'I would learn from you, sir,' said that gentle lady,
If the question was not irksome, what the reason was
That someone as young and valiant as yourself,   1510
So courteous and chivalrous as you are known far and wide —
And of all the aspects of chivalry, the thing most praised
Is the true practice of love, knighthood's very lore;
For to speak of the endeavours of true knights,
The written heading and text of their deeds is that: 1515

How ledes for her lel lufe hor lyvez han auntered,
Endured for her drury dulful stoundez,
And after wenged with her walour and voyded her care,
And broght blysse into boure with bountees hor awen —
1520 And ye ar knyght comlokest kyd of your elde,
Your worde and your worchip walkez ayquere,
And I haf seten by yourself here sere twyes,
Yet herde I never of your hed helde no wordez
That ever longed to luf, lasse ne more;
1525 And ye, that are so cortays and coynt of your hetes,
Oghe to a yonke thynk yern to schewe
And teche sum tokenez of trweluf craftes.
Why, ar ye lewed, that alle the los weldez?
Other elles ye demen me to dille your dalyaunce to herken?
1530   For schame!
     I com hider sengel, and sitte
     To lerne at yow sum game;
     Dos, techez me of your wytte
     Whil my lorde is fro hame.'

1535 'In goud faythe,' quoth Gawayn, 'God yow foryelde!'
Gret is the gode gle, and gomen to me huge,
That so worthy as ye wolde wynne hidere,
And pyne yow with so pouer a man, as play wyth your knyght
With anyskynnez countenaunce, hit keverez me ese;
1540 Bot to take the torvayle to myself to trwluf expoun,
And towche the temez of tyxt and talez of armez
To yow that, I wot wel, weldez more slyght
Of that art, bi the half, or a hundreth of seche
As I am, other ever schal, in erde ther I leve,
1545 Hit were a folé felefolde, my fre, by my trawthe.
I wolde yowre wylnyng worche at my myght,
As I am hyghly bihalden, and evermore wylle
Be servaunt to yourselven, so save me Dryghtyn!'
Thus hym frayned that fre, and fondet hym ofte,
1550 For to haf wonnen hym to woghe, what-so scho thoght ellez;
Bot he defended hym so fayr that no faut semed,
Ne non evel on nawther halve, nawther thay wysten
          bot blysse.
     Thay laghed and layked long;
1555   At the last scho con hym kysse,

86

How knights have ventured their lives for true love,
Suffered for their love-longings dismal times,
And later taken revenge on their misery through valour,
Bringing joy to their ladies through their personal merits.
And you are the outstanding knight of your time,   *1520*
Your fame and your honour are known everywhere,
And I have sat by you here on two separate occasions
Yet never heard from your mouth a solitary word
Referring to love, of any kind at all.
And you, who make such courteous and elegant vows,   *1525*
Should be eager to instruct a youthful creature,
And teach her some elements of skill in true love.
What, are you ignorant, who enjoy such great fame?
Or do you think me too silly to take in courtly chat?
         For shame!   *1530*
      I come here alone, and sit
      To learn your special play;
      Show me your expertise
      While my husband is away.'

'In good faith,' said Gawain, 'may God reward you!   *1535*
It gives me great gladness and pleases me hugely
That one as noble as yourself should make your way here,
And trouble yourself with a nobody, trifling with your knight
With any kind of favour: it gives me delight.
But to take the task on myself of explaining true love,   *1540*
And treat the matter of romance and chivalric tales
To you whom — I know well — have more expertise
In that subject by half than a hundred such men
As myself ever can, however long I may live,
Would be absolute folly, noble lady, on my word.   *1545*
I will carry out your desires with all my power,
As I am in all duty bound, and always will be
The servant of your wishes, may God preserve me!'
Thus that lady made trial of him, tempting him many times
To have led him into mischief, whatever her purpose;   *1550*
But he defended himself so skilfully that no fault appeared,
Nor evil on either side, nor anything did they feel
        but delight.
      They laughed and bantered long;
      Then she kissed her guest;   *1555*

Hir leve fayre con scho fonge,
And went hir waye, iwysse.

Then ruthes hym the renk and ryses to the masse,
And sithen hor diner watz dyght and derely served.
1560 The lede with the ladyez layked alle day,
Bot the lorde over the londez launced ful ofte,
Swez his uncely swyn, that swyngez bi the bonkkez
And bote the best of his braches the bakkez in sunder
Ther he bode in his bay, tel bawemen hit breken,
1565 And madee hym mawgref his hed for to mwe utter,
So felle flonez ther flete when the folk gedered.
Bot yet the styffest to start bi stoundez he made,
Til at the last he watz so mat he myght no more renne,
Bot in the hast that he myght he to a hole wynnez
1570 Of a rasse bi a rokk ther rennez the boerne.
He gete the bonk at his bak, bigynez to scrape,
The frothe femed at his mouth unfayre bi the wykez,
Whettez his whyte tuschez; with hym then irked
Alle the burnez so bolde that hym by stoden
1575 To nye hym on-ferum, bot neghe hym non durst
    for wothe;
    He hade hurt so mony byforne
    That al thught thenne ful lothe
    Be more wyth his tusches torne
1580   That breme watz and braynwode bothe.

Til the knyght com hymself, kachande his blonk,
Sygh hym byde at the bay, his burnez bysyde;
He lyghtes luflych adoun, levez his corsour,
Braydez out a bryght bront and bigly forth strydez,
1585 Foundez fast thurgh the forth ther the felle bydez.
The wylde watz war of the wyghe with weppen in honde,
Hef heghly the here, so hetterly he fnast
That fele ferde for the freke, lest felle hym the worre.
The swyn settez hym out on the segge even,
1590 That the burne and the bor were both upon hepez
In the wyghtest of the water: the worre hade that other,
For the mon merkkez hym wel, as thay mette fyrst,
Set sadly the scharp in the slot even,
Hit hym up to the hult, that the hert schyndered,

> Charmingly took her leave,
> And went her way at last.

Then Gawain rouses himself and dresses for mass,
And afterwards dinner was cooked and splendidly served.
The knight diverted himself with the ladies all day,   1560
But the lord raced ceaselessly over the countryside,
After his menacing boar, that scurries over the hills,
And bit the backs of his bravest hounds asunder
Where he stood at bay, until archers broke it,
And forced him unwillingly to move into the open;   1565
So thickly the arrows flew when the hunters gathered.
But yet he made the bravest of them flinch at times,
Until at last he was so tired that he could run no more,
And as fast as he can he makes his way to a hole
By a rocky ledge overlooking the stream.   1570
He gets the river-bank at his back, begins to scrape —
The froth foamed hideously at the corners of his mouth —
And whets his white tusks. Then it grew irksome
For all the bold men who surrounded him trying
To wound him from afar, but for the danger none dared   1575
> to get close;
> So many had been hurt
> That no one wished to risk
> To be more savaged by
> A maddened boar's tusk.   1580

Until the lord himself came, spurring his horse,
Saw the boar standing at bay, ringed by his men;
He nimbly dismounts, leaving his courser,
Unsheathes a bright sword and mightily strides,
Hastens quickly through the stream towards the waiting boar. 1585
The beast saw the man with his weapon in hand,
Raised his bristles erect, and so fiercely snorted
That many feared for the man, lest he got the worst of it.
The boar charged out, straight at the man,
So that he and the beast were both in a heap   1590
Where the water was swiftest. The other had the worse;
For the man takes aim carefully as the two met,
And thrust the sword firmly straight into his throat,
Drove it up to the hilt, so that the heart burst open,

1595 And he yarrande hym yelde, and yedoun the water
     ful tyt.
   A hundreth houndez hym hent,
   That bremely con hym bite,
   Burnez him broght to bent,
1600 And doggez to dethe endite.

 There watz blawyng of prys in mony breme horne,
 Heghe halowing on highe with hathelez that myght;
 Brachetes bayed that best, as bidden the maysterez
 Of that chargeaunt chace that were chef huntes.
1605 Thenne a wyghe that watz wys upon wodcraftez
 To unlace this bor lufly bigynnez.
 Fyrst he hewes of his hed and on highe settez,
 And sythen rendez him al roghe bi the rygge after,
 Braydez out the boweles, brennez hom on glede,
1610 With bred blent therwith his braches rewardez.
 Sythen he britnez out the brawen in bryght brode cheldez,
 And hatz out the hastlettez, as hightly bisemez;
 And yet hem halchez al hole the halvez togeder,
 And sythen on a stif stange stoutly hem henges.
1615 Now with this ilk swyn thay swengen to home;
 The bores hed watz borne bifore the burnes selven
 That him forferde in the forthe thurgh forse of his honde
     so stronge.
   Til he seye Sir Gawayne
1620 In halle hym thoght ful longe;
   He calde, and he com gayn
   His feez ther for to fonge.

 The lorde ful lowde with lote and laghter myry,
 When he seye Sir Gawayn, with solace he spekez;
1625 The goude ladyez were geten, and gedered the meyny,
 He schewez hem the scheldez, and schapes hem the tale
 Of the largesse and the lenthe, the lithernez alse
 Of the were of the wylde swyn in wod ther he fled.
 That other knyght ful comly comended his dedez,
1630 And praysed hit as a gret prys that he proved hade,
 For suche a brawne of a best, the bolde burne sayde,
 Ne such sydes of a swyn segh he never are.
 Thenne hondeled thay the hoge hed, the hende mon hit praysed,

And squawling he gave up, and was swept through the water   *1595*
      downstream.
      Seized by a hundred hounds
      Fierce and sharp of tooth,
      Men dragged him to the bank,
      And dogs do him to death.   *1600*

There was sounding of capture from many brave horns,
Proud shouting by knights as loud as they could,
Hounds bayed at that beast, as bidden by the masters
Who were the chief huntsmen of that wearisome chase.
Then a man who was expert in hunting practice   *1605*
Skilfully begins to dismember this boar.
First he cuts off the head and sets it on high,
And then roughly opens him along the spine,
Throws out the entrails, grills them over embers,
And rewards his hounds with them, mixed with bread.   *1610*
Next he cuts out the boar's-meat in broad glistening slabs,
And takes out the haslets, as properly follows;
Yet he fastens the two sides together unbroken,
And then proudly hangs them on a strong pole.
Now with this very boar they gallop towards home;   *1615*
Carrying the boar's head before the same man
Who had killed it in the stream by force of his own
      strong hand.
      Until he saw Gawain
      It seemed a tedious time,   *1620*
      He gladly came when called,
      His due reward to claim.

The lord, noisy with speech and merry laughter,
Joyfully exclaims at the sight of Sir Gawain.
The good ladies were brought down and the household assembled;   *1625*
He shows them the sides of meat, and gives an account
Of the boar's huge size and the ferocity
Of the fight with the beast in the wood where he fled.
The other knight warmly commended his deeds,
And praised his action as proof of his excellence,   *1630*
For such boar's-meat, the brave knight declared,
And such sides of wild boar he had never seen before.
Then they picked up the huge head, the polite man praised it

And let lodly therat the lorde for to here.
1635 'Now, Gawayn,' quoth the godmon, 'this gomen is your awen
By fyn forwarde and faste, faythely ye knowe.'
'Hit is sothe,' quoth the segge, 'and as siker trwe
Alle my get I schal gif agayn, bi my trawthe.'
He hent the hathel aboute the halse, and hendely hym kysses,
1640 And eftersones of the same he served hym there.
'Now ar we even,' quoth the hathel, 'in this eventide,
Of alle the covenauntes that we knyt, sythen I com hider,
    bi lawe.'
    The lorde sayde, 'Bi saynt Gile,
1645   Ye ar the best that I knowe!
    Ye ben ryche in a whyle,
    Such chaffer and ye drowe.'

Thenne thay teldet tablez trestes alofte,
Kesten clothez upon; clere lyght thenne
1650 Wakned by wowes, waxen torches;
Segges sette and served in sale al aboute;
Much glam and gle glent up therinne
Aboute the fyre upon flet, and on fele wyse
At the soper and after, mony athel songez,
1655 As coundutes of Krystmasse and carolez newe,
With al the manerly merthe that mon may of telle.
And ever oure luflych knyght the lady bisyde,
Such a semblaunt to that segge semly ho made
Wyth stille stollen countenaunce, that stalworth to plese,
1660 That al forwondered watz the wyghe, and wroth with hymselven,
Bot he nolde not for his nurture nurne hir agaynez,
Bot dalt with hir al in daynté, how-se-ever the dede turned
    towrast.
    Quen thay hade played in halle
1665   As longe as hor wylle hom last,
    To chambre he con hym calle,
    And to the chemné thay past.

Ande ther thay dronken, and dalten, and demed eft nwe
To norne on the same note on Nwe Yerez even;
1670 Bot the knyght craved leve to kayre on the morn,
For hit watz neghe at the terme that he to schulde.
The lorde hym letted of that, to lenge hym resteyed,

And pretended to feel horror, to honour the lord.
'Now, Gawain,' said his host, 'this quarry is all yours,   1635
By fully ratified covenant, as you well know.'
'That is so,' said the knight, 'and just as truly indeed
I shall give you all I gained in return, by my pledged word.'
He grasped the lord round the neck and graciously kisses him,
And then a second time treated him in the same way.   1640
'Now we are quit,' said Gawain, 'at the end of the day,
Of all the agreements we have made since I came here,
        in due form.'
            The lord said, 'By St Giles,
            You're the best man I know!
            You'll be a rich one soon   1645
            If you keep on trading so.'

Then tables were set up on top of trestles,
And tablecloths spread on them: bright light then
Glittered on the walls from waxen torches.   1650
Attendants laid table and served throughout hall.
A great noise of merry-making and joking arose
Round the fire in the centre; and of many kinds,
At supper and afterwards, noble songs were sung,
Such as Christmas carols and the newest dances,   1655
With all the fitting amusement that could be thought;
Our courteous knight sitting with the lady throughout.
Such a loving demeanour she displayed to that man,
Through furtive looks of affection to give him delight,
That he was utterly astonished and angry inside;   1660
But he could not in courtesy rebuff her advances,
But treated her politely, even though his actions might be
        misconstrued.
            When the revelry in hall
            Had lasted long enough,
            To the fireside in his room   1665
            The lord took Gawain off.

And there they drank and chatted, and spoke once again
To repeat the arrangement on New Year's Eve;
But the knight begged leave to depart the next day,   1670
For it was near time for the appointment that he had to keep.
The lord held him back, begging him to remain,

And sayde, 'As I am trwe segge, I siker my trawthe
Thou schal cheve to the grene chapel thy charres to make,
1675   Leude, on Nw Yeres lyght, longe bifore pryme.
Forthy thow lye in thy loft and lach thyn ese,
And I schal hunt in this holt, and halde the towchez,
Chaunge wyth the chevisaunce, bi that I charre hider;
For I haf fraysted the twys, and faythful I fynde the.
1680   Now 'thrid tyme throwe best' thenk on the morne,
Make we mery quyl we may and mynne upon joye,
For the lur may lach when-so mon lykez.'
This watz graythely graunted, and Gawayn is lenged,
Blithe broght watz hym drynk, and thay to bedde yeden
1685   with light.
      Sir Gawayn lis and slepes
      Ful stille and softe al night;
      The lorde that his craftez kepes,
      Ful erly he watz dight.

1690   After messe a morsel he and his men token;
Miry watz the mornyng, his mounture he askes.
Alle the hatheles that on horse schulde helden hym after
Were boun busked on hor blonkkez bifore the halle gatez.
Ferly fayre watz the folde, for the forst clenged;
1695   In red rudede upon rak rises the sunne,
And ful clere castez the clowdes of the welkyn.
Hunteres unhardeled bi a holt syde,
Rocheres roungen bi rys for rurde of her hornes;
Summe fel in the fute ther the fox bade,
1700   Traylez ofte a traveres bi traunt of her wyles;
A kenet kryes therof, a hunt on hym calles;
His felawes fallen hym to, that fnasted ful thike,
Runnen forth in a rabel in his ryght fare,
And he fyskez hem byfore; thay founden hym sone,
1705   And quen thay seghe hym with syght thay sued hym fast,
Wreghande hym ful weterly with a wroth noyse;
And he trantes and tornayeez thurgh mony tene greve,
Havilounez, and herkenez bi hegges ful ofte.
At the last bi a littel dich he lepez over a spenne,
1710   Stelez out ful stilly bi a strothe rande,
Went half wylt of the wode with wylez fro the houndes;
Thenne watz he went, er he wyst, to a wale tryster,

And said, 'As I am an honest man, I give you my word
That you shall reach the Green Chapel to settle your affairs,
Dear sir, on New Year's Day, well before nine.   *1675*
Therefore lie in your bed enjoying your ease,
And I shall hunt in the woods, and keep the compact,
Exchange winnings with you when I return here;
For I have tested you twice, and find you trustworthy.
Now tomorrow remember, 'Best throw third time';   *1680*
Let us make merry while we can and think only of joy,
For misery can be found whenever a man wants it.'
This was readily agreed, and Gawain is stayed;
Drink was gladly brought to him, and with torches they went
        to their beds.   *1685*
      Sir Gawain lies and sleeps
      All night taking his rest;
      While eager for his sport
      By dawn the lord was dressed.

After mass he and his men snatched a mouthful of food: *1690*
The morning was cheerful, he calls for his horse.
All the knights who would ride after him on horses
Were ready arrayed in the saddle outside the hall doors.
The countryside looked splendid, gripped by the frost;
The sun rises fiery through drifting clouds,   *1695*
And then dazzling bright drives the rack from the sky.
At the edge of a wood hunters unleashed the hounds;
Among the trees rocks resounded with the noise of their horns.
Some picked up the scent where a fox was lurking,
Search back and forwards in their cunning practice.   *1700*
A small hound gives tongue, the huntsman calls to him,
His fellows rally around, panting loudly,
And dash forward in a rabble right on the fox's track.
He scampers ahead of them, they soon found his trail,
And when they caught sight of him followed fast,   *1705*
Abusing him furiously with an angry noise.
He twists and dodges through many a dense copse,
Often doubling back and listening at the hedges.
At last he jumps over a fence by a little ditch,
Creeps stealthily by the edge of a bush-covered marsh,   *1710*
Thinking to escape from the wood and the hounds by his wiles.
Then he came, before he knew it, to a well-placed station,

Ther thre thro at a thrich thrat hym at ones,
    al graye.
1715   He blenched agayn bilyve,
      And stifly start on-stray,
      With alle the wo on lyve
      To the wod he went away.

Thenne watz hit list upon lif to lythen the houndez,
1720 When alle the mute hade hym met, menged togeder:
Such a sorwe at that syght thay sette on his hede
As alle the clamberande clyffes hade clatered on hepes;
Here he watz halawed, when hathelez hym metten,
Loude he watz yayned with yarande speche;
1725 Ther he watz threted and ofte thef called,
And ay the titleres at his tayl, that tary he ne myght.
Ofte he watz runnen at, when he out rayked,
And ofte reled in agayn, so Reniarde watz wylé.
And ye, he lad hem bi lagmon, the lorde and his meyny,
1730 On this maner bi the mountes quyle mid-over-under,
Whyle the hende knyght at hom holsumly slepes
Withinne the comly cortynes, on the colde morne.
Bot the lady for luf let not to slepe,
Ne the purpose to payre that pyght in hir hert,
1735 Bot ros hir up radly, rayked hir theder,
In a mery mantyle, mete to the erthe,
That watz furred ful fyne with fellez wel pured;
No howez goud on hir hede bot the hagher stones
Trased aboute hir tressour by twenty in clusteres;
1740 Hir thryven face and hir throte throwen al naked,
Hir brest bare bifore, and bihinde eke.
Ho comez withinne the chambre dore, and closes hit hir after,
Wayvez up a wyndow, and on the wyghe callez,
And radly thus rehayted hym with hir riche wordes,
1745   with chere:
      'A, mon, how may thou slepe,
      This morning is so clere?'
      He watz in drowping depe,
      Bot thenne he con hir here.

1750 In dregh droupyng of dreme draveled that noble,
As mon that watz in morning of mony thro thoghtes,

Where three fierce greyhounds flew at him at once
      in a rush.
        Undaunted changing course   *1715*
        He quickly swerved away,
        Pursued into the woods
        With hideous outcry.

Then it was joy upon earth to hear the hounds giving tongue
When all the pack had come upon him, mingled together: *1720*
Such a cursing at that sight they called down on his head
As if all the clustering cliffs had crashed down in a mass.
Here he was yelled at when hunters happened upon him,
Loudly he was greeted with chiding speech;
There he was reviled and often called thief,   *1725*
And always the hounds at his tail, that he could not pause.
Many times he was run at when he made for the open,
And many times doubled back, so cunning was Reynard.
And yes! strung out he led them, the lord and his followers,
Across the hills in this manner until mid-afternoon,   *1730*
While the knight in the castle takes his health-giving sleep
Behind splendid bed-curtains on the cold morn.
But out of love the lady did not let herself sleep,
Nor the purpose to weaken that was fixed in her heart;
But rose from her bed quickly and hastened there   *1735*
In a charming mantle reaching to the ground,
That was richly lined with well-trimmed furs:
No modest coif on her head, but skilfully cut gems
Arranged about her hair-fret in clusters of twenty;
Her lovely face and throat displayed uncovered,   *1740*
Her breast was exposed, and her shoulders bare.
She enters the chamber and shuts the door after her,
Throws open a window and calls to the knight,
Rebuking him at once with merry words
      in play: *1745*
        'Ah, sir, how can you sleep?
        The morning is so clear!'
        Deep in his drowsiness
        Her voice broke in his ear.

In the stupor of a dream that nobleman muttered,   *1750*
Like a man overburdened with troublesome thoughts;

How that destiné schulde that day dele hym his wyrde
At the grene chapel, when he the gome metes,
And bihoves his buffet abide withoute debate more;

1755   Bot quen that comly com he kevered his wyttes,
Swenges out of the swevenes, and swarez with hast.
The lady luflych com laghande swete,
Felle over his fayre face, and fetly hym kyssed;
He welcumez hir worthily with a wale chere.

1760   He sey hir so glorious and gayly atyred,
So fautles of hir fetures and of so fyne hewes,
Wight wallande joye warmed his hert.
With smothe smylyng and smolt thay smeten into merthe,
That al watz blis and bonchef that breke hem bitwene,

1765   and wynne.
       Thay lanced wordes gode,
       Much wele then watz therinne;
       Gret perile bitwene hem stod,
       Nif Maré of hir knyght mynne.

1770   Fo that prynces of pris depresed hym so thikke,
Nurned hym so neghe the thred, that nede hym bihoved
Other lach ther hir luf other lodly refuse.
He cared for his cortaysye, lest crathayn he were,
And more for his meschef yif he schulde make synne,

1775   And be traytor to that tolke that that telde aght.
'God schylde,' quoth the schalk, 'that schal not befalle!'
With luf-laghyng a lyt he layd hym bysyde
Alle the spechez of specialté that sprange of her mouthe.
Quoth that burde to the burne, 'Blame ye disserve

1780   Yif ye luf not that lyf that ye lye nexte,
Bifore alle the wyghez in the worlde wounded in hert,
Bot if ye haf a lemman, a lever, that yow lykez better,
And folden fayth to that fre, festned so harde
That yow lausen ne lyst — and that I leve nouthe;

1785   And that ye telle me that now trwly I pray yow,
For alle the lufez upon lyve layne not the sothe
          for gile.'
       The knyght sayde, 'Be sayn Jon,'
       And smethely con he smyle,

1790   'In fayth I welde right non,
       Ne non wil welde the quile.'

How destiny would deal him his fate on the day
When he meets the man at the Green Chapel,
And must stand the return blow without any more talk:
But when that lovely one spoke he recovered his wits,   *1755*
Broke out of his dreaming and hastily replied.
The gracious lady approached him, laughing sweetly,
Bent over his handsome face and daintily kissed him.
He welcomes her politely with charming demeanour;
Seeing her so radiant and attractively dressed,   *1760*
Every part of her so perfect, and in colour so fine,
Hot passionate feeling welled up in his heart.
Smiling gently and courteously they made playful speech,
So that all that passed between them was happiness, joy
        and delight.   *1765*
        Gracious words they spoke,
        And pleasure reached its height.
        Great peril threatened, should
        Mary not mind her knight.

For that noble lady so constantly pressed,   *1770*
Pushed him so close to the verge, that either he must
Take her love there and then or churlishly reject it.
He felt concerned for good manners, lest he behaved like a boor,
And still more lest he shame himself by an act of sin,
And treacherously betray the lord of the castle.   *1775*
'God forbid!' said the knight, 'That shall not come about!'
With affectionate laughter he put to one side
All the loving inducements that fell from her mouth.
Said that lady to the knight, 'You deserve rebuke
If you feel no love for the person you are lying beside,   *1780*
More than anyone on earth wounded in her heart;
Unless you have a mistress, someone you prefer,
And have plighted troth with that lady, so strongly tied
That you wish not to break it — which now I believe;
And I beg you now to confess that honestly: *1785*
For all the loves in the world hide not the truth
        in guile.'
        The knight said, 'By St John,'
        And gave a pleasant smile,
        'In truth I have no one,   *1790*
        Nor seek one for this while.'

'That is a worde,' quoth that wyght, 'that worst is of alle,
Bot I am swared for sothe, that sore me thinkkez.
Kysse me now comly, and I schal cach hethen,
1795   I may bot mourne upon molde, as may that much lovyes.'
Sykande ho sweghe doun and semly hym kyssed,
And sithen ho severes hym fro, and says as ho stondes,
'Now, dere, at this departyng do me this ese,
Gif me sumquat of thy gifte, thi glove if hit were,
1800   That I may mynne on the, mon, my mournyng to lassen.'
'Now iwysse,' quoth that wyghe, 'I wolde I hade here
The levest thing for thy luf that I in londe welde,
For ye haf deserved, for sothe, sellyly ofte
More rewarde bi resoun then I reche myght;
1805   Bot to dele yow for drurye that dawed bot neked,
Hit is not your honour to haf at this tyme
A glove for a garysoun of Gawaynez giftez;
And I am here an erande in erdez uncouthe,
And have no men wyth no males with menskful thingez;
1810   That mislykez me, ladé, for luf at this tyme,
Iche tolke mon do as he is tan, tas to non ille
        ne pine.'
      'Nay, hende of hyghe honours,'
      Quoth that lufsum under lyne,
1815   'Thagh I hade noght of yourez,
      Yet schulde ye have of myne.'

Ho raght hym a riche rynk of red golde werkez,
With a starande ston stondande alofte
That bere blusshande bemez as the bryght sunne —
1820   Wyt ye wel, hit watz worth wele ful hoge.
Bot the renk hit renayed, and redyly he sayde,
'I wil no giftez, for God, my gay, at this tyme;
I haf none yow to norne, ne noght wyl I take.'
Ho bede hit hym ful bysily, and he hir bode wernes,
1825   And swere swyfte by his sothe that he hit sese nolde,
And ho soré that he forsoke, and sayde therafter,
'If ye renay my rynk, to ryche for hit semez,
Ye wolde not so hyghly halden be to me,
I schal gif yow my girdel, that gaynes yow lasse.'
1830   Ho lacht a lace lyghtly that leke umbe hir sydez,

'That remark,' said the lady, 'is the worst you could make,
But I am answered indeed, and painfully, I feel.
Kiss me now lovingly, and I will hasten from here,
I must spend my life grieving, as a woman deeply in love.'   *1795*
Sighing she stooped down and kissed him sweetly,
And then moves away from him and says, standing there,
'Now, dear sir, do me this kindness at parting,
Give me something as a present, for instance your glove,
That I may remember you by, to lessen my sorrow.'   *1800*
'Now truly,' said that man, 'I wish I had here
The dearest thing in the world I possess for your love,
For you have truly deserved, wonderfully often,
More recompense by right than I could repay.
But to give you as love-token something worth little   *1805*
Would do you no honour, or to have at this time
A glove for a keepsake, as Gawain's gift.
I am here on a mission in unknown country,
And have no servants with bags full of precious things,
That grieves me, lady, for your sake at this time,   *1810*
But each man must do as conditions allow; take no offence
              or pain.'
              'No, most honoured sir,'
              Then said that lady free,
              'Though I get no gift from you,   *1815*
              You shall have one from me.'

She held out a precious ring of finely worked gold
With a sparkling jewel standing up high,
Its facets flashing as bright as the sun:
Take my word, it was worth an enormous sum.   *1820*
But the knight would not accept it, and straightaway said,
'I want no gifts, I swear, dear lady, at this time;
I have nothing to offer you, and nothing will I take.'
She pressed him insistently, and he declines her request,
Swearing quickly on his word that he would never touch it,   *1825*
And she was grieved that he refused it, and said to him then,
'If you reject my ring because you think it too precious,
And wish not to be so deeply indebted to me,
I shall give you my girdle, that profits you less.'
Quickly she unbuckled a belt clipped round her waist,   *1830*

101

Knit upon hir kyrtel under the clere mantyle;
Gered hit watz with grene sylke and with golde schaped,
Noght bot arounde brayden, beten with fyngrez;
And that ho bede to the burne, and blythely bisoght,
1835 Thagh hit unworthi were, that he hit take wolde.
And he nay that he nolde neghe in no wyse
Nauther golde ne garysoun, er God hym grace sende
To acheve to the chaunce that he hade chosen there.
'And therfore, I pray yow, displese yow noght,
1840 And lettez be your bisinesse, for I baythe hit yow never
    to graunte.
   I am derely to yow biholde
   Bicause of your sembelaunt,
   And ever in hot and colde
1845   To be your trwe servaunt.'

'Now forsake ye this silke,' sayde the burde thenne,
'For hit is symple in hitself? and so wel hit semez.
Lo, so hit is littel, and lasse hit is worthy;
But who-so knew the costes that knit ar therinne,
1850 He wolde hit prayse at more prys, paraventure.
For quat gome so is gorde with this grene lace,
While he hit hade hemely halched aboute,
Ther is no hathel under heven tohewe hym that myght,
For he myght not be slayn for slyght upon erthe.'
1855 Then kest the knyght, and hit come to his hert
Hit were a juel for the jopardé that hym jugged were:
When he acheved to the chapel his chek for to fech,
Myght he haf slypped to be unslayn, the sleght were noble.
Thenne he thulged with hir threpe and tholed hir to speke,
1860 And ho bere on hym the belt and bede hit hym swythe —
And he granted and hym gafe with a goud wylle —
And bisoght hym, for hir sake, discever hit never,
Bot to lelly layne fro hir lorde; the leude hym acordez
That never wyghe schulde hit wyt, iwysse, bot thay twayne
1865   for noghte.
   He thonkked hir oft ful swythe,
   Ful thro with hert and thoght.
   Bi that on thrynne sythe
   Ho hatz kyst the knyght so toght.

Fastened over her kirtle beneath the fine mantle;
It was woven of green silk and trimmed with gold,
Embroidered at the edges and decorated by hand;
And this she offered to the knight, and sweetly implored him
That despite its slight value he would accept it.   1835
And he declared absolutely that he would never agree
To take either gold or keepsake before God gave him grace
To finish the task he had undertaken.
'And therefore I beg you, do not be displeased,
And cease your insisting, for I shall never be brought   1840
          to consent.
     I am deeply in your debt
     Because of your kind favour,
     And will through thick and thin
     Remain your servant ever.'   1845

'Now, do you refuse this belt,' the lady said then,
'Because it is worth little? and so truly it appears.
See, it is indeed a trifle, and its worth even less;
But anyone who knew the power woven into it
Would put a much higher price on it, perhaps.   1850
For whoever is buckled into this green belt,
As long as it is tightly fastened about him
There is no man on earth who can strike him down,
For he cannot be killed by any trick in the world.'
Then the knight reflected, and it flashed into his mind   1855
This would be a godsend for the hazard he must face
When he reached the chapel to receive his deserts;
Could he escape being killed, the trick would be splendid.
Then he suffered her pleading and allowed her to speak,
And she pressed the belt on him, offering it at once —   1860
And he consented and gave way with good grace —
And she begged him for her sake never to reveal it,
But loyally hide it from her husband. Gawain gives his word
That no one should ever know of it, not for anything,
          but themselves.   1865
     He gave her heartfelt thanks
     With earnest mind and sense;
     By then she has three times
     Kissed that valiant prince.

1870 Thenne lachchez ho hir leve, and levez hym there,
For more myrthe of that mon moght ho not gete,
When ho watz gon, Sir Gawayn gerez hym sone,
Rises and riches him in araye noble,
Lays up the luf-lace the lady hym raghte,
1875 Hid hit ful holdely, ther he hit eft fonde.
Sythen chevely to the chapel choses he the waye,
Prevély aproched to a prest, and prayed hym there
That he wolde lyste his lyf and lern hym better
How his sawle schulde be saved when he schuld seye hethen.
1880 There he schrof hym schyrly and schewed his mysdedez,
Of the more and the mynne, and merci besechez,
And of absolucioun he on the segge calles;
And he asoyled hym surely and sette hym so clene
As domezday schulde haf ben dight on the morn.
1885 And sythen he mace hym as mery among the fre ladyes,
With comelych caroles and alle kynnes joye,
As never he did bot that daye, to the derk nyght,
          with blys.
          Uche mon hade daynté thare
1890   Of hym, and sayde, 'Iwysse,
          Thus mery he watz never are,
          Syn he com hider, er this.'

Now hym lenge in that lee, ther luf hym bityde!
Yet is the lorde on the launde ledande his gomnes.
1895 He hatz forfaren this fox that he folwed longe;
As he sprent over a spenne to spye the schrewe,
Ther as he herd the howndes that hasted hym swythe,
Renaud com richchande thurgh a roghe greve,
And alle the rabel in a res ryght at his helez.
1900 The wyghe watz war of the wylde, and warly abides,
And braydez out the bryght bronde, and at the best castez.
And he schunt for the scharp, and schulde haf arered;
A rach rapes hym to, ryght er he myght,
And ryght bifore the hors fete thay fel on hym alle,
1905 And woried me this wyly wyth a wroth noyse.
The lorde lyghtez bilyve, and lachez hym sone,
Rased hym ful radly out of the rach mouthes,
Haldez heghe over his hede, halowez faste,
And ther bayen aboute hym mony brath houndez.

Then she takes her departure, leaving him there,   *1870*
For more pleasure from that man was not to be had.
When she had gone, Gawain quickly makes himself ready,
Gets up and dresses himself in splendid array,
Puts away the love-token the lady gave him,
Hid it carefully where he could find it again.   *1875*
Then quickly to the chapel he makes his way,
Approached a priest privately, and besought him there
To hear his confession and instruct him more clearly
How his soul could be saved when he leaves this world.
There he confessed himself honestly and admitted his sins,   *1880*
Both the great and the small, and forgiveness begs,
And calls on the priest for absolution.
And the priest absolved him completely, and made him as clean
As if the Judgement were appointed for the next day.
And then Gawain makes merry with the noble ladies,   *1885*
With charming dance-songs and gaiety of all kinds,
As he never did before that day, until darkness fell,
      with joy.
      Each man had courtesy
      From him, and said, 'Sure,   *1890*
      So merry since he came
      He never was before'.

Let him stay in that shelter, and love come his way!
But still the lord is afield, enjoying his sport.
He has headed off the fox that he pursued so long;   *1895*
As he leapt over a hedge to look for the villain,
Where he heard the hounds barking as they chased him fast,
Reynard came running through a rough thicket
With the pack howling behind him, right at his heels.
The man caught sight of the fox, and warily waits,   *1900*
Unsheathes his bright sword and slashes at the beast;
And he swerved away from the blade and would have turned back.
A hound rushed at him before he could turn,
And right at the horse's feet the pack fell on him all,
Tearing at the wily one with an enraged noise.   *1905*
The lord swiftly dismounts, grabs the fox at once,
Lifted it quickly out of the hounds' mouths,
Holds it high over his head, halloos loudly,
And many fierce hounds surround him there, baying.

1910   Huntes hyghed hem theder with hornez ful mony,
Ay rechatande aryght til thay the renk seyen.
Bi that watz comen his compeyny noble
Alle that ever ber bugle blowed at ones,
And alle thise other halowed that had no hornes;
1915   Hit watz the myriest mute that ever men herde,
The rich rurd that ther watz raysed for Renaude saule
        with lote.
        Hor houndez thay ther rewarde,
        Her hedez thay fawne and frote,
1920   And sythen thay tan Reynarde
        And tyrven of his cote.

And thenne thay helden to home, for hit watz niegh nyght,
Strakande ful stoutly in hor store hornez.
The lorde is lyght at last at hys lef home,
1925   Fyndez fire upon flet, the freke ther-byside,
Sir Gawayn the gode, that glad watz withalle,
Among the ladies for luf he ladde much joye.
He were a bleaunt of blwe that bradde to the erthe,
His surkot semed hym wel that softe watz forred,
1930   And his hode of that ilke henged on his schulder,
Blande al of blaunner were bothe al aboute.
He metez me this godmon inmyddez the flore,
And al with gomen he hym gret, and goudly he sayde,
'I schal fylle upon fyrst oure forwardez nouthe,
1935   That we spedly han spoken, ther spared watz no drynk.'
Then acoles he the knyght and kysses hym thryes,
As saverly and sadly as he hem sette couthe.
'Bi Kryst,' quoth that other knyght, 'ye cach much sele
In chevisaunce of this chaffer, yif ye hade goud chepez.'
1940   'Ye, of the chepe no charg,' quoth chefly that other,
'As is pertly payed the porchaz that I aghte.'
'Mary,' quoth that other man, 'myn is bihynde,
For I haf hunted al this day, and noght haf I geten
Bot this foule fox felle — the fende haf the godez!
1945   And that is ful pore for to pay for suche prys thinges
As ye haf thryght me here thro, suche thre cosses
        so gode.'
        'Inogh,' quoth Sir Gawayn,
        'I thonk yow, bi the rode';

Hunters hurried towards him with many horns blowing,   *1910*
Sounding rally in proper fashion until they saw the lord.
When his noble company was all assembled,
Everyone carrying a bugle blew it at once,
And the others, without horns, raised a great shout.
It was the most glorious baying that man ever heard,   *1915*
The noble clamour set up there for Reynard's soul
> with din.
> > Hunters reward their hounds,
> > Heads they rub and pat;
> > And then they took Reynard   *1920*
> > And stripped him of his coat.

And then they set off for home, for it was nearly night,
Stridently sounding their mighty horns.
At last the lord dismounts at his well-loved home,
Finds a fire burning in hall, the knight waiting beside,   *1925*
Sir Gawain the good, completely content,
Taking great pleasure from the ladies' affection.
He wore a blue mantle of rich stuff reaching the ground;
His softly furred surcoat suited him well,
And his hood of the same stuff hung on his shoulder,   *1930*
Both trimmed with ermine along the edges.
He meets his host in the middle of the hall,
Laughingly greeted him, and courteously said,
'Now I shall first carry out the terms of our covenant,
Which we readily agreed on when wine was not spared.'   *1935*
Then he embraces the lord and gives him three kisses,
With as much relish and gravity as he could contrive.
'By God,' said that other knight, 'you had much luck
In winning this merchandise, if the price was right.'
'Oh, never mind the price,' replied the other quickly,   *1940*
'So long as the goods I got have been honestly paid.'
'Marry,' said the other man, 'mine don't compare,
For I have hunted all day, and yet have caught nothing
But this stinking fox pelt — the devil take the goods!
And that is a meagre return for such precious things   *1945*
As you have warmly pressed on me, three such kisses
> so good.'
> > 'Enough,' said Gawain,
> > 'I thank you, by the Rood';

1950
        And how the fox watz slayn
        He tolde hym as thay stode.

With merthe and mynstralsye, wyth metez at hor wylle,
Thay maden as mery as any men moghten
With laghyng of ladies, with lotez of bordez.
1955   Gawayn and the godemon so glad were thay bothe
Bot if the douthe had doted, other dronken ben other.
Both the mon and the meyny maden mony japez
Til the sesoun watz seghen that thay sever moste;
Burnez to hor bedde behoved at the laste.
1960   Thenne lowly his leve at the lorde fyrst
Fochchez this fre mon, and fayre he hym thonkkez:
'Of such a selly sojorne as I haf hade here,
Your honour at this hyghe fest, the hyghe kyng yow yelde!
I gef yow me for on of yourez, if yowreself lykez,
1965   For I mot nedes, as ye wot, meve to-morne,
And ye me take sum tolke to teche, as ye hyght,
The gate to the grene chapel, as God wyl me suffer
To dele on Nw Yerez day the dome of my wyrdes.'
'In god faythe,' quoth the godmon, 'wyth a goud wylle
1970   Al that ever I yow hyght halde schal I redé.'
Ther asyngnes he a servaunt to sette hym in the waye,
And coundue hym by the downez, that he no drechch had,
For to ferk thurgh the fryth and fare at the gaynest
        bi greve.
1975
        The lorde Gawayn con thonk,
        Such worchip he wolde hym weve.
        Then at tho ladyez wlonk
        The knyght hatz tan his leve.

With care and wyth kyssyng he carppez hem tille,
1980   And fele thryvande thonkkez he thrat hom to have,
And thay yelden hym agayn yeply that ilk.
Thay bikende hym to Kryst with ful colde sykyngez.
Sythen fro the meyny he menskly departes;
Uche mon that he mette, he made hem a thonke
1985   For his servyse and his solace and his sere pyne,
That thay wyth busynes had ben aboute hym to serve;
And uche segge as soré to sever with hym there
As thay hade wonde worthyly with that wlonk ever.

And how the fox was killed   *1950*
He heard as there they stood.

With mirth and minstrelsy, and all the food they would wish,
They made as much merriment as any men could
With laughter of ladies and jesting remarks.
Both Gawain and the lord were ravished with joy   *1955*
As if the company had gone crazy or taken much drink.
Both the lord and his retainers played many tricks
Until the time came round when they must separate:
Folk to their beds must betake them at last.
Then humbly this noble knight first takes leave   *1960*
Of the lord, and graciously gives him thanks:
'For such a wonderful stay as I have had here,
Honoured by you at this holy feast, may God repay you!
I offer myself as your servant, if you agree,
For I am compelled, as you know, to leave tomorrow,   *1965*
If you will assign someone to show me, as you promised,
The road to the Green Chapel, as God will allow me,
To get what fate ordains for me on New Year's Day.'
'In good faith,' said the lord, 'very willingly,
Everything I ever promised you I shall readily give.'   *1970*
There he appoints a servant to put Gawain on the road
And guide him over the fells, so that he would not be delayed,
To ride through the woods and take the shortest path
     in the trees.
    Gawain thanked the lord   *1975*
    Paying him great respect;
    Then from those noble ladies
    Took leave, as was correct.

With tears and with kisses he addresses them both,
And begged them to accept many profuse thanks,   *1980*
And they immediately returned the same words to him.
They commended him to Christ with many deep sighs.
Then from the household he takes courteous leave;
To each man whom he met he expressed his thanks
For his service and kindness and the personal pains   *1985*
They had taken in busying themselves for his sake;
And each man was as sorry to part from him there
As if they had honourably lived with that nobleman ever.

Then with ledes and lyght he watz ladde to his chambre,
1990   And blythely broght to his bedde to be at his rest.
Yif he ne slepe soundyly say ne dar I,
For he hade muche on the morn to mynne, yif he wolde,
        in thoght.
      Let hym lyghe there stille,
1995   He hatz nere that he soght;
      And ye wyl a whyle be stylle
      I schal telle yow how thay wroght.

Then with attendants and torches he was led to his room,
And cheerfully brought to his bed and his rest.   *1990*
Whether or not he slept soundly I dare not say,
For he had much about the next day to turn over, if he wished,
       in his mind.
    Let him lie there undisturbed,
    He is close to what he sought;   *1995*
    Be quiet a short while,
    And I'll tell how things turned out.

Fitt 4

Part 4

Now neghez the Nw Yere, and the nyght passez,
The day dryvez to the derk, as Dryghtyn biddez;
2000 Bot wylde wederez of the worlde wakned theroute,
Clowdes kesten kenly the colde to the erthe,
Wyth nyghe innoghe of the northe the naked to tene.
The snawe snitered ful snart, that snayped the wylde;
The werbelande wynde wapped fro the hyghe,
2005 And drof uche dale ful of dryftes ful grete.
The leude lystened ful wel that ley in his bedde,
Thagh he lowkez his liddez, ful lyttel he slepes;
Bi uch kok that crue he knwe wel the steven.
Deliverly he dressed up, er the day sprenged,
2010 For there watz lyght of a laumpe that lemed in his chambre;
He called to his chamberlayn, that cofly hym swared,
And bede hym bryng hym his bruny and his blonk sadel;
That other ferkez hym up and fechez hym his wedez,
And graythez me Sir Gawayn upon a grett wyse.
2015 Fyrst he clad hym in his clothez the colde for to were,
And sythen his other harnays, that holdely watz keped,
Bothe his paunce and his platez, piked ful clene,
The ryngez rokked of the roust of his riche bruny;
And al watz fresch as upon fyrst, and he watz fayn thenne
2020   to thonk.
            He hade upon uche pece,
            Wypped ful wel and wlonk;
            The gayest unto Grece
            The burne bede bryng his blonk.

2025 Whyle the wlonkest wedes he warp on hymselven —
His cote wyth the conysaunce of the clere werkez
Ennurned upon velvet, vertuus stonez
Aboute beten and bounden, enbrauded semez,
And fayre furred withinne wyth fayre pelures —
2030 Yet laft he not the lace, the ladiez gifte,
That forgat not Gawayn for gode of hymselven.

Now the New Year approaches and the night wears away,
The dawn presses against the darkness, as the Creator bids,
But rough weather blows up in the country outside,   *2000*
Clouds empty their bitter cold contents on the earth,
With enough malice from the north to torment the ill-clad.
Snow pelted down spitefully, stinging the wild creatures;
The wind shrilly whistled down from the fells,
Choking the valleys with enormous drifts.   *2005*
The knight lay in bed listening intently,
Although his eyelids are shut very little he sleeps;
Each cock-crow reminded him of his undertaking.
He got up quickly before the day dawned,
For there was light from a lamp burning in his room;   *2010*
He called to his chamberlain, who answered him promptly,
Bade him bring his mail-shirt and saddle his horse.
The man leaps out of bed and fetches him his clothes,
And gets Gawain ready in splendid attire.
First he puts clothing on him to keep out the cold,   *2015*
And then the rest of his gear, that had been well looked after,
His body-armour and his plate, all polished clean,
The rings of his fine mail-shirt rocked free of rust;
Everything unstained as at first, for which he gladly
          gave thanks.   *2020*
      Wearing each metal piece
      Rubbed clean of stain and spot,
      The best-dressed man on earth
      Ordered his horse be brought.

While he dressed himself in his noblest clothes —   *2025*
His coat with its finely embroidered badge
Set upon velvet, with stones of magical power
Inlaid and clasped round it, with embroidered seams,
And richly lined on the inside with beautiful furs —
He did not leave out the belt, the lady's present: *2030*
For his own good Gawain did not forget that.

Bi he hade belted the bronde upon his balghe haunchez,
Thenn dressed he his drurye double hym aboute,
Swythe swethled umbe his swange swetely that knyght
2035 The gordel of the grene silk, that gay wel bisemed,
Upon that ryol red clothe that ryche watz to schewe.
Bot wered not this ilk wyghe for wele this gordel,
For pryde of the pendauntez, thagh polyst thay were,
And thagh the glyterande golde glent upon endez,
2040 Bot for to saven hymself, when suffer hym byhoved,
To byde bale withoute dabate of bronde hym to were
　　　　　　other knyffe.
　　　　　Bi that the bolde mon boun
　　　　　Wynnez theroute bilyve,
2045 　　　　Alle the meyny of renoun
　　　　　He thonkkez ofte ful ryve.

Thenne watz Gryngolet graythe, that gret watz and huge,
And hade ben sojourned saverly and in a siker wyse,
Hym lyst prik for poynt, that proude hors thenne.
2050 The wyghe wynnez hym to and wytez on his lyre,
And sayde soberly hymself and by his soth swerez:
'Here is a meyny in this mote that on menske thenkkez,
The mon hem maynteines, joy mot thay have;
The leve lady on lyve luf hir bityde;
2055 Yif thay for charyté cherysen a gest,
And halden honour in her honde, the hathel hem yelde
That haldez the heven upon hyghe, and also yow alle!
And yif I myght lyf upon londe lede any quyle,
I schuld rech yow sum rewarde redyly, if I myght.'
2060 Thenn steppez he into stirop and strydez alofte;
His schalk schewed hym his schelde, on schulder he hit laght,
Gordez to Gryngolet with his gilt helez,
And he startez on the ston, stod he no lenger
　　　　　　to praunce.
2065 　　　　His hathel on hors watz thenne,
　　　　　That bere his spere and launce.
　　　　　'This kastel to Kryst I kenne':
　　　　　He gef hit ay god chaunce.

The brygge watz brayed doun, and the brode gatez
2070 Unbarred and born open upon bothe halve.

When he had buckled his sword on his curving hips,
That noble knight bound his love-token twice
Closely wrapped round his middle, with delight;
The girdle of green silk, whose colour went well   *2035*
Against that splendid red surcote that showed so fine.
But the knight did not wear the belt for its costliness,
Or for pride in its pendants, however they shone,
Or because its edges gleamed with glittering gold,
But to safeguard himself when he had to submit,   *2040*
To await death without sword to defend himself
        or blade.
      When he was fully dressed
      The knight hurries outside,
      And pays that noble household   *2045*
      His debt of gratitude.

Then Gringolet was ready, that great horse and huge,
Who had been stabled securely, keeping him safe;
In such fine condition that he was eager to gallop.
The knight walks up to him and examines his coat,   *2050*
And said gravely to himself, swearing by his true word,
'There is a company in the castle that keeps courtesy in mind;
And a lord who supports them, may he have joy,
And may the dear lady be loved all her life!
If out of kindliness they cherish a guest   *2055*
And dispense hospitality, may the noble lord
Who holds up heaven repay them, and reward you all!
And were I to live any long time on earth
I would gladly recompense you, if I could.'
Then he sets foot in stirrup and vaults on to his horse,   *2060*
His servant gave him his shield, he slung it on his shoulder,
Strikes spurs into Gringolet with his gilt heels,
And he leaps forward on the paving, he waited no longer
        to prance.
      His man was mounted then,   *2065*
      Carrying his spear and lance.
      'I commend this house to God,
      May it never meet mischance.'

The drawbridge was lowered, and the broad gates
Unbarred and pushed open upon both sides.   *2070*

The burne blessed hym bilyve, and the brede passed —
Prayses the porter bifore the prynce kneled,
Gef hym God and goud day, that Gawayn he save —
And went on his way with his wyghe one,
2075 That schulde teche hym to tourne to that tene place
Ther the ruful race he schulde resayve.
Thay bowen bi bonkkez ther boghez ar bare,
Thay clomben bi clyffez ther clengez the colde.
The heven watz uphalt, bot ugly ther-under;
2080 Mist muged on the mor, malt on the mountez,
Uche hille hade a hatte, a myst-hakel huge.
Brokez byled and breke bi bonkkez about,
Schyre schaterande on schorez ther thay doun showved.
Wela wylle watz the way ther thay bi wode schulden,
2085 Til hit watz sone sesoun that the sunne ryses
            that tyde.
                Thay were on a hille ful hyghe,
                The quyte snaw lay bisyde;
                The burne that rod hym by
2090   Bede his mayster abide.

'For I haf wonnen yow hider, wyghe, at this tyme,
And now nar ye not fer fro that note place
That ye han spied and spuryed so specially after;
Bot I schal say yow for sothe, sythen I yow knowe,
2095 And ye are a lede upon lyve that I wel lovy,
Wolde ye worch bi my wytte, ye worthed the better.
The place that ye prece to ful perelous is halden;
Ther wonez a wyghe in that waste, the worst upon erthe,
For he is stiffe and sturne, and to strike lovies,
2100 And more he is then any mon upon myddelerde,
And his body bigger then the best fowre
That ar in Arthurez hous, Hestor, other other.
He chevez that chaunce at the chapel grene,
Ther passes non bi that place so proude in his armes
2105 That he ne dyngez hym to dethe with dynt of his honde;
For he is a mon methles, and mercy non uses,
For be hit chorle other chaplayn that bi the chapel rydes,
Monk other masseprest, other any mon elles,
Hym thynk as queme hym to quelle as quyk go hymselven.
2110 Forthy I say the, as sothe as ye in sadel sitte,

The knight blessed himself quickly and rode over the planks,
Praises the porter who knelt before him
Commending Gawain to God, that he should the knight save,
And went on his way with his single guide,
Who would show him the way to that perilous place   2075
Where he must submit to a fearful stroke.
They struggled up hillsides where branches are bare,
They climbed up past rock-faces gripped by the cold.
The clouds were high up, but murky beneath them,
Mist shrouded the moors, melted on the hills.   2080
Each summit wore a hat, a huge cloak of mist.
Streams foamed and splashed down the slopes around them,
Breaking white against the banks as they rushed downhill.
Very wandering was the way they must take to the wood,
Until soon it was time for sunrise at that point   2085
           of the year.
       They were high up in the hills,
       By snow surrounded then;
       The servant at his side
       Bade Gawain draw rein.   2090

'For I have guided you here, sir, on this day,
And now you are not far from that notorious place
That you have searched and enquired for so specially.
But I shall tell you truly — since I know who you are,
And you are a man whom I love dearly —   2095
If you would follow my advice, it would be better for you.
The place you are going to is extremely dangerous;
There lives a man in that wilderness, the worst in the world,
For he is powerful and grim, and loves dealing blows,
And is bigger than any other man upon earth: 2100
His body is mightier than the four strongest men
In Arthur's household, Hector or any other.
He so brings it about at the Green Chapel
That no one passes that place, however valiant in arms,
Who is not battered to death by force of his hand;   2105
For he is a pitiless man who never shows mercy.
For whether peasant or churchman passes his chapel,
Monk or mass-priest, or whatever man else,
To him killing seems as pleasant as enjoying his own life.
Therefore I tell you, as sure as you sit in your saddle,   2110

Com ye there, ye be kylled, I may the knyght rede;
Trawe ye me that trwely, thagh ye had twenty lyves
        to spende.
    He hatz wonyd here ful yore,
2115   On bent much baret bende,
    Agayn his dyntez sore
    Ye may not yow defende.

'Forthy, goude Sir Gawayn, let the gome one,
And gotz away sum other gate, upon Goddez halve!
2120 Cayrez bi sum other kyth, ther Kryst mot yow spede,
And I schal hygh me hom agayn, and hete yow fyrre
That I schal swere bi God and alle his gode halwez,
As help me God and the halydam, and othez innoghe,
That I schal lelly yow layne, and lance never tale
2125 That ever ye fondet to fle for freke that I wyst.'
'Grant merci,' quoth Gawayn, and gruchyng he sayde,
'Wel worth the, wyghe, that woldez my gode,
And that lelly me layne I leve wel thou woldez.
Bot helde thou hit never so holde, and I here passed,
2130 Founded for ferde for to fle, in fourme that thou tellez,
I were a knyght kowarde, I myght not be excused.
Bot I wyl to the chapel, for chaunce that may falle,
And talk wyth that ilk tulk the tale that me lyste,
Worthe hit wele other wo, as the wyrde lykez
2135   hit hafe.
    Thaghe he be a sturn knape
    To stightel, and stad with stave,
    Ful wel con Dryghtyn schape
    His servauntez for to save.'

2140 'Mary!' quoth that other man, 'now thou so much spellez
That thou wylt thyn awen nye nyme to thyselven,
And the lyste lese thy lyf, the lette I ne kepe.
Haf here thi helme on thy hede, thi spere in thi honde,
And ryde me doun this ilke rake bi yon rokke syde,
2145 Til thou be broght to the bothem of the brem valay;
Thenne loke a littel on the launde, on thy lyfte honde,
And thou schal se in that slade the self chapel,
And the borelych burne on bent that hit kepez.
Now farez wel, on Godez half, Gawayn the noble!

If you go there you'll be killed, I warn you, sir knight,
Believe that for certain, though you had twenty lives
       to lose.
    He has dwelt there long,
    And brought about much strife;   2115
    Against his brutal blows
    Nothing can save your life.

'Therefore, good Sir Gawain, let the man be,
And for God's sake get away from here by some other road!
Ride through some other country, where Christ be your help,   2120
And I will make my way home again, and further I vow
That I shall swear by God and all his virtuous saints —
As help me God and the holy thing, and many more oaths —
That I shall keep your secret truly, and never reveal
That ever you took flight from a man that I knew.'   2125
'Many thanks,' replied Gawain, and grudgingly he spoke,
'Good luck to you, man, who wishes my good,
And that you would loyally keep my secret I truly believe.
But however closely you kept it, if I avoided this place,
Took to my heels in fright, in the way you propose,   2130
I should be a cowardly knight, and could not be excused.
But I will go to the chapel, whatever may chance,
And discuss with that man whatever matter I please,
Whether good or ill come of it, as destiny
          decides.   2135
    Though an opponent grim
    To deal with, club in hand,
    His faithful servants God
    Knows well how to defend.'

'Marry!' said the other man, 'since your words make it clear   2140
That you will deliberately bring harm on yourself,
And lose your life by your own wish, I won't hinder you.
Put your helmet on your head, take your spear in your hand,
And ride down this track beside the rock over there
Until it brings you to the bottom of the wild valley;   2145
Then look to your left, some way off in the glade,
And you will see in that dale the chapel itself,
And the giant of a man who inhabits the place.
Now in God's name, noble Gawain, farewell!

2150   For alle the golde upon grounde I nolde go wyth the,
        Ne bere the felaghschip thurgh this fryth on fote fyrre.'
        Bi that the wyghe in the wod wendez his brydel,
        Hit the hors with the helez as harde as he myght,
        Lepez hym over the launde, and levez the knyght there
2155   al one.
           'Bi Goddez self,' quoth Gawayn,
           'I wyl nauther grete ne grone;
           To Goddez wylle I am ful bayn,
           And to hym I haf me tone.'

2160   Thenne gyrdez he to Gryngolet, and gederez the rake,
        Schowvez in bi a schore at a schawe syde,
        Ridez thurgh the roghe bonk ryght to the dale;
        And thenne he wayted hym aboute, and wylde hit hym thoght,
        And seye no syngne of resette bisydez nowhere,
2165   Bot hyghe bonkkez and brent upon bothe halve,
        And rughe knokled knarrez with knorned stonez;
        The skwez of the scowtes skayned hym thoght.
        Thenne he hoved, and wythhylde his hors at that tyde,
        And ofte chaunged his cher the chapel to seche:
2170   He seye non suche in no syde, and selly hym thoght,
        Save, a lyttle on a launde, a lawe as hit were;
        A balgh berw bi a bonke the brymme bysyde,
        Bi a forgh of a flode that ferked thare;
        The borne blubred therinne as hit boyled hade.
2175   The knyght kachez his caple and com to the lawe,
        Lightez doun luflyly, and at a lynde tachez
        The rayne and his riche with a roghe braunche.
        Thenne he bowez to the berwe, aboute hit he walkez,
        Debatande with hymself quat hit be myght.
2180   Hit hade a hole on the ende and on ayther syde,
        And overgrowen with gresse in glodes aywhere,
        And al watz holw inwith, nobot an olde cave,
        Or a crevisse of an olde cragge, he couthe hit noght deme
           with spelle.
2185   'We, lorde!' quoth the gentyle knyght,
           'Whether this be the grene chapelle?
           Here myght aboute mydnyght
           The dele his matynnes telle!'

For all the wealth in the world I would not go with you,   *2150*
Nor keep you company through this wood one further step.'
With that the man at his side tugs at his bridle,
Struck his horse with his heels as hard as he could,
Gallops over the hillside and leaves the knight there
          alone.   *2155*
      Said Gawain, 'By God himself,
      I shall not moan or cry;
      My life is in his hands,
      His will I shall obey'.

Then he sets spurs to Gringolet and picks up the path,   *2160*
Makes his way down a slope at the edge of a wood,
Rides down the rugged hillside right to the valley,
And then looked about him, and it seemed a wild place,
And saw no sign of a building anywhere near,
But high and steep hillsides upon both sides,   *2165*
And rough rocky crags of jagged stones:
The clouds grazing the jutting rocks, as it seemed.
Then he halted, and checked his horse for a while,
Often turning his face to look for the chapel.
He saw nothing of the kind anywhere, which he thought strange,   *2170*
Except a way off in a glade, something like a mound;
A rounded hillock on the bank of a stream,
Near the bed of a torrent that tumbled there;
The water foamed in its course as though it had boiled.
The knight urges his horse and comes to the mound,   *2175*
Alights nimbly, and makes fast to a tree
The reins and his noble steed with a rough branch.
Then he goes to the mound and walks around it,
Wondering to himself what it could be.
It had a hole at the end and on either side,   *2180*
And was covered all over with patches of grass,
And was all hollow inside; nothing but an old cave,
Or a fissure in an old rock: what to call it he hardly
          could tell.
      'Good lord!' said the noble knight,   *2185*
      'Can the Green Chapel be this place?
      Here probably at midnight
      The devil his matins says!'

'Now iwysse,' quoth Wowayn, 'wysty is here;
2190   This oritore is ugly, with erbez overgrowen;
Wel bisemez the wyghe wruxled in grene
Dele here his devocioun on the develez wyse.
Now I fele hit is the fende, in my fyve wyttez,
That hatz stoken me this steven to strye me here.
2195   This is a chapel of meschaunce, that chekke hit bytyde!
Hit is the corsedest kyrk that ever I com inne!'
With hegh helme on his hede, his launce in his honde,
He romez up to the roffe of the rogh wonez.
Thene herde he of that hyghe hil, in a harde roche
2200   Biyonde the broke, in a bonk, a wonder breme noyse:
Quat! hit clatered in the clyff, as hit cleve schulde,
As one upon a gryndelston hade grounden a sythe.
What! hit wharred and whette, as water at a mulne;
What! hit rusched and ronge, rawthe to here.
2205   Thenne 'Bi Godde,' quoth Gawayn, 'that gere, as I trowe,
Is ryched at the reverence me, renk, to mete
          bi rote.
        Let God worche! "We loo"
        Hit helppez me not a mote.
2210   My lif thagh I forgoo,
        Drede dotz me no lote.'

Thenne the knyght con calle ful hyghe,
'Who stightlez in this sted me steven to holde?
For now is gode Gawayn goande ryght here.
2215   If any wyghe oght wyl, wynne hider fast,
Other now other never, his nedez to spede.'
'Abyde,' quoth on on the bonke aboven his hede,
And thou schal haf al in hast that I the hyght ones.'
Yet he rusched on that rurde rapely a throwe,
2220   And wyth quettyng awharf, er he wolde lyght;
And sythen he keverez bi a cragge, and comez of a hole,
Whyrlande out of a wro wyth a felle weppen,
A denez ax nwe dyght, the dynt with to yelde,
With a borelych bytte bende bi the halme,
2225   Fyled in a fylor, fowre foot large —
Hit watz no lasse, bi the lace that lemed ful bryght —
And the gome in the grene gered as fyrst,
Bothe the lyre and the leggez, lokkez and berde,

'Now truly,' said Gawain, 'this is a desolate place;
This chapel looks evil, with grass overgrown;   2190
Here fittingly might the man dressed in green
Perform his devotions, in devilish ways.
Now all my senses tell me that the devil himself
Has forced this agreement on me, to destroy me here!
This is a chapel of disaster, may ill-luck befall it!   2195
It is the most damnable church I was ever inside.'
With tall helmet on head, his lance in his hand,
He climbs to the top of that primitive dwelling.
Then he heard up the hillside, from behind a great rock,
On the slope across the stream, a deafening noise: 2200
What! it echoed in the cliffs, as though they would split,
As if someone with a grindstone were sharpening a scythe.
What! it whirred and sang, like water at a mill;
What! it rasped and it rang, terrible to hear.
Then said Gawain, 'By God, these doings, I suppose,   2205
Are a welcoming ceremony, arranged in my honour
               as a knight.
      God's will be done: "Alas"
      Helps me no whit here.
      Although my life be lost,   2210
      Noise cannot make me fear.'

Then the knight shouted at the top of his voice,
'Who is master of this place, to keep tryst with me?
For now is good Gawain waiting right here.
If anyone wants something, let him hurry here fast,   2215
Either now or never, to settle his affairs.'
'Wait,' said someone on the hillside above,
'And you shall quickly have all that I promised you once.'
Yet he kept making that whirring noise for a while,
And turned back to his whetting before he would come down;   2220
And then makes his way among the rocks, bursting out of a hole,
Whirling out of a nook with a fearsome weapon —
A Danish axe newly made — for dealing the blow,
With a massive blade curving back on the shaft,
Honed with a whetstone, four feet across —   2225
No less than that, despite the gleaming green girdle —
And the man in the green, dressed as at first,
Both his flesh and his legs, hair and beard,

Save that fayre on his fote he foundez on erthe,
2230   Sette the stele to the stone, and stalked bysyde.
When he wan to the watter, ther he wade nolde,
He hypped over on hys ax, and orpedly strydez,
Bremly brothe on a bent that brode watz aboute,
          on snawe.
2235   Sir Gawayn the knyght con mete,
        He ne lutte hym nothyng lowe;
        That other sayde, 'Now, sir swete,
        Of steven mon may the trowe.

'Gawayn,' quoth that grene gome, 'God the mot loke!'
2240   Iwysse thou art welcom, wyghe, to my place,
And thou hatz tymed thi travayl as truee mon schulde,
And thou knowez the covenauntez kest uus bytwene:
At this tyme twelmonyth thou toke that the falled,
And I schulde at this Nwe Yere yeply the quyte.
2245   And we ar in this valay verayly oure one;
Here are no renkes us to rydde, rele as uus lykez.
Haf thy helme of thy hede, and haf here thy pay.
Busk no more debate then I the bede thenne
When thou wypped of my hede at a wap one.'
2250   'Nay, bi God,' quoth Gawayn, 'that me gost lante,
I schal gruch the no grwe for grem that fallez.
Bot styghtel the upon on strok, and I schal stonde stylle
And warp the no wernyng to worch as the lykez,
          nowhare.'
2255   He lened with the nek, and lutte,
        And schewed that schyre al bare,
        And lette as he noght dutte;
        For drede he wolde not dare.

Then the gome in the grene graythed hym swythe,
2260   Gederez up hys grymme tole Gawayn to smyte;
With alle the bur in his body he ber hit on lofte,
Munt as maghtyly as marre hym he wolde;
Hade hym dryven adoun as dregh as he atled,
Ther hade ben ded of his dynt that doghty watz ever.
2265   Bot Gawayn on that giserne glyfte hym bysyde,
As hit com glydande adoun on glode hym to schende,
And schranke a lytel with the schulderes for the scharp yrne.

Except that grandly on foot he stalked on the earth,
Set the handle to the ground and walked beside it.   2230
When he came to the stream he refused to wade:
He hopped over on his axe and forcefully strides,
Fiercely grim on a clearing that stretched wide about,
      under snow.
      Sir Gawain met the knight,   2235
      Made him a frosty bow;
      The other said, 'Good sir,
      'A man may trust your vow.

'Gawain,' said that green man, 'may God protect you!
You are indeed welcome, sir, to my place;   2240
You have timed your journey as a true man should,
And you know the agreement settled between us:
A twelvemonth ago you took what fell to your lot,
And I was to repay you promptly at this New Year.
And we are in this valley truly by ourselves,   2245
With no knights to separate us, so we can fight as we please.
Take your helmet off your head, and here get your pay.
Make no more argument than I offered you then,
When you slashed off my head with a single stroke.'
'No, by God,' said Gawain, 'who gave me a soul,   2250
I shall bear you no grudge at all, whatever hurt comes about.
Just limit yourself to one blow, and I will stand still
And not resist whatever it pleases you to do
      at all.'
      He bent his neck and bowed,   2255
      Showing the flesh all bare,
      And seeming unafraid;
      He would not shrink in fear.

Then the man dressed in green quickly got ready.
Raised his terrible axe to give Gawain the blow;   2260
With all the strength in his body he heaved it in the air,
Swung it as fiercely as if meaning to mangle him.
Had he brought the axe down as forcibly as he acted,
That courageous knight would have been killed by the blow;
But Gawain glanced sideways at that battle-axe   2265
As it came sweeping down to destroy him there,
And hunched his shoulders a little to resist the sharp blade.

That other schalk wyth a schunt the schene wythhaldez,
And thenne repreved he the prynce with mony prowde wordez:
2270 'Thou art not Gawayn,' quoth the gome, 'that is so goud halden,
That never arghed for no here by hylle ne be vale,
And now thou fles for ferde er thou fele harmez!
Such cowardise of that knyght cowthe I never here.
Nawther fyked I ne flaghe, freke, quen thou myntest,
2275 Ne kest no cavelacioun in kyngez hous Arthor.
My hede flagh to my fote, and yet flagh I never;
And thou, er any harme hent, arghez in hert.
Wherfore the better burne me burde be called
                    therfore.'
2280   Quoth Gawayn, 'I schunt onez,
            And so wyl I no more;
            Bot thagh my hede falle on the stonez,
            I con not hit restore.

'But busk, burne, bi thi fayth, and bryng me to the poynt.
2285 Dele to me my destiné, and do hit out of honde,
For I schal stonde the a strok, and start no more
Til thy ax have me hitte: haf here my trawthe.'
'Haf at the thenne!' quoth that other, and hevez hit alofte,
And waytez as wrothely as he wode were.
2290 He myntez at hym maghtyly, bot not the mon rynez,
Withhelde heterly his honde er hit hurt myght.
Gawayn graythely hit bydez, and glent with no membre,
Bot stode stylle as the ston, other a stubbe auther
That ratheled is in roché grounde with rotez a hundreth.
2295 Then muryly efte con he mele, the mon in the grene,
'So, now thou hatz thi hert holle, hitte me bihovs.
Halde the now thy hyghe hode that Arthur the raght,
And kepe thy kanel at this kest, yif hit kever may.'
Gawayn ful gryndelly with greme thenne sayde:
2300 'Wy! thresch on, thou thro mon, thou thretez to longe;
I hope that thi hert arghe wyth thyn awen selven.'
'For sothe,' quoth that other freke, 'so felly thou spekez,
I wyl no lenger on lyte lette thin ernde
                    right nowe.'
2305   Thenne tas he hym strythe to stryke,
            And frounsez bothe lyppe and browe,
            No mervayle thagh hym myslyke

128

The other man checked the bright steel with a jerk,
And then rebuked the prince with arrogant words:
'You're not Gawain,' said the man, 'who is reputed so good,   2270
Who never quailed from an army, on valley or on hill,
And now flinches for fear before he feels any hurt!
I never heard of such cowardice shown by that knight.
I neither flinched nor fled, sir, when you aimed one at me,
Nor raised any objections in King Arthur's house.   2275
My head fell to the floor, yet I gave no ground;
But you, though not wounded, are trembling at heart,
So I deserve to be reckoned the better man
       for that.'
      Gawain said, 'I flinched once,   2280
      But won't twice hunch my neck,
      Though if my head should fall
      I cannot put it back.

'But hurry up, man, by your faith, and come to the point.
Deal out my fate to me, and do it out of hand,   2285
For I shall let you strike a blow, and not move again
Until your axe has hit me, take my true word.'
'Have at you then!' said the other, and raises it up,
Contorting his face as though he were enraged.
He swings the axe at him savagely, without harming the man,   2290
Checked his blow suddenly before it could inflict hurt.
Gawain awaits it submissively, not moving a limb,
But stood as still as a stone, or the stump of a tree
Anchored in rocky ground by hundreds of roots.
Then the man in green spoke mockingly again,   2295
'So, now you have found courage it is time for the blow.
Now may the order of knighthood given you by Arthur
Preserve you and your neck this time, if it has power!'
Then Gawain replied angrily, mortified deeply,
'Why, strike away, you fierce man, you waste time in threats;   2300
I think you have frightened yourself with your words.'
'Indeed,' said that other man, 'you speak so aggressively
That I will no longer delay or hinder your business
      at all.'
      He takes his stance to strike,   2305
      Puckering mouth and brow;
      No wonder if Gawain feels

That hoped of no rescowe.

He lyftes lyghtly his lome, and let hit doun fayre
2310   With the barbe of the bitte bi the bare nek;
Thagh he homered heterly, hurt hym no more
Bot snyrt hym on that on syde, that severed the hyde.
The scharp schrank to the flesche thurgh the schyre grece,
That the schene blod over his schulderes schot to the erthe;
2315   And quen the burne sey the blode blenk on the snawe,
He sprit forth a spenne-fote more then a spere lenthe,
Hent heterly his helme, and his hed cast,
Schot with his schulderes his fayre schelde under,
Braydez out a bryght sworde, and bremly he spekez —
2320   Never syn that he watz burne borne of his moder
Watz he never in this worlde wyghe half so blythe —
'Blynne, burne, of thy bur, bede me no mo!
I haf a stroke in this sted withoute stryf hent,
And if thow rechez me any mo, I redyly schal quyte,
2325   And yelde yederly agayn — and therto ye tryst —
        and foo.
        Bot on stroke here me fallez —
        The covenaunt schop so,
        Fermed in Arthurez hallez —
2330   And therfore, hende, now hoo!'

The hathel heldet hym fro, and on his ax rested,
Sette the schaft upon schore, and to the scharp lened,
And loked to the leude that on the launde yede,
How that doghty, dredles, dervely ther stondez
2335   Armed, ful aghles: in hert hit hym lykez.
Thenn he melez muryly wyth a much steven,
And with a rynkande rurde he to the renk sayde:
'Bolde burne, on this bent be not so gryndel.
No mon here unmanerly the mysboden habbez,
2340   Ne kyd bot as covenaunde at kyngez kort schaped.
I hyght the a strok and thou hit hatz, halde the wel payed;
I relece the of the remnaunt of ryghtes alle other.
Iif I deliver had bene, a boffet paraunter
I couthe wrotheloker haf waret, to the haf wroght anger.
2345   Fyrst I mansed the muryly with a mynt one,
And rove the wyth no rofe-sore, with ryght I the profered

No hope of rescue now.

He swiftly raises his weapon, and brings it down straight
With the cutting edge of the blade over Gawain's bare neck;   2310
Although he struck fiercely, he hurt him no more
Than to slash the back of his neck, laying open the skin.
The blade cut into the body through the fair flesh
So that bright blood shot over his shoulders to the ground.
And when the knight saw his blood spatter the snow   2315
He leapt forward with both feet more than a spear's length,
Snatched up his helmet and crammed it on his head,
Jerked his shoulders to bring his splendid shield down,
Drew out a gleaming sword and fiercely he speaks —
Never since that man was born of his mother   2320
Had he ever in the world felt half so relieved —
'Hold your attack, sir, don't try it again!
I have passively taken a blow in this place,
And if you offer me another I shall repay it promptly
And return it at once — be certain of that —   2325
                    with force.
          One single blow is due;
          The contract is my proof,
          Witnessed in Arthur's hall;
          And therefore, sir, enough!'   2330

The knight kept his distance, and rested on his axe,
Set the shaft on the ground and leant on the blade,
Contemplating the man before him in the glade;
Seeing how valiant, fearlessly bold he stood there
Armed and undaunted, he admired him much.   2335
Then he spoke to him pleasantly in a loud voice,
And said to the knight in a resounding tone,
'Brave sir, don't act so wrathfully in this place.
No one has discourteously mistreated you here,
Or acted contrary to the covenant sworn at the king's court.   2340
I promised you a blow and you have it; think yourself well paid;
I free you from the rest of all other obligations.
Had I been more dextrous, maybe I could
Have dealt you more spiteful blow, to have roused your anger.
First I threatened you playfully with a pretence,   2345
And avoided giving you a gash, doing so rightly

For the forwarde that we fest in the fyrst nyght,
And thou trystyly the trawthe and trwly me haldez,
Al the gayne thow me gef, as god mon schulde.
2350 That other munt for the morne, mon, I the profered,
Thou kyssedes my clere wyf — the cosses me raghtez.
For bothe two here I the bede bot two bare myntes
boute scathe.
Trwe mon trwe restore,
2355 Thenne thar mon drede no wathe.
At the thrid thou fayled thore,
And therfore that tappe ta the.

'For hit is my wede that thou werez, that ilke woven girdel,
Myn owen wyf hit the weved, I wot wel for sothe.
2360 Now know I wel thy cosses, and thy costes als,
And the wowyng of my wyf: I wroght it myselven.
I sende hir to asay the, and sothly me thynkkez
On the fautlest freke that ever on fote yede;
As perle bi the quite pese is of prys more,
2365 So is Gawayn, in god fayth, bi other gay knyghtez.
Bot here yow lakked a lyttel, sir, and lewté yow wonted;
Bot that watz for no wylyde werke, ne wowyng nauther,
Bot for ye lufed your lyf; the lasse I yow blame.'
That other stif mon in study stod a gret whyle,
2370 So agreved for greme he gryed withinne;
Alle the blod of his brest blende in his face,
That al he schranke for schome that the schalk talked.
The forme worde upon folde that the freke meled:
'Corsed worth cowarddyse and covetyse bothe!
2275 In yow is vylany and vyse that vertue disstryez.'
Thenne he kaght to the knot, and the kest lawsez,
Brayde brothely the belt to the burne selven:
'Lo, ther the falssyng, foule mot hit falle!
For care of thy knokke cowardyse me taght
2380 To acorde me with covetyse, my kynde to forsake,
That is larges and lewté that longez to knyghtez.
Now am I fawty and falce, and ferde haf ben ever
Of trecherye and untrawthe: bothe bityde sorwe
and care!
2385 I biknowe yow, knyght, here stylle,
Al fawty is my fare;

Because of the agreement we made on the first night,
When you faithfully and truly kept your pledged word,
Gave me all your winnings, as an honest man should.
That other feint, sir, I gave you for the next day,   2350
When you kissed my lovely wife and gave me those kisses.
For both occasions I aimed at you two mere mock blows
            without harm.
        True man must pay back truly,
        Then he need nothing fear;   2355
        You failed me the third time
        And took that blow therefore.

'For it is my belt you are wearing, that same woven girdle,
My own wife gave it to you, I know well in truth.
I know all about your kisses, and your courteous manners,   2360
And my wife's wooing of you: I arranged it myself.
I sent her to test you, and to me truly you seem
One of the most perfect men who ever walked on the earth.
As pearls are more valuable than the white peas,
So is Gawain, in all truth, before other fair knights.   2365
Only here you fell short a little, sir, and lacked fidelity,
But that was not for fine craftsmanship, nor wooing either,
But because you wanted to live: so I blame you the less.'
That other brave man stood speechless a long while,
So mortified and crushed that he inwardly squirmed;   2370
All the blood in his body burned in his face,
So that he winced with shame at what the man said.
The first words that the knight uttered there
Were, 'A curse upon cowardice and coveteousness!
You breed boorishness and vice that ruin virtue.'   2375
Then he took hold of the knot and looses the buckle,
Flung the belt violently towards that man:
'There it is, the false thing, may the devil take it!
For fear of your blow taught me cowardice,
To give way to covetousness, be false to my nature,   2380
The generosity and fidelity expected of knights.
Now I am false and unworthy, and have always dreaded
Treachery and deceit: may misfortune and grief
            befall both!
        Sir, humbly I confess   2385
        My good name is marred.

>Letez me overtake your wylle
>And efte I schal be ware.'

The loghe that other leude and luflyly sayde,
2390 'I halde hit hardily hole, the harme that I hade.
Thou art confessed so clene, beknowen of thy mysses,
And hatz the penaunce apert of the poynt of myn egge,
I halde the polysed of that plyght, and pured as clene
As thou hadez never forfeted sythen thou watz fyrst borne;
2395 And I gif the, sir, the gurdel that is golde-hemmed;
For hit is grene as my goune, Sir Gawayn, ye maye
Thenk upon this ilke threpe, ther thou forth thryngez
Among prynces of prys, and this a pure token
Of the chaunce of the grene chapel at chevalrous knyghtez.
2400 And ye schal in this Nwe Yer agayn to my wonez,
And we schyn revel the remnaunt of this ryche fest
>ful bene.'
>Ther lathed hym fast the lorde
>And sayde, 'Wyth my wyf, I wene,
2405 >We schal yow wel acorde,
>That watz your enmy kene.'

'Nay, for sothe,' quoth the segge, and sesed hys helme,
And hatz hit of hendely, and the hathel thonkkez,
'I haf sojorned sadly; sele yow bytyde
2410 And he yelde hit yow yare that yarkkez al menskes!
And comaundez me to that cortays, your comlych fere,
Bothe that on and that other, myn honoured ladyez,
That thus hor knyght wyth hor kest han koyntly bigyled.
Bot hit is no ferly thagh a fole madde,
2415 And thurgh wyles of wymmen be wonen to sorwe,
For so watz Adam in erde with one bygyled,
And Salamon with fele sere, and Samson eftsonez —
Dalyda dalt hym hys wyrde — and Davyth therafter
Watz blended with Barsabe, that much bale tholed.
2420 Now these were wrathed wyth her wyles, hit were a wynne huge
To luf hom wel and leve hem not, a leude that couthe.
For thes wer forne the freest, that folwed alle the sele
Exellently of alle thyse other, under hevenryche
>that mused;
2425 >And alle thay were biwyled

134

                Let me regain your trust,
                Next time I'll be on guard.'

Then the other man laughed, and graciously said,
'The wrong you did me I consider wiped out.   2390
You have so cleanly confessed yourself, admitted your fault,
And done honest penance on the edge of my blade.
I declare you absolved of that offence, and washed as clean
As if you had never transgressed since the day you were born.
And I make you a gift, sir, of my gold-bordered belt;   2395
Since it is green like my gown, Sir Gawain, you may
Remember this meeting in the world where you mingle
With princes of rank: it will be a true token
Of the exploit of the Green Chapel among chivalrous knights.
And you shall come back to my castle at this New Year,   2400
And we will see out the revelry of this high feast
                with joy.'
                He pressed him earnestly
                And said, 'We shall, I know,
                Reconcile you with my wife,   2405
                Who was your cunning foe.'

'No, indeed,' said the knight, and seizing his helmet
Takes it off politely and gives the lord thanks;
'I have stayed long enough: good fortune attend you,
And may he who gives all honours soon send you reward!   2410
And commend me to that gracious one, your lovely wife,
Both the one and the other of those honourable ladies
Who have so cleverly deluded their knight with their game.
But it is no wonder if a fool acts insanely
And is brought to grief through womanly wiles;   2415
For so was Adam beguiled by one, here on earth,
Solomon by several women, and Samson was another —
Delilah was cause of his fate — and afterwards David
Was deluded by Bathsheba, and suffered much grief.
Since these were ruined by their wiles, it would be a great gain   2420
To love women and not trust them, if a man knew how.
For these were the noblest of old, whom fortune favoured
Above all others on earth, or who dwelt
                under heaven.
                Beguiled were they all   2425

135

With wymmen that thay used.
Thagh I be now bigyled
Me think me burde be excused.

'Bot your gordel,' quoth Gawayn, 'God yow foryelde!
2430 That wyl I welde wyth goud wylle, not for the wynne golde,
Ne the saynt, ne the sylk, ne for syde pendaundes,
For wele ne for worchyp, ne for the wlonk werkkez,
Bot in syngne of my surfet I schal se hit ofte,
When I ride in renoun, remorde to myselven
2435 The faut and the fayntyse of the flesche crabbed,
How tender hit is to entyse teches of fylthe;
And thus, quen pryde schal me pryk for prowes of armes,
The loke to this luf-lace schal lethe my hert.
Bot on I wolde yow pray, displeses yow never:
2440 Syn ye be lorde of the yonder londe her I haf lent inne
Wyth yow wyth worschyp — the wyghe hit yow yelde
That uphaldez the heven and on hygh sittez —
How norne ye yowre ryght nome, and thenne no more?'
'That schal I telle the trwly,' quoth that other thenne,
2445 'Bertilak de Hautdesert I hat in this londe.
Thurgh myght of Morgne la Faye, that in my hous lenges,
And koyntyse of clergye, bi craftes wel lerned,
The maystrés of Merlyn mony hatz taken —
For ho hatz dalt drwry ful dere sumtyme
2450 With that conable klerk, that knowes alle your knyghtez
            at hame.
      Morgne the goddes
      Therfore hit is hir name:
      Weldez non so hyghe hawtesse
2455   That ho ne con make ful tame —

'Ho wayned me upon this wyse to your wynne halle
For to assay the surquidré, yif hit soth were
That rennes of the grete renoun of the Rounde Table.
Ho wayned me this wonder your wyttez to reve,
2460 For to have greved Gaynour and gart hir to dyghe
With glopnyng of that ilke gome that gostlych speked
With his hede in his honde bifore the hyghe table.
That is ho that is at home, the auncian lady;
Ho is even thyn aunt, Arthurez half-suster,

By women they thought kind.
Since I too have been tricked
Then I should pardon find.

'But for your belt,' said Gawain, 'God repay you for that!
I accept it gratefully, not for its wonderful gold,   2430
Nor for the girdle itself nor its silk, nor its long pendants,
Nor its value nor the honour it confers, nor its fine workmanship,
But I shall look at it often as a sign of my failing,
And when I ride in triumph, recall with remorse
The corruption and frailty of the perverse flesh,   2435
How quick it is to pick up blotches of sin.
And so, when pride in my knightly valour stirs me,
A glance at this girdle will humble my heart.
Just one thing I would ask, if it would not offend you,
Since you are the lord of the country that I have dwelt in,   2440
Honourably treated in your house — may he reward you
Who holds up the heavens and sits upon high! —
What do you call yourself rightly, and then no more demands?'
'I will tell you that truthfully,' replied that other man,
'Bertilak of Hautdesert I am called in this land.   2445
Through the power of Morgan le Fay, who lives under my roof,
And her skill in learning, well taught in magic arts,
She has acquired many of Merlin's occult powers —
For she had love-dealings at an earlier time
With that accomplished scholar, as all your knights know   2450
            at home.
            Morgan the goddess
            Therefore is her name;
            No one, however haughty
            Or proud she cannot tame.   2455

'She sent me in this shape to your splendid hall
To make trial of your pride, and to judge the truth
Of the great reputation attached to the Round Table.
She sent me to drive you demented with this marvel,
To have terrified Guenevere and caused her to die   2460
With horror at that figure who spoke like a spectre
With his head in his hand before the high table.
That is she who is in my castle, the very old lady,
Who is actually your aunt, Arthur's half-sister,

2465 The duches doghter of Tyntagelle, that dere Uter after
Hade Arthur upon, that athel is nowthe.
Therfore I ethe the, hathel, to com to thyn aunt,
Make myry in my hous; my meny the lovies,
And I wol the as wel, wyghe, bi my faythe,
2470 As any gome under God for thy grete trauthe.'
And he nikked hym naye, he nolde bi no wayes.
Thay acolen and kyssen and kennen ayther other
To the prynce of paradise, and parten ryght there
on coolde;
2475   Gawayn on blonk ful bene
    To the kyngez burgh buskez bolde,
    And the knyght in the enker-grene
    Whiderwarde-so-ever he wolde.

Wylde wayez in the worlde Wowen now rydez
2480 On Gryngolet, that the grace hade geten of his lyve;
Ofte he herbered in house and ofte al theroute,
And mony aventure in vale, and venquyst ofte,
That I ne tyght at this tyme in tale to remene.
The hurt watz hole that he hade hent in his nek,
2485 And the blykkande belt he bere theraboute
Abelef as a bauderyk bounden by his syde,
Loken under his lyfte arme, the lace, with a knot,
In tokenyng he watz tane in tech of a faute.
And thus he commes to the court, knyght al in sounde.
2490 Ther wakned wele in that wone when wyst the grete
That gode Gawayn watz commen; gayn hit hym thoght.
The kyng kysses the knyght, and the whene alce,
And sythen mony syker knyght that soght hym to haylce,
Of his fare that hym frayned; and ferlyly he telles,
2495 Biknowez alle the costes of care that he hade,
The chaunce of the chapel, the chere of the knyght,
The luf of the ladi, the lace at the last.
The nirt in the neck he naked hem schewed
That he laght for his unleuté at the leudes hondes
2500   for blame.
    He tened quen he schulde telle,
    He groned for gref and grame;
    The blod in his face con melle,
    When he hit schulde schewe, for schame.

The duchess of Tintagel's daughter, whom noble Uther   2465
Afterwards begot Arthur upon, who now is king.
So I entreat you, good sir, to visit your aunt
And make merry in my house: my servants all love you,
And so will I too, sir, on my honour,
As much as any man on earth for your great truth.'   2470
But Gawain told him no, not for any persuasion.
They embrace and kiss, and commend each other
To the prince of paradise, and separate there
              in the cold;
        On his great horse Gawain   2475
        To the king's court quickly goes,
        And the knight in emerald green
        Went wheresoever he chose.

Over wild country Gawain now makes his way
On Gringolet, after his life had been mercifully spared.   2480
Sometimes he lodged in a house and often out of doors,
And was vanquisher often in many encounters
Which at this time I do not intend to relate.
The injury he had received in his neck was healed,
And over it he wore the gleaming belt   2485
Across his body like a baldric, fastened at his side,
And this girdle tied under his left arm with a knot,
To signify he had been dishonoured by a slip.
And so safe and sound he arrives at the court.
Joy spread through the castle when the nobles learnt   2490
That good Gawain had returned: they thought it a wonder.
The king kisses the knight, and the queen too,
And then many true knights who came to embrace him,
Asking how he had fared; he tells a marvellous story,
Describes all the hardships he had endured,   2495
What happened at the chapel, the Green Knight's behaviour,
The lady's wooing, and finally the belt.
He showed them the scar on his bare neck
That he received for his dishonesty at the lord's hands
              in rebuke.   2500
        Tormented by his tale
        He groaned for grief and hurt;
        The blood burned in his face
        When he showed the shameful cut.

2505 'Lo, lorde,' quoth the leude, and the lace hondeled,
'This is the bende of this blame I bere in my nek,
This is the lathe and the losse that I laght have
Of cowardise and covetyse that I haf caght thare,
This is the token of untrawthe that I am tane inne,
2510 And I mot nedez hit were wyle I may last;
For mon may hyden his harme, bot unhap ne may hit,
For ther hit onez is tachched twynne wil hit never.'
The kyng comfortez the knyght, and alle the court als
Laghen loude therat, and luflyly acorden
2515 That lordes and ladis that longed to the Table,
Uche burne of the brotherhede, a bauderyk schulde have,
A bende abelef hym aboute of a bryght grene,
And that, for sake of that segge, in swete to were.
For that watz acorded the renoun of the Rounde Table,
2520 And he honoured that hit hade evermore after,
As hit is breved in the best boke of romaunce.
Thus in Arthurus day this aunter bitidde,
The Brutus bokez therof beres wyttenesse;
Sythen Brutus, the bolde burne, bowed hider fyrst,
2525 After the segge and the asaute watz sesed at Troye,
iwysse,
Mony aunterez here-biforne
Haf fallen suche er this.
Now that bere the croun of thorne
2530 He bryng uus to his blysse! AMEN.

HONY SOYT QUI MAL PENCE.

'See, my lord,' said the man, and held up the girdle,   *2505*
'This belt caused the scar that I bear on my neck;
This is the injury and damage that I have suffered
For the cowardice and covetousness that seized me there;
This is the token of the dishonesty I was caught committing,
And now I must wear it as long as I live.   *2510*
For a man may hide his misdeed, but never erase it,
For where once it takes root the stain can never be lifted.'
The king consoles the knight, and the whole court
Laughs loudly about it, and courteously agrees
That lords and ladies who belong to the Table,   *2515*
Each member of the brotherhood, should wear such a belt,
A baldric of bright green crosswise on the body,
Similar to Sir Gawain's and worn for his sake:
And that became part of the renown of the Round Table,
And whoever afterwards wore it was always honoured,   *2520*
As is set down in the most reputable books of romance.
So in the time of Arthur this adventure happened,
And the chronicles of Britain bear witness to it;
After the brave hero Brutus first arrived here,
When the siege and the assault were ended at Troy,   *2525*
        indeed.
      Many exploits before now
      Have happened much like this.
      Now may the thorn-crowned God
      Bring us to his bliss! AMEN.   *2530*

HONI SOIT QUI MAL Y PENSE.

Notes on the text

5   *Ennias the athel* Here *athel* is used as a title appropriate to a prince (Aeneas), but at 2065 the word is applied to Gawain's guide. See the note on p. 153.

31   *as I in toun herde* It seems unlikely that the poet had either read or heard this particular tale recited. Although the beheading-game figures in an Irish legend and the test of chastity has many analogues, no other surviving story combines them in a single narrative. But originality was not expected of medieval story-tellers.

32   *with tonge* Emphasises the oral nature of the tale. Compare *wyth syght*, 197 and 226, and *meled with his muthe*, 447, for similar constructions.

33   *stad and stoken* Set down and fixed, but perhaps not before the Gawain poet himself did so.

54   *in her first age* In their youth. The youthfulness of the courtly folk and the fashionable novelty of their dress and manners is marked throughout the story.

60   *hit watz nwe cummen* The first day of the new year is still in progress.

66-7   Andrew and Waldron suggest that *hondeselle* are given to servants and *yeres giftes* to equals. But Arthur is said figuratively to have received a *hanselle* at 491.

69-70   The lines refer to some kind of Christmas game, perhaps involving guesses and paying a forfeit of kisses when the guess is wrong.

73   *the best burne ay abof* Members of the court are seated according to social degree, at the *hyghe table*, 107, or at *sidbordez*, 115. The reference to *lordes and ladis that longed to the Table*, 2515, suggests that the poet saw the Round Table as a social institution.

79   *preved of prys* Proved of value. A theme of the poem makes its first appearance.

80   *in daye* Ever.

82   *yghen gray* Virtually obligatory in medieval heroines.

109   *gode Gawan* So characterised throughout the story, even after his disgrace. The spelling of the hero's name varies considerably. He is *Gawan* consistently throughout Part 1. Later the poet or his scribe prefers the form *Gawayn* or *Gawayne*, which is used throughout Part 4. For alliterative purposes he is occasionally referred to as *Wawan*, *Wawen*, *Wowayn*, or *Wowen*. Less frequently he is *Gavan* or *Gavayn*.

112   *abof biginez the table* Sits in the place of honour.

133   *haf leve liflode to cache* Arthur will not eat until he has *sen a selly* 475, which is about to arrive.

137   *on the most* Not 'one of the biggest' but 'the very biggest.'

160   *scholes under schankes* Meaning that he was not wearing the steel shoes belonging to a suit of armour; see 574. The Green Knight's feet are covered by the *well-haled hose* of 157.

165   *tryfles* Decorative emblems, such as are embroidered on Gawain's silk uryson, 611-2, and on the old lady's headdress 960.

206-9   The incongruity of the holly-bob and the terrifying axe symbolises two major aspects of the pagan midwinter festival from which Christmas is descended, merry-making and blood-sacrifice. Like other evergreen plants, the holly was regarded as the winter retreat of the vegetation spirit, which had to be encouraged to revive the earth by the example of human licentiousness and the blood of a victim.

227 *raysoun* Words, implicit in *speke* but evidently idiomatic.

246 *I deme hit not al for doubte* The narrator puts in a comment, assuring his audience that not all the knights were too frightened to reply.

277 *batayl bare* Either 'without armour' (compare 290) or — as suggested by *thre bare mote* 1141 — 'in single combat.'

283 *a Crystemas gomen* In earlier times the midwinter festival included many games and sports now forgotten. Many of them involved mock-violence, of which traces remained in Blind Man's Buff, played by striking a blindfold victim and inviting him to guess who had struck him. Others exposed a victim to ridicule by playing a trick on him. Gawain's angry response to his humiliation is out of keeping with the Christmas spirit.

286 *brayn* Crazy, reckless; usually *braynwod*, as at 1461.

290 *as bare as I sitte* Without the protection of armour.

296 *barlay* An obscure term, possibly meaning 'by law,' or here, 'by agreement.'

316 *the lorde greved* Arthur was offended.

331 *sturez hit aboute* Brandishes the axe to get the feel of it.

336 *for hys mayn dintez* Because of Arthur's great practice blows.

342 *this melly mot be myne* Let this be my combat. The two lines 341–2 should probably be regarded as a summary of what Gawain is about to say. The exemplary speech that follows approaches the request to act as Arthur's substitute with great deference and circumlocution, which would be pointless if Gawain had already made his plea in blunt and forthright terms.

345 *withoute vylanye* Without discourtesy or bad manners, since a meal is in progress.

346 *that my legge lady lyked not ille* That the Queen (beside whom Gawain is sitting) would not be offended if I left her side. Gawain comes into the story with an impressive display of good manners, perhaps in implicit rebuke of the Green Knight's boisterous rudeness.

354 *the wakkest...and of wyt feblest* Gawain's extreme modesty is less commendable, since it is patently insincere. His later behaviour proves him very conscious of his reputation.

374 *thou schal byden the bur* You'll be kept waiting for his blow. Arthur does not foresee the Green Knight's ability to survive decapitation.

387–9 The bob and wheel again summarises what the speaker is about to say at greater length.

390–1 The Green Knight does not explain why he is especially pleased that Gawain accepts the challenge. Presumably Gawain's reputation as a virtuous knight makes him the appropriate man for the test.

404 *innogh in Nwe Yer* Literally, 'enough for this New Year's Day'; meaning that Gawain need say nothing more, as the Green Knight goes on to say. New Year is probably mentioned to make up the alliteration on *innogh* and *needes no*.

408   *myn owen nome* The Green Knight does not reveal his name until 2445, after a second request.

426   *broun* Burnished.

447   *meled…with his muthe* Spoke with his mouth; a means of intensifying the verb.

454   *men knowen me mony* But Gawain meets no one who has heard of him.

471   *such craft* A display of skill. Arthur conceals his true feelings from the Queen and speaks as though the beheading had been a conjuring trick.

477   *heng up thyn ax* Arthur *gaynly* or aptly quotes a proverbial saying, meaning 'end your strife.'

493   *wordez were wane* Because the Green Knight had taken their breath away.

504   *wyth wynter hit threpez* The seasons do not simply follow each other quietly but fight for succession: see 525, where autumn wind *wrastelez with the sunne*. The poet sees natural life in dynamic terms, not as picturesque scenery.

505   *colde clengez adoun* Winter is driven down into the earth, waiting to emerge again. The poet's year begins and ends with the lifelessness of winter, when everything that had previously sprung up decays (529).

546   *the cost of this cace* The nature of this affair.

566–591   The description of Gawain's arming, like the detailed account of the dismembering of the slaughtered deer at 1330-63, shows the poet's keen interest in ritual process. The intricate form and symbolism of the pentangle evidently has a similar fascination for him.

618   *bryght and broun* Clear and coloured.

619   *the schelde* The shield has a Christian icon on one side (649) and a pagan emblem on the other. In this respect it is typical of its age. Many medieval English churches are decorated with pagan symbols — unknowingly, one supposes.

624   *thof tary hyt me schulde* Even if it should hold up my story; as it does. Since the pentangle plays no part in Gawain's adventure, and since the symbolism claimed for it is at best dubious, it is difficult to understand why the poet introduced it in this admitted digression. But, as suggested above, he has a great liking for elaborate contrivances.

630   *the endeles knot* No other use of this phrase is known. Like the poet's claim to have heard the story recited, and his closing reference to its place in *the best boke of romaunce* 2521, the remark should probably be regarded as poetic licence. The line does not alliterate.

638   *tale most trwe* Truest in speech (though not at the third exchange of winnings).

652   *fraunchyse and felawschyp* The story gives Gawain no opportunity to demonstrate either generosity or good fellowship. Judged by his refusal to give the lady a parting gift, and by the admitted *covetise* that makes him hold back Bertilak's winnings, Gawain does not seem over-generous.

       forbe al thyng The whole passage is characterised by extremes: *alle his afyaunce, alle other thyngez, his belde never payred, croked were never, harder…then on any other.* The result is an impersonal ideal of moral perfection not borne out in Gawain's actual behaviour.

654   *pité* cannot be translated in one word, as it means both pity and piety. But the five virtuous qualities are weakly associated with Gawain, who at 2381 laments

that he has failed in the *lewté that longez to knyghtez*, a crucial attribute not mentioned here.

673   *sothly* A dialect term meaning 'quietly.'

682   *Who knew ever any kyng...?* The courtiers criticise Arthur for having encouraged Gawain to keep his word when it means his certain death.

690   *the bok as I herde say* Another reference to the narrator's supposed source, heard rather than read.

726-32   The poet begins to display his feeling for winter, repeated at several later points of the poem; most impressively at 2000-5

750   *carande for his costes* Concerned about his religious observances.

761   *in sythes sere* Every time he prayed.

772   *hit schemered and schon* See also *that blenked ful quyte*, 799. In medieval romance, shining buildings are characteristic of the otherworld: compare the castle in *Sir Orfeo*, which 'Gan schyne as doth the crystalle' (Ashmole 61, 361). Hautdesert, which includes a witch among its occupants, is an ironic answer to Gawain's prayer.

776   *bone hostel* Good lodging; a traditional invocation to St Julian, *Sayn Gilyan* 774, the patron saint of hospitality.

797   *craftyly sleghe* The castle architecture abounds with craftsmanship. *Sleghe*, meaning skilful, intricate, subtle, is a term of some significance in the poem. Gawain's fellow-guests hope to see *sleghtez of thewez* 916, skilful displays of good manners; and after creeping into his bedchamber the lady calls him *a sleper unslyghe* 1209 or unwary, a related term. On being told that he cannot be killed *for slyght upon erthe* 1854 while wearing the belt, Gawain tells himself that such a *sleght were noble* 1858. Here the word shades off towards modern 'sleight,' with overtones of trickery or deceit appropriate to the story. But many passages of the poem illustrate the poet's fondness for the elaborate craftsmanship or *wylyde werke* that is evident in his own writing, particularly in the *entrelacement* of Part 3.

798   *ches he innoghe* He saw enough of them, meaning there were very many.

802   *papure* Paper, a word newly introduced into English, perhaps by the poet.

835-7   This courteous encouragement to make use of everything *at yowre wylle* may hint at the freedom later offered to Gawain by the lady.

847   *fre of hys speche* Noble in speech, unlike his boastful counterpart.

875   *a cheyer* Chairs were relatively rare, and to be given one was a mark of respect. The usual form of seat is indicated by the Green Knight's reference to knights *aboute on this bench* 280, and by Gawain's request for permission to *boghe fro this benche* 344.

883   *his cher mended* His expression improved. Gawain begins to relax after his strenuous journey.

890   *fele kyn fischez* Many kinds of fish. Because Christmas Eve is a fast-day no red meat is served. The meal is jokingly referred to as penance 897, and Gawain is promised something better on the next day 898.

912   *alle prys and prowes and pured thewes* Great excellence, military valour, and refined manners.

918   *Wich spede is in speche unspurd may we lerne* We may learn without asking what success in conversation consists of.

919   *that fyne fader of nurture* Gawain is excitedly welcomed not as a renowned warrior but as the recognised authority on cultured behaviour, especially *luf-talkyng* 927, flirtatious chat.

934   *a cumly closet* An attractive closed pew.

943   *the fayrest in felle* Literally, the most beautiful in skin. Compare *lufsum under lyne* 1814, where 'linen' indicates a woman. The present phrase means 'the most beautiful woman.'

950-69   The striking contrast between the lovely young woman and the raddled old one invites interpretation. The poet may be returning to the theme of the passing year, suggesting that, like spring, womanly beauty must succumb to old age; but the passage implies the triumph of youth rather than its destruction. The close association of the two figures seems symbolic, however, and may embody a warning for Gawain. While the *auncian wyf* has the witchlike appearance, it is the young one who may enchant him.

971   *he lent hem agaynes* He went towards them.

979   *spycez* Spiced cakes, still a Christmas tradition. Cloves, ginger, and cinnamon were available.

983-5   Another Christmas game, evidently a jumping contest, typically boisterous in character.

999   *messes ful quaynt* Finely prepared meals, set out (*drest*) on the high table. Elsewhere *koynt* (877) is a variant spelling, again indicating skilfully made things.

1009   *And to poynte hit* Even if I described it in detail.

1018   *Uche mon tented hys* Each man attended to his own needs or pleasures.

1022   *Sayn Jonez day* 27 December, but three days later it is New Year's Eve — a day too early. The poet seems to have overlooked 28 December.

1025   *wonderly thay woke* They stayed up a remarkably long time — making a night of it. The poet does not explain why the festivities do not continue until Twelfth Night, 6 January. Is he clearing the stage for Gawain's encounters with the lady?

1028   *wyghe straunge* A stranger or visitor to the castle. The manuscript reading *stronge* obscures the sense.

1034   *enbelyse, bele chere* Bertilak makes an uncharacteristic sortie into courtly French terms.

1045   *Bi non way that he myght* He could not by any means.

1049   *Er the halidayez holly were halet* Before the holidays were completely over. A curious remark. Gawain reaches Hautdesert after a long journey (*towen fro ferre*, 1093) as the festivities are reaching their height, having left Camelot long before the holiday season began.

1074   *in spenne* There.

1082   *and ellez do quat ye demen* And do whatever you think fit. A typical rash promise, which Bertilak immediately takes advantage of.

1096   *ye schal lenge in your lofte* Gawain should be suspicious when his promise has such an undemanding outcome.

1107   *quat chek so ye acheve* Whatever fortune you win. The remark is equivocal. *Chek* also has the sense of misfortune — see 1857 and 2195 — and although Bertilak is politely suggesting that he will be the loser in the exchange, Gawain's winnings will in fact prove very unlucky for him.

1109   *Quether leude so lymp lere other better* Whichever man wins something worthless or better. The literal sense of *lymp* is 'falls to his lot.'

1116   *frenkysch fare* Refined manners, modelled on courtly French behaviour.

1141   *thre bare mote* Three single notes on the horn, ordering the release of the hounds.

1146   *to trystors vewters yod* Keepers of hounds went to their hunting-stations.

1180   *Lurkkez* Lay snug; but the term has pejorative overtones that are heard again at 1195. Unlike Bertilak, who is in the saddle before daylight (1137), Gawain lies in bed *quyl the daylyght lemed on the wowes.* The contrast seems deliberate, and unfavourable to *the god mon.*

1189   *and the burne schamed* And the knight was embarrassed. Gawain begins to come alive as a character with human foibles not previously admitted. In the next line *and let as he slepte* is still less heroic.

1201   *and let as hym wondered* Pretended to be astonished. From this point onwards Gawain repeatedly dissembles, concealing his true feelings under a veneer of politeness.

1210   *Now ar ye tan astyt!* Now are you captured in a moment! There may be a suggestion here of another traditional game, played by women on Hock Monday, immediately after Easter. It consisted of seizing and binding men, who were released after paying a small sum of money. The lady's threat of binding Gawain in his bed unless they agree on terms (*true* = truce), and his acknowledgement of being her prisoner (*prysoun*, 1219), encourage the possibility.

1214   *that me wel lykez* that pleases me very much. Obviously it doesn't, as Gawain shows by wishing to leave his bed and dress himself 1220, but courtesy does not allow him to protest.

1237   *ye are welcum to my cors* A suggestive ambiguity that cannot be translated. *My cors* may mean 'me,' just as 'your honour' or 'your worship' mean 'you.' But the literal sense of the phrase, 'my body,' is present, and *Youre awen won to wale* in the next line makes the lady's implicit purpose plain.

1242   *I be not now he that ye of speken* More modesty; but the question of Gawain's true nature is raised more than once subsequently, and remains problematic.

1247   *To the plesaunce of your prys* To pleasing you, or to carrying out your wishes; *your prys* meaning your noble self.

1253   *your daynté wordez* The lady emphasises the pleasure of listening to Gawain's courteous conversation, as though that were all she wanted.

1276   *ye haf waled wel better* You have made a much better choice; reminding the lady that she has a husband.

1283   *Thagh ho were burde bryghtest the burne in mynde hade* The frightening prospect facing Gawain (*the lur that he soght* 1284) does not allow him to become distracted by the lady's beauty, though her loveliness surpasses anything he can remember. The manuscript reading of this line, *Thagh I were burde bryghtest the burde in mynde hade,* is usually amended as shown.

1293   *Bot that ye be Gawan hit gotz in mynde* The suggestion that he is not Gawain but an impostor immediately suggests to him that he has *fayled in fourme of his castes*, been guilty of a breach of good manners. In his mind, his identity is inseparable from his courtesy, an attribute not innate but assumed.

1355   *the corbeles fee* A piece of gristle thrown to the crows as part of the ritual.

1362   *blw prys* A blast on the horn when the quarry is taken.

1377   *the tayles* Left on the carcasses to facilitate the tally, or count.

1379   *Haf I prys wonnen?* Do I deserve praise?

1395   *frayst me no more* Ask no more questions. Gawain sticks to the letter of their agreement, prompted by the need for secrecy in liaisons between knights and ladies.

1412   *crowen...bot thryse* Cocks supposedly crowed at midnight, 3am, and 6am.

1421   After the hounds give tongue, nothing indicates what has excited them until the boar breaks out of cover at 1439. The poet's audience shares the suspense and the eventual surprise.

1469   *Whyle oure luflych lede lys in his bedde* As before and subsequently, a single sentence links one activity with the other, inviting comparison. Although *luflych* and *in gerez ful ryche* seem approving, the flat statement *lys in his bedde* set against the picture of Bertilak *Suande this wylde swyn til the sunne schafted* 1467 makes Gawain appear slothfully inert.

1474   *watz hym ate* At him in one of two senses or both: in his bedchamber, and bothering him.

1483   *compaynye* Andrew and Waldron suggest that the term may have amorous connotations, as does the Wife of Bath's *compaignye in youthe*.

1490   *Quereso countenaunce is couthe* Wherever looks of favour are shown.

1493   *devayed* denied, refused: a neologism from Old French, repeated by the lady at 1497.

1513   *the lel layk of luf, the lettrure of armes* The lady elevates the importance of faithful love by arguing that it is the central doctrine of chivalry. Her remark suggests to what an extent the masculine world of the heroic warrior is giving way to a new cultural tradition.

1519   *into boure* Into the lady's bower.

1522   *sere twyes* On two separate occasions.

1525   *coynt of your hetes* Gracious in your promises of knightly service.

1539   *hit keverez me ese* It delights me. But again the exaggerated terms of Gawain's speech suggest the opposite, and its sheer verbosity covers a very small measure of sense: see particularly 1542-5.

1550   *to haf wonnen hym to woghe* It is uncertain whether *woghe* means 'wrong' or 'woo.'

1561   *Bot the lorde* The poet underlines the contrast: 'But Bertilak, on the other hand...'

1565   *mawgref his hed* Do what he might.

1571   *bigynez to scrape* Angrily scrapes the earth with his feet.

1575   *to nye hym on-ferum* To hurt him from a distance. Only Bertilak dares approach him.

1584-5   The pace of the narrative quickens and gathers energy from its verbs: *braydez out, forth strydez, foundez fast.*

1634   *let lodly therat* Pretended to be horrified by it.

1638   *Alle my get I schal yow gif agayn* When not addressing the lady, Gawain is capable of simple unaffected speech.

1647   *Such chaffer and ye drowe* If you carry on such a trade, since on the second day Gawain has doubled his takings. Bertilak makes another joking allusion to marketing at the third exchange: see 1938-9.

1653   *Aboute the fyre upon flet* Round a central fire in the hall.

1658   *Such semblaunt* Such affectionate looks. Although *wroth with hymselven*, angry inside himself at being compromised, Gawain continues to treat the lady courteously.

1674-5   *Thou schal cheve to the grene chapel...longe bifore pryme.* Prime begins either at 6 am or at sunrise. At 1073 Bertilak promises that Gawain will *cum to that merk at mydmorn*, meaning at 9 am. In fact the sun rises when he is on the way to the Green Chapel 2085-6. In northwest England midwinter sunrise would not occur before 8 am. Two hours earlier it would be completely dark.

1677   *halde the towchez* Keep the terms of the agreement.

1688   *that his craftez kepes* Who attends to his pursuits; with a tacit allusion to the crafty game being played on Gawain without his knowledge.

1700   *Traylez ofte atraveres* Tracks the scent by working back and forth across the line.

1711   *Went haf wylt of the wood* Thought to have escaped out of the wood.

1716   *onstray* In a different direction.

1729   *he lad hem bi lagmon* Norman Davis explains *lagmon* as 'the last man in a line of reapers,' who would advance diagonally across a field; hence 'strung out.'

1730   *quyle myd over under* Variously explained as mid-morning, midday, or afternoon. When the fox is killed it is *niegh nyght* 1922.

1731   Again as the story returns to Gawain it comments on the attractiveness of his position, sleeping *holsumly* at home behind *comly cortynes*. 1750 gives a different impression.

1738   *hwez* So the manuscript; Andrew and Waldron prefer *hwef*. The sense of the passage is that the lady is not wearing the headdress of a married woman.

1750   *In dregh droupyng of dreme draveled that noble* A literal translation — 'In a heavy troubled sleep that nobleman muttered' — misses the grinding effect of the alliterated words.

1751   *in mornyng of mony thro thoghtes* The first admission that Gawain is oppressed by the fearful prospect that he must face *when he the gome metes*. In sleep he cannot repress the thoughts that his waking self puts aside in assuming his courtly manner.

1769   *Nif Maré of hir knyght mynne* Unless the Virgin be mindful of her knight. The suggestion that Mary might intervene is uncalled for, since the temptation is a test of moral character which Gawain must resolve by his own strength.

1798   *at this departyng* At the moment when Gawain believes he has safely emerged from his ordeal for the last time, the lady launches an attack more difficult to recognise or resist.

1806-12   Gawain's reasons for excusing himself do not include his true motive — an unwillingness to compromise himself by giving a love-token to a married woman.

1823   *I haf none yow to norne ne noght wyl I take* Gawain's argument, that it would be wrong to accept a gift without giving one in return, is a sound principle — particularly at Christmas. But when the lady's offer proves irresistible he forgets this resolution.

1833   *Noght bot arounde brayden* No part of which was not embroidered at the edges.

1836   *And he nay that he nolde neghe in no wyse / Nauther gold ne garysoun* The succession of negatives, *nay, nolde, no, nauther*, expresses Gawain's absolute refusal. For the moment he is concerned only with the evident value of the belt, whose gold trimmings do not attract him.

1855   *hit come to his hert* It flashed into his mind. Unlike the sexual temptation which originates in the lady, the idea of accepting the belt comes from Gawain himself, and is not recognised as a moral failing.

1858   *the sleght were noble* It would be a fine trick; but the literal sense of *noble* clashes with Gawain's acceptance of trickery.

1863   *to lelly layne fro hir lorde* To faithfully conceal it from her husband, which must involve dishonouring Gawain's promise to exchange winnings truly.

1864-5   *never...for noghte* Not under any circumstances.

1878   *lyste his lyf* Hear his confession. Much ink has been spilt over the passage. If Gawain tells the priest about his love-token he would be obliged to return it: if he does not reveal the liaison he cannot be *schrof schyrly* or given absolution. The courtly code of secrecy and the requirements of his religious faith seem to be in conflict. The poet may have chosen to ignore the fact for the sake of the story, giving Gawain credit both for his piety and for his fidelity to the code of *fine amour*.

1881   *the more and the mynne* the greater and lesser sins. It is difficult to see what mortal sin Gawain thinks he may have committed, unless accepting a married woman's love-present is one.

1889   *hade daynté* Admired, though elsewhere meaning courteous treatment (1250).

1896   *the schrewe* The villain.

1902   *And he schunt for the scharp* Reynard's attempt to dodge Bertilak's sword anticipates Gawain's flinching under the first axe-blow, when he *schranke with the schulderes for the scharp yrne*, 2267. The parallel is confirmed by Gawain's admission at 2280, '*I schunt ones.*'

1905   *woried me this wyly* Tore at the fox. The ethic dative *me* is colloquial, and remains so for Shakespeare, e.g., 'It ascends me into the brain... The vital commoners muster me all to their captain': *Henry IV* Part 2, iv. 3. Other examples occur at 2014 and 2144.

1921   *and tyrven of his cote* And stripped off his coat. The third day's hunting is significantly unlike the other two. The fox is vermin, useless as food; there is no ritual breaking-up of the quarry, and nothing to bring back as winnings but a smelly fox-skin. The differences are appropriate to Gawain's falseness.

1934   *I schal fylle upon fyrst* Gawain breaks with precedent, and possibly with good manners, by taking over his host's privilege of initiating the process.

1939   *yif ye hade goud chepez* If you struck a good bargain. Gawain might think he did, since he got the belt for nothing, but he will pay for it dearly.

1940-1   *'Ye, of the chepe no charg,' quoth chefly that other,*
       'As is pertly payed the chepez that I aghte.'

The defective alliteration of the second line suggests a transcription error, caused by carrying down *chepe* from the previous line instead of a word now lost. As Tolkien and Gordon pointed out, *chepez* is plural but the verb *is payed* is singular. A singular noun alliterating on p- seems to be required. The same editors suggested *porchaz*, meaning 'gain,' which is generally adopted.

1945   *ful pore for to pay for suche prys thinges* A wretched return for such precious things (the kisses). In fact *the foule fox felle* is an appropriate response to Gawain's deceitful behaviour.

1955-6   The syntax of these two lines seems erratic. Instead of following *so glad* with a comparison 'as if' the poet continues *bot if,* meaning unless. The intended sense of the passage seems to be, 'They could only have been more deliriously happy if the whole company had gone crazy or got drunk.'

1964-8   Gawain politely offers to become Bertilak's servant (*on of yourez*) if he will give him a man (*take sum tolke*) to guide him to the Green Chapel.

1968   *the dome of my wyrdes* The judgement of my fate.

1972   *downez* Hills, a term still in use, as in the South Downs of Sussex.

1973   *to ferk thurgh the fryth* To ride through the wood, as Gawain does at 2084. *Bi greve* refers to it again.

1991   *Yif he ne slepe soundyly say ne dar I* Though it soon becomes clear that Gawain slept very little; see 2006-8.

1994, 1996   *stille, stylle* French literary convention allows homonyms to be used as rhyme-words different in sense; here 'without moving,' 1994 and 'without noise,' 1996.

2008   *he knwe wel the steven* He remembered the appointment; as at 2194, 2213, 2238.

2021   *He hade upon uche pece* He was wearing all his armour.

2031   *That forgat not Gawayn, for gode of hymselven* One of the poet's many ironic touches. Gawain may think that the belt will protect him, but it does not prevent *the nirt in the nek* 2498 and it dishonours him.

2037-40   More irony. The poet seems anxious to assure the audience that Gawain did not wear the belt for the wrong reason — *pryde of the pendauntes*. The fact that he wears it from fear of death is much less to his credit as a knight.

2068   *He gef hit ay god chaunce* Either Gawain wishes the castle lasting good fortune or, continuing his prayer in the previous line, hopes that Christ will do so, *He gef* then meaning 'May he give.'

2084   *the way ther thay bi wod schulden* The path which they had to take through the woods.

2106   *he is a mon methles and mercy non uses* This description of the Green Knight is markedly unlike the exuberantly playful figure who demands a Christmas game of Arthur.

2112   *I may the knyght rede* I can tell you, knight. The original text does not include the first personal pronoun, which was supplied by Sisam. The manuscript would have the guide refer to Gawain impersonally as *the knyght*, an unlikely form of address in view of the familiarity of *Forthy I say the* in the previous line.

2124   *I schal lelly yow layne* The guide repeats Gawain's promise to the lady at 1863. Gawain does not doubt her secrecy, since her own reputation is involved, but the guide would lose nothing by telling the story.

2137   *stad with stave* Armed with a club. The agreement requires Gawain to accept a return blow *wyth what weppen so thou wylt* 384, not specifically with an axe. The guide may be misleading him out of ignorance, or setting up Gawain for the unpleasant shock of discovering that the Green Knight's weapon is a battle-axe with a four-foot blade. *Stave* solves two practical problems: the need to alliterate on st- and to rhyme with *hafe* and *save*.

2138–9   In fact Gawain is not relying on God but on the belt to save him.

2182   *nobot an olde cave* An unlikely guess. The hollow mound half-covered with grass, with *a hole on the ende and on ayther syde*, has the characteristic form of a prehistoric burial chamber. If so, the poet himself could not have known what he was describing, or why it was an appropriate place for decapitation.

2206–7   *Is ryched at the reverence me renk to mete / bi rote* Is intended in honour of me, in order to meet a knight with due ceremony; or, if *renk* means a field of combat or a duelling-place, the noise is intended to mark [*mete*] it out ceremoniously. I have taken the simpler of the alternatives proposed by Andrew and Waldron.

2214   *goande ryght here* Walking right here, with a suggestion of being ready to take off if no one answers.

2226   *Hit watz no lasse bi that lace that lemed ful bryght* Commentators disagree about which lace the poet is referring to. The axe used by Gawain has *a lace lapped aboute, that louked at the hede* 217 as part of its decoration. But the axe which the Green Knight has just finished sharpening is a different weapon, newly made and not apparently decorated. The other lace is the green girdle or *luf-lace*: see 1830, *a lace…that leke umbe hir sydez*, and 2030, *the lace, the ladiez gifte*. The belt is so designated at least eight times between 1830 and 2505, while lace in the first sense is not clearly mentioned again after 217. The more likely reading of the line is that the axe seemed enormous to Gawain, despite the assurance of the green belt, whose *glyterande golde* decoration explains *lemed ful bryght*.

2238   *Of steven mon may the trowe* One can trust you to keep an appointment.

2254   *Nowhare* Anywhere you like. Gawain is only concerned that the Green Knight shall restrict himself to one stroke (2253).

2264   *that doghty watz ever* The man who was always brave.

2271   *That never arghed for no here* Who never quailed for any army: the only reference to Gawain's reputation as a warrior.

2285   *out of honde* At once. The first recorded use of the phrase.

2297   *the hyghe hode that Arthur the raght* The knighthood bestowed on you by Arthur.

2303   *I wyl no lenger on lyte lette thin ernde* Literally: I will no longer in delay hinder your mission; in other words, I will finish off the matter *right nowe* 2304.

2316   *spenne-fote* With feet together.

2328   *The covenaunt schop ryght so* Gawain insists that the Green Knight respect their agreement, forgetting that he had been false to his undertaking with Bertilak.

2345   *I mansed the muryly with a mynt one* I jokingly threatened you with a pretended blow.

2347   *the forwarde that we fest in the fyrst nyght* The Green Knight begins unobtrusively to reveal his identity with Bertilak. By *fyrst nyght* he means the night before the first hunt.

2353   *Boute scathe* Without injury, unscathed.

2354   *Trwe mon trwe restore* A true man must repay faithfully. This simple basic principle, which contrasts with Gawain's elaborate code of behaviour, raises echoes within the poem: of repaying one stroke with another, of exchanging Christmas presents, love-tokens, and winnings, and of keeping one's pledged word. The expressions *Kryst yow foryelde* (may Christ repay you) used at 839, 1279, and *God yow foryelde* 1535, 2429, help to underline the idea.

2362   *I sende hir to asay the* The testing of Gawain's chastity is arranged by Bertilak, and carried out by his wife. The suggestion that Morgan le Fay was behind the testing of the Round Table, put into effect by the victim of her enchantment (2456-62) confuses the motivation of the story.

2367   *wylyde werke* Intricate workmanship (of the belt).

2369   *in study* Lost in thought, speechless.

2379   *For care of thy knokke* Because of anxiety about your blow.

2380   *my kynde to forsake* To be untrue to my nature. Gawain thinks of himself as having *larges and lewté* (2381) as innate qualities of his being: vices have no natural place in his character.

2390   *the harme that I hade* Being cheated of his winnings.

2399   *at chevalrous knyghtez* Where chivalrous knights live.

2403   *lathed hym fast* Invited him eagerly.

2414-26   In his embarrassment and humiliation at being found dishonest Gawain transfers the blame to his hostess, and makes a moral attack on women that reverses his previous courteous respect for them. This spiteful reaction and his refusal to continue the Christmas revels reveal an inability to laugh at himself that reduces Gawain's attractiveness.

2421   *To luf hom wel and leve hem not, a leude that couthe* To love them well and not trust them, if that were possible: the expression of a newly acquired bitterness.

2430-2   Like the narrator earlier, Gawain is anxious to deny that the value or the beauty of the belt attracts him.

2435   *The faut and the fayntyse of the flesche crabbed* The weakness and frailty of the perverse flesh. Gawain is making another attempt to excuse himself by blaming his body, which he speaks about as though it were not an integral part of himself.

2438   *lethe my hert* Humble me. But wearing the belt for the rest of his life may be an inverted form of pride, or a masochistic refusal to let himself forget that he once acted dishonestly.

2456-62   The disclosure that the old lady at the castle is Morgan le Fay, and that the Green Knight has been carrying out her orders, is a blemish on an otherwise perfect story. At this point it is too late to erase the impression of the Green

Knight's great power and authority in Part I, or to raise the importance of a background figure who is given no dialogue. The plan of frightening Guenevere to death cannot have been in the poet's mind when he described the Green Knight's intrusion, for the Queen's reactions are not mentioned. The poet's reasons for introducing this unconvincing last minute surprise are hard to fathom.

2478   *Whiderwarde-so-evere he wolde* Wherever he wished (and not where Morgan told him to go).

2514   *laghen loude therat* Unless the other knights think that Gawain is making too much of his disgrace, which has been excused and forgiven by the Green Knight, it is not certain what amuses them; but the story of a Christmas game ends appropriately with laughter.

2523   *The Brutus bokez therof beres wyttenesse* A final attempt by the poet to persuade his audience that the story exists in written form.

2525   *After the segge and the asaute watz sesed at Troye* The last long line of the poem repeats the first one, as though bringing the story full circle after its hundred and one stanzas.

    Honi soit qui mal y pense Evil be to him who evil thinks: the motto embroidered on the blue velvet garter worn by Knights of the Garter, the highest order of English knighthood bestowed by the sovereign. According to Froissart, the order was instituted about 1344. The poet's use of the motto has not been accounted for.

A Note on Some Words

Two features of the poet's vocabulary create particular problems for translators of *Sir Gawain and the Green Knight*. The first is the surprisingly large number of words which can be translated as 'man.' The list includes *burn, freke, gome, hathel, leude, mon, renk, schalk, segge,* and *wyghe,* all derived from Old English, and *tulk,* which comes from Old Norse. This wide choice allows the poet to pick whichever term suits his alliterative needs. Thus the guide warns Gawain,

> Ther wonez a wyghe in that waste, the worst upon erthe, (2098)

before adding a few lines later,

> And more he is then any mon upon myddelerde, (2100)

and finally appeals,

> Forthy, goude Sir Gawayn, let the gome one! (2118)

Since in this passage *wyghe, mon,* and *gome* all refer to the Green Knight, the three terms would appear to have the same meaning; but it seems unlikely that all eleven words are exact synonyms. However, distinguishing between them is not easy. *Hathel* is usually taken to mean 'knight,' but at line 2065 the servant who carries Gawain's spear and lance is given that title before being referred to successively as *schalk, wyghe,* and *burne.* He then addresses Gawain as *wyghe* and *lede,* evidently without disrespect for his princely rank. Perhaps we should assume that if the words were differentiated in ways now lost, the poet treated them all alike for the purposes of alliteration; but a translator must fear that he is missing some shade of meaning that would have been apparent to a medieval audience. The second problem is exactly opposite. In some respects the poet seems to have a very limited supply of adjectives and adverbs, and to use the same term in a number of obviously different contexts. *Lufly,* which is both adjective and adverb, is an example of the adaptability of such words, as these instances show:

laght to his lufly head (433)
lachez lufly his leve (595)
Lowande and lufly alle his lymmez (868)
The lorde lufly her by lent (1002)

ful lufly con ho lete (1206)
To unlace this bor lufly bigynnez (1606)

All that seems certain about these six instances is that *lufly* indicates praise or approval of some kind, and that although 'lovely' may be the appropriate trans-lation in line 1206 it is unsuitable elsewhere. In lines 595 and 1002 it means po-litely or courteously, but which adjective fittingly describes the Green Knight's decapitated head in line 433? Fine, handsome, splendid? The general impres-sion is clear, but the translator is left to judge which term suits the context. The line about unlacing the boar seems to require a further extension of meaning. Evidently the ritual task – performed by *a wyghe that watz wys upon wodcraftez* – is carried out in such a way that *lufly* conveys admiration of his work; so per-haps 'expertly' is the right translation. Dismounting from a horse attracts the same approving adverb. *Lyght luflych adoun*, Arthur invites the intruder, Berti-lak *lyghtes luflych adoun* before attacking the wild boar, and Gawain *lyghtez doun luflyly* at the Green Chapel. The similarity of the three phrases suggests that it is a conventional tag, but lacking an equivalent the translator must treat it re-spectfully and find a suitable modern term. 'Gracefully,' 'nimbly,' and 'quickly' are all possible. The alternative to this somewhat arbitrary choice of a word is to settle on one adjective or adverb that will fit every context. That would show the poet's fondness for the same term, but although 'politely' is certainly one of the senses of *luflych*, Gawain's greaves and the loop-holes in the castle require some such description as 'neat,' 'well-made,' or 'attractive.' A modern word that covered every possibility would be too imparticular to mean any-thing specific. In the present translation *luflych* has been variously rendered, and the original text has been left to show how frequently the term is used.

A second variable term stands in the text as *game, gomen,* and the plural forms *gamnez* and *gomnez*. Its more familiar sense is used when the Green Knight proposes *a Crystemas gomen* 283, but a different meaning must be found for the court's decision to *gif Gawan the game* 365, the remark about the pentan-gle *whereever the gomen bygan* 661, the lady's wish to learn *sum game* from Gawain 1532, and Bertilak's comment in presenting the boar's meat to Gawain: *This gomen is your awen* 1635. Bertilak's *gamnez* 1319 we should call his sport, but the sense of this variable term cannot always be confidently deter-mined. A reader who keeps an eye on the Middle English text will recognise how frequently the word occurs, together with other terms appropriate to the midwinter festival – *bourdez, laghter, layke, japez, joye, myry, play* – and to the se-ries of practical jokes played on Gawain.

The poet's use of the second personal singular presents a further problem for the translator. The pronouns *thou, thee,* and *thine* are no longer in common

use, and to reintroduce them would be false to the spirit of a modern translation. A more serious objection is that these terms of address had nuances of
meaning that are now lost or obscure. As Gawain's reply to the guide shows,
thou was used in speaking to servants:

> 'Bot helde thou hit never so holde, and I here passed
> Founded for ferde for to fle, in fourme that thou tellez,
> I were a knyght kowarde.' (2129-31)

It was also used to convey insult or contempt, and although the OED does not
recognise this use before 1440 the Green Knight's mocking rebuke, *Thou art
not Gawayn*, when the hero flinches under the axe at line 2270, appears to be an
earlier example. The terms are used throughout the Green Knight's appearance
at Camelot, again probably in this sense; in Arthur's angry response, for example,

> 'Hathel, by heven thy askyng is nys,
> And as thou foly hatz frayst, fynde the behoves.' (323-4)

At the Green Chapel both speakers address each other in this way, both before
and after the blow; the Green Knight telling Gawain, for instance, *I hyght the a
strok and thou hit hatz, halde the wel payed.* Here the use is not disrespectful. On
the other hand Gawain's relationship to Arthur does not lead him to address
the king in the way that we might think justified by their kinship. *Sythen this
note is so nys that noght hit yow falles,* he tells the king,

> And I have frayned hit at yow fyrst, foldez hit to me.' (359)

To make the matter more complicated the lady alternates between both
forms of address, promising Gawain, *I schal gif yow my girdel, that gaynes yow
lasse,* but then adopting what now seems the intimate form in reproaching him,
Thou hatz foryeten yederly that yisterday I taghtte. On her third visit she bursts in
with an exclamation that sounds like another rebuke, *How may thou slepe?*
Modern readers may notice these variations but cannot be expected to recognise their significance, which the translator has no means of representing even
when the speaker's preference for 'thou' over 'you' presents no difficulty.

Appendix A: From Fled Bricend/Bricriu's Feast

Once, when the Ulaid were at Emuin Machae, tired after the fair and the games, Conchubur and Fergus and the other Ulaid chieftains returned from the playing field to sit in Conchubur's Cráebrúad. Lóegure and Conall and Cú Chulaind were not there that evening, but the best of the other warriors of Ulaid were. As night drew on, they saw a huge, ugly churl coming towards them in the house, and it seemed to them that there was not in all Ulaid a warrior half as tall. His appearance was frightful and terrifying: a hide against his skin, and a dun cloak round him, and a great bushy tree overhead where a winter shed for thirty calves could fit. Each of his two yellow eyes was the size of an ox-cauldron; each finger was as thick as a normal man's wrist. The tree trunk in his left hand would have been a burden for twenty yoked oxen; the axe in his right hand, whence had gone three fifties of glowing metal pieces, had a handle that would have been a burden for a team of oxen, yet it was sharp enough to cut hairs against the wind.

He came in this guise and stood beneath the forked beam at one end of the fire. 'Do you find the house so narrow,' said Dubthach Dóeltenga, 'that there is no place to stand but under the forked beam? You may wish to contest the position of house candlebearer, but you are more likely to burn the house than to illuminate the company inside?' 'Although that is my gift,' the churl replied, 'perhaps you will grant that, despite my height, the entire household may be lit without the house's being burnt. But that is not my primary gift, and I have others. That which I have come to seek I have not found in Ériu or the Alps or Europe or Africa or Asia or Greece or Scythia or Inis Orc or the Pillars of Hercules or Tor mBregoind or Inis Gaid. Nowhere have I found a man to keep my bargain. Since you Ulaid surpass the hosts of every land in anger and prowess and weaponry, in rank and pride and dignity, in honour and generosity and excellence, let one of you keep faith with me in the matter over which I have come.'

'It is not right,' said Fergus, 'to dishonour a province because of one man's failure to keep his word – perhaps death is no nearer to him than it is to you.' 'It is not I who shirk death,' replied the churl. 'Then let us hear your proposal,' said Fergus. 'Only if I am allowed fair play,' said the churl. 'It is right to allow him that,' said Senchae son of Ailill, 'for it would be no fair play if a great host broke faith with a completely unknown individual. Besides, it would seem to us that if you are to find the man you seek, you will find him here.' 'I exempt Conchubur, for he is the king, and I exempt Fergus, for he is of equal rank,' said the churl. 'Whoever else may dare, let him come that I may cut off his head tonight, he mine tomorrow.'

'After those two,' said Dubthach, 'there is certainly no warrior here worthy of that.' 'Indeed, there is,' said Muinremur son of Gerrgend, and he sprang into the centre of the house. Now, Muinremur had the strength of one hundred warriors, and each arm had the strength of one hundred. 'Bend down, churl,' he said, 'that I may cut off your head tonight – you may cut off mine tomorrow night.' 'I could make that bargain anywhere,' said the churl. 'Let us rather make the bargain I proposed: I will cut off your head tonight, and you will avenge that by cutting off my head tomorrow night,' 'I swear by what my people swear by,' said Dubthach Dóeltenga, 'such a death would not be pleasant if the man you killed tonight clung to you tomorrow. But you alone have the power to be killed one night and to avenge it the next.' 'Then whatever conditions you propose I will fulfil, surprising as you may find that,' said the churl, whereupon he made Muinremur pledge to keep his part of the bargain the following night.

With that, Muinremur took the churl's axe, whose two edges were seven feet apart. The churl stretched his neck out on the block, and Muinremur so swung the axe that it stuck in the block underneath; the head rolled to the foot of the forked beam, and the house was filled with blood. At once, the churl rose, gathered his head and his block and his axe and clutched them to his chest, and left the house, blood streaming from the neck and filling the Cráebrúad on every side. The household were horrorstruck by the wondrousness of the event they had witnessed. 'I swear by what my people swear by,' said Dubthach Dóeltenga, 'if that churl returns tomorrow after having been killed tonight, not a man in Ulaid will be left alive.'

The following night, the churl returned, but Muinremur avoided him. The churl complained, saying 'Indeed, it is not fair of Muinremur to break his part of the bargain.' Lóegure Búadach, however, was present that night, and, when the churl continued 'Who of the warriors who contest the champion's portion of Ulaid will fulfil this bargain with me tonight? Where is Lóegure Búadach?', Lóegure said 'Here I am!' The churl pledged Lóegure as he had pledged Muinremur, but Lóegure, like Muinremur, failed to appear the following night. The churl then pledged Conall Cernach, and he too failed to appear and keep his pledge.

When he arrived on the fourth night, the churl was seething with rage. All the women of Ulaid had gathered there that night to see the marvel that had come to the Cráebrúad, and Cú Chulaind had come as well. The churl began to reproach them, then, saying 'Men of Ulaid, your skill and courage are no more. Your warriors covet the champion's portion, yet they are unable to contest it. Where is that pitiful stripling you call Cú Chulaind? Would his word be better than that of his companions?' 'I want no bargain with you,' said Cú

Chulaind. 'No doubt you fear death, wretched fly,' said the churl. At that, Cú Chulaind sprang towards the churl and dealt him such a blow with the axe that his head was sent to the rafters of the Cráebrúad, and the entire house shook. Cú Chulaind then struck the head with the axe once more, so that he shattered it into fragments. The churl rose nonetheless.

The following day, the Ulaid watched Cú Chulaind to see if he would avoid the churl the way his companions had done; they saw that he was waiting for the churl, and they grew very dejected. It seemed to them proper to begin his death dirge, for they feared greatly that he would live only until the churl appeared. Cú Chulaind, ashamed, said to Conchubur 'By my shield and by my sword, I will not go until I have fulfilled my pledge to the churl – since I am to die, I will die with honour.'

Towards the end of the day, they saw the churl approaching them. 'Where is Cú Chulaind?' he asked. 'Indeed, I am here,' said Cú Chulaind. 'You speak low, tonight, wretch, for you fear death greatly,' said the churl. 'Yet for all that, you have not avoided me.' Cú Chulaind rose and stretched his neck out on the block, but its size was such that his neck reached only halfway across. 'Stretch out your neck, you wretch,' said the churl. 'You torment me,' said Cú Chulaind. 'Kill me quickly. I did not torment you last night. Indeed, I swear, if you torment me now, I will make myself as long as a heron above you.' 'I cannot dispatch you, not with the length of the block and the shortness of your neck,' said the churl.

Cú Chulaind stretched himself, then, until a warrior's foot would fit between each rib, and he stretched his neck until it reached the other side of the block. The churl raised his axe so that it reached the rafters of the house. What with the creaking of the old hide that he wore and the swish of his axe as he raised it with the strength of his two arms, the sound he made was like that of a rustling forest on a windy night. the churl brought the axe down, then, upon Cú Chulaind's neck – with the blade turned up. All the chieftains of Ulaid saw this.

'Rise, Cú Chulaind!' the churl then said. 'Of all the warriors in Ulaid and Ériu, whatever their merit, none is your equal for courage and skill and honour. You are the supreme warrior of Ériu, and the champion's portion is yours, without contest; moreover, your wife will henceforth enter the drinking house before all the other women of Ulaid. Whoever might dispute this judgement, I swear by what my people swear by, his life will not be long.' After that, the churl vanished. It was Cú Rui son of Dáre, who in that guise had come to fulfil the promise he had made to Cú Chulaind.

[**Source**: *Fled Bricend. Bricriu's Feast*, trans., Jeffrey Gantz, *Early Irish Myths and Sagas* (Penguin, 1981): 251-55. Translation © 1981 by Jeffrey Gantz. Reprinted with permission.]

Appendix B: *From* Le Chevalier à L'Epée / The Knight of the Sword

One summer King Arthur was at his city of Carlisle. With him were the Queen and Gawain, but of the others, only Kay the Seneschal and Yvain came too. Every day Gawain indulged his inclination to go and amuse and enjoy himself. When he had made ready his horse, he equipped himself elegantly. He put on a pair of spurs made of gold over his cut-away hose of well-embroidered silken cloth. He put on breeches, very white and very fine, a shortish, wide shirt of linen finely pleated, and donned his fur-lined cloak. He was very richly dressed. Then he went out of the town. He took the way which went to the right, so that he entered the forest. He listened to the song of the birds, which were singing very sweetly. For a long time he listened to them, for he heard a great many of them, and so he fell into a reverie about an adventure that he called to mind that had happened to him. So long he lingered there that he went astray in the forest and so lost his way. The sun went down as he began to think; and evening was coming on when he came out of his reverie. He had no idea where he was, and so he thought that he would turn back. Then he came to a cart-track which continually went on before him; and it grew still darker, so that he did not know where to go. He began to look intently before him down the track through a clearing, and there he saw a great fire lighted. He went slowly in that direction because he thought that he might find a man who would put him on his way, a wood-cutter or a charcoal-burner. Then he saw near the fire a warhorse, which was tied up to a tree. He went over to the fire and there he saw a knight sitting. He greeted him at once:

"May that God who has made the world and placed the souls in our bodies," he said, "grant you, good sir, a large share in Him."

"Friend," replied the knight, "may God protect you, too. Tell me whence you have come, you who go alone at such an hour."

And Gawain told him the whole truth from beginning to end: how he went out to enjoy himself, and then how he got lost in the forest because of his daydream, in which he so completely forgot everything that he lost his way. And the knight undertook to put him back on his way in the morning with a good will, provided only that he would stay and bear him company until the night was past. This request was granted. He lay down his lance and shield, got down from his horse and tied it to a small tree, covered himself with his cloak and then sat down beside the fire. The knight asked him how he had travelled that day, and Gawain told him everything – he never deigned to lie to him. However, the knight acted treacherously; never a word of truth did he tell him – you will hear in full why he did it. When they had watched long enough and talked of many things, they fell asleep by the fire. At daybreak Sir Gawain woke first, and then the other knight.

"My house is very close to here – two leagues away and no more – and so I beg you to come to it. You may be sure of very fine lodging there, and welcome to it," he said.

Then they mounted their warhorses, took their shields, their lances and their swords and set out at once on a metalled road. They had not gone very far before they were out of the forest and in the open countryside. Then the knight spoke to Gawain:

"Sir," he said, "listen to this. It is always the custom and indeed the accepted thing, when a courteous and worthy knight brings another with him, that he should go ahead of him to make his lodging ready, so that he will find everything there, and so that on his arrival he will not find anything which might displease him. I have no-one to send, as you can clearly see, apart from myself. So I beg you, if it is not displeasing to you, to come along at your own pace, and I will go ahead with all haste. You will see my house beside an enclosure straight ahead, in a valley."

Gawain knew well that what he said was right and proper, and so he went at a slow pace while the other went on with great speed. On this direct route, Sir Gawain came upon four shepherds who had stopped beside the track. They greeted him courteously, and he returned their greeting in the name of God, went past them, and said no more.

"Ah, what a misfortune" said one of them, "for such a noble, handsome, elegant knight! Indeed, it is a great shame that he should be wounded or injured."

Gawain was completely amazed at this when he had heard these words. He immediately began to wonder greatly to himself why they lamented for him when they did not know him at all. Quickly he returned to them and greeted them all once again, then courteously asked them to tell him the truth about why they had said that he was unlucky. One of them answered him:

"Sir," he said, "we are sorry because we see that you are following the knight who went ahead on an iron-grey horse. Before our very eyes he has led many off, but we have never yet seen any who have ever returned."

And Gawain said,

"Friend, do you know if he did any good to them or not?"

"Sir, it is said in this countryside that the man who gainsays him in anything, whatever it is, either bad or good, he kills in his own house. We only know what we have heard tell, for nobody ever saw anyone who has returned from there; and if you will believe us, do not follow him a foot further forward if you value your life. You are an extremely fair knight, and it would be a pity if he killed you."

And Sir Gawain said to them:

"Shepherds, I commend you to God. I do not intend to abandon my route through his territory for a child's tale."

If it became known in his country that he had hesitated for such a thing, he would have been reproached to the end of his days. He journeyed on with his horse at a walking pace, thinking of this, until he came to a valley which the other knight had pointed out to him. Beside a great enclosure, surmounting a mound, he saw a fine castle which had recently been fortified. He saw a wide, deep ditch, and the bailey in front of the bridge had very fine outbuildings. Never in his life had Gawain ever seen anything richer belonging either to a prince or a king. But I do not wish to stop to describe the outbuildings, except to say that they were very fine and costly. He came up to the tilting-ground but then went in through the gate and crossed the courtyard and came to the end of the bridge. The lord hurried up to meet him, making a great appearance of being delighted at his coming. A squire received his weapons, another took Gringalet, a third removed his spurs. Then his host took him by the hand and led him over the bridge, and they found a very fine fire in the room facing the tower, and a very rich seat covered with silken fabric all round. They stabled his horse on one side (in such a way that he could see it) and someone brought it plenty of fodder and hay. Gawain thanked them for everything, and in nothing did they wish to oppose his wishes. The host said to him:

"Good sir, your dinner is being prepared, and I can assure you that the servants are hurrying as much as they can to get it ready for you. Now if meanwhile you will amuse yourself, you can be quite free and at your ease. If there is anything that displeases you, say so without hesitation."

Gawain said that the lodging was arranged entirely according to his liking. The lord went into one of the rooms to look for his daughter – there was no girl in all the land who came anywhere near her for excellence. I could not describe in a day all the beauty or even half of it, with which she was filled and adorned, nor do I wish to pass it over, so I will describe it in a few words. Everything that nature knew how to make that ought to be pleasing in a human body in the way of grace and beauty was united in her. The host, who was no peasant, took her by the right hand and led her to the hall. And Gawain when he had gazed on her great beauty, was very nearly overwhelmed, yet nevertheless he jumped up. The girl, even more, when she had looked at Gawain, was overwhelmed by his good looks and by his noble bearing. And meanwhile, courteously and in brief words he greeted her. At once the host presented her by the hand to Sir Gawain, and he said to him:

"I bring you my daughter, if it does not displease you, for I have no more splendid entertainment to charm and please you. She well knows how to keep you excellent company if she wishes. It is my wish that she should not refuse. There is so much feeling and spirit in you that if she were to fall in love with you, she would find in it nothing but honour. As for me, I give you this assurance, that I will never be jealous of you; on the contrary, I command her in your hearing that she shall never oppose you in anything."

Gawain thanked him politely, not wishing to gainsay him; and the other went out forthwith towards the kitchen to ask if it was possible to dine fairly soon. Gawain sat down beside the girl, very worried because of his host, whom he greatly feared, but nevertheless he immediately spoke courteously and without a trace of impoliteness to the girl with the fair hair. He spoke neither too much nor too little, talked discreetly with her, and very handsomely offered her his service, and spoke so much of his feelings that she, who was sensible and wise, understood and fully realised that he would love her above all else if it should be to her pleasure. Then she did not know what to do, whether to refuse or to accept him: he had spoken so courteously to her and she had seen such good manners in him that she would have quite fallen in love with him, had she dared to reveal it; but on no account would she consent to make her feelings known to him when he could not carry it any further. She well knew that she would be acting in an uncourtly way if she caused him to suffer from love-sickness from which he could never escape successfully; but to refuse him was difficult for her, so much was her heart drawn towards him. Then she spoke courteously to him:

"Sir," she said, "I understand that my father has forbidden me to oppose you in anything. Now I only know that I say to you that, if I do consent to do your wish I shall never bring it to a successful conclusion, and I shall have killed and betrayed you. But of one thing I warn you, and in good faith I say it to you, that you beware of base conduct; in nothing that my father says to you, whatever it may be, whether good or bad, can you oppose him in the slightest without peril, for if you do, you will be dead on the spot. You would be ill-advised even to give a hint of being aware of anything."

And now the host, who had gone to the kitchen, returned and the food was ready, and the water called for; he had no wish to wait any longer. When they had washed they sat down and the servants laid the overcloths above the white and beautiful tablecloths, the dishes and the knives, then the bread, and then the wine and cups of silver and fine gold. But I do not wish to stop longer, to specify the dishes one by one; for they had plenty of meat and fish, roast birds and venison, and joyfully they ate their fill, and the host absolutely insisted that Gawain and the girl should drink, and so he said to the girl that she should urge the knight. And he said:

"You should deeply appreciate that I intend her to love you."

Gawain thanked him politely.

When they had eaten enough the servants were in readiness, and they removed the tablecloths and the overcloths, and they brought them water and the towel to dry on. After the meal the host said that he wished to go to see his woods and so he asked Gawain to sit and amuse himself with the lady; and at the same time he called Gawain and spoke to him, ordering him not to go away until he came back, and he instructed a servant that if he appeared to want anything, he should provide it immediately. Gawain, who was noble and courteous, saw clearly that he must remain and that he could not do otherwise, so he said immediately that he had no desire to go, since he wished to stay there. The host mounted his horse and went off at top speed. He went to seek another adventure, for he was certain of this one that he had enclosed within his walls. The girl took Gawain by the hand, and they sat on one side so as to discuss how he could protect himself. Sweetly and charmingly she comforted him, but she was worried to death about it, because she knew the idea that her father had in mind, If she knew how, she would have shown him by what device he could escape, but her father never wished to say anything about it. But she took care not to oppose him, so that Gawain could by some means escape.

"Now let us stay here," he said. "It will do me no harm. He brought me to his house and has given me a very warm welcome. Since he had done me honour and good, never from now onwards will I fear anything at all unless I should discover to see any reason for which I ought to fear him."

She said to him, "It is of no use. There was a common saying, and many people still say, that you must praise the day in the evening when you see that it has come to a good end, and the same about one's host in the morning. And may God, just as I desire, grant that you may leave your host in joy and without ill-will."

When they had talked for a long time and spoken much of this and that, the host returned to his castle. Gawain sprang up to welcome him, with the girl, hand in hand; they greeted him very sweetly. He told them that he was in a great hurry because he was afraid that if he had lingered, Gawain would have gone away already, not wishing to remain longer. It began to get dark and the host asked the servants what there was for supper. His daughter said to him:

"At your pleasure you can ask for wine and fruit, but nothing else by right. You have eaten enough already." He then ordered it. They first washed, and then the fruit was set before him, and the servants brought wine, in plenty, of every kind.

"Sir, take your pleasure," he said to sir Gawain. "Of one thing you may be certain: it grieves me and often distresses me when I give hospitality to some one who does not enjoy it and who does not express his desires."

"Know the truth, sir," said Gawain: "I am delighted."

When they had eaten the fruit the host ordered the beds to be made and said,

"I will lie down in this room, and this knight in my bed; do not make it too small, because my daughter will lie with him. With so good a knight I think that she will be well occupied. She should be very happy at what he has promised her."

Both of them thanked him for it and pretended that it pleased them very much. Gawain was now very anxious because he believed that if he went to bed the host would have him cut in pieces, and he also realised that if he refused, he would kill him in his castle.

The host hurried to go to bed; he took Gawain by the hand and led him into the room immediately. The girl with the fresh face went with him too. The room was well adorned with tapestries and twelve candles were burning there, completely encircling the bed and giving forth a very great brightness. The bed, too, was well adorned with rich quilts and white sheets – but I do not wish to linger in describing the richness of the silken hangings from Palermo and Rome with which the room was decorated, or the sables, the light-coloured and the grey furs. To put it in a single word: whatever was fitting for a knight, or to adorn the person of a lady both in winter and in summer, was there in very great quantity – it had very rich furnishings. Gawain was very much astonished at the richness that he saw, and the knight said to him:

"Sir, this room is very beautiful. Both you and this girl shall lie there, and nobody else. Shut the doors, my girl, and do what he tells you, for I know very well that such nobles have no need of a crowd. But this much I want to warn you: do not extinguish the candles or I shall be very angry. I wish, since I have commanded it, that he may see your great beauty when you lie in his arms, so that he shall have greater pleasure and so that you may see his handsome body." Then he withdrew from the room and the girl shut the doors. Sir Gawain lay down, and she returned to the bed and lay down beside him naked – no request was necessary. And she lay all night long between his arms, very sweetly. He kissed and hugged her often, and in fact had gone so far that he would have accomplished his desire when she said:

"Sir, enough! Things must not go on like this. I am not without consideration for you."

Gawain looked all round but he could not see a living thing there.

"Darling," he said, "I want to know what it is that you say prevents me from having my desire of you."

She replied:

"I will most willingly tell you what I know about it. Do you see this sword which hangs here, which has this silver ornamentation, and a pommel and hilt of fine gold? I am not guessing about this thing that you will hear me tell you of now; rather, I have seen it well tried out. My father is very fond of this device, with which he has frequently killed very good and valued knights. Believe me, in here alone, he has killed more than twenty of them; but I do not know whence it came to them. Never shall there enter through this door a knight who shall escape alive. My father makes them very welcome, but if he catches one in the smallest fault he kills him. One must beware of base deeds; well it becomes one to steer aright. He immediately inflicts justice on him if he can catch him out in the slightest thing. And if a man takes such good care that he is not caught out in anything, he is made to spend the night with me. Then he meets his death; do you know why there is no escape? If he appears in any way to fulfil with me the desire by which he is seized, at once the sword strikes him on his body. And if he wants to go and grasp it and to snatch it away, it immediately jumps out of its sheath at him and gives him one on the body. So you realise that the sword which guards me all the time in this way is indeed in some way enchanted. Now you should be forewarned by me, for you are so courteous and wise that it would be a very great pity and it would grieve me ever afterwards if you were killed for me."

Now Gawain did not know what to do. Never before in the whole of his life had he ever heard tell of such a dire threat, and so he suspected that she had told him all to protect herself, so that he could not satisfy his desire. On the other hand, he reflected, it could not be concealed – indeed was everywhere known – that he had lain with her all alone, both of them naked, in her bed, and that he had, on account of a single word, desisted from making love to her. It is more becoming to die in honour than to live long in shame.

"Darling," he said, "that's nothing. Since I am here, I just want to be your lover. You can't avoid it."

"You can't blame me for it from now on," she said.

He came so close to her that she cried out, and the sword leapt from the sheath and dealt him a glancing blow on the side so that he was struck on the skin but not severely wounded. It pierced through the quilt and through all the sheets as far as the mattress, then went back into its scabbard. Gawain was left completely amazed and quite lost all his desire, as he lay beside her utterly taken aback.

"Sir," she said, "for God's sake, enough! You think that I told you because I wanted to defend myself from you in this situation, but in fact I have never told any knight about this but you. And you can be sure that it is a great wonder that you are not utterly dead on the spot from the first blow. For God's sake now, do lie down in peace and take care from now on not to touch me in any way. A wise man may easily undertake something which turns out to his disadvantage."

Gawain remained dejected and cast down because he did not know how to behave. If God granted that he should return to his land again, this affair could never be concealed, and it would be known everywhere that he had lain all alone at night with such a beautiful and charming girl, and yet had never done anything to her. And she had not opposed him with anything more than the threat of a sword wielded by nobody! So now he would be shamed all his days, if she eluded him thus. And so the candles that he saw around him which gave a very bright light caused him very great irritation, for by them he saw her great beauty. Her hair was blonde, her forehead broad and her eyebrows delicate; her eyes were sparkling, her nose well shaped and her complexion fresh and bright, with a small and laughing mouth. Her neck was long and graceful, her hands white and her sides soft and curved – under the sheets her body was white and tender. No-one could have found any fault in her, she had so graceful and well-made a figure. He drew close to her very gently because he was not a peasant. He was playing a certain game when the sword jumped from its scabbard and made another attack on him; the flat struck him on the neck. He very nearly took himself for a fool. But the sword was deflected a little and turned to his right shoulder so that it cut three fingers' breadths in the skin and caused a piece to be cut out of the silken quilt. Then it thrust itself back into its sheath. When Gawain felt himself wounded in the shoulder and on the side, and saw that he could not achieve success, he was much grieved and did not know what to do, and he was very exasperated at his situation.

"Sir," she said "are you dead?"

"Lady," he replied, "I am not; but for the rest of this night I give you this assurance, that you shall have a truce with me."

"Sir," said she, "by my faith, if it had been given when it was asked for it would now be much pleasanter for you."

Gawain was much anguished by this, and the girl as well. Neither the one nor the other slept, but watched in great grief all night long until morning.

Prompt and early the host got up when it was day, and came into the bedroom. He was far from being silent or dumb, but called very loudly, and the girl immediately opened the door and then came back, so she was beside Gawain lying naked. And the knight came in after. He saw them both lying in peace, and asked them how they were, and Sir Gawain replied:

"Very well, thank you, sir."

When the knight heard that he spoke so clearly, you may guess that he was most upset, since he was wicked and ill-natured.

"What!" he said, "Are you alive?"

"Indeed," said Sir Gawain, "I am perfectly well and healthy. I assure you that I have not done anything for which I ought to be done to death, and if in your own house, without a reason, you do me evil and harm, it would be very wrong."

"What!" said he, "So you are not dead? It much annoys me that you are alive."

Then he came forward a little, so that he plainly saw the quilt which had been cut and the blood-stained bed-linen.

"Fellow," he said, "now tell me straightaway where this blood comes from?"

And Sir Gawain paused, because he did not want to lie to him, and because he knew no explanation under which he could well shield himself, that the host would not see through. The host soon spoke:

"Fellow," he said, "listen here. You can conceal nothing from me. You wished to have your desire of this girl, but you could not succeed because of the sword which prevented it."

And Sir Gawain said to him:

"Sir, you speak truth: the sword has wounded me in two places, but has not injured me severely."

And when the knight heard that he was not mortally wounded, he said:

"You have come to a good place, good sir. But now if you want to get off completely, tell me, your country and your name, of what family, of what reputation and of what rank you are, so that all your wishes may be fulfilled. I want to be quite certain."

"Sir," he said, "I am called Gawain and I am the nephew of good King Arthur. You can be sure of this, that I have never changed my name."

"Indeed," said the host, "I know very well, that in you he has a very good knight. I find none better spoken of. Neither in your land as far as Majorca, nor in all the kingdom of Logres could a better be found. I will tell you how I have proved it. All the knights in the world who go to seek adventures, could they have lain in this bed, would all have had to die one after the other, until it chanced that the very best should come. The sword would choose him for me, because it would not kill the best knight when he came. And now one has truly stood the test, for the sword has chosen you as the best; and when God bestows honour on you, I do not know how to choose or to find one who would be worthier to have my daughter. I grant her to you and bestow her on you. No evil whatsoever from now on need you fear from me. And so I give you the command of this castle, in good faith, for all the days of your life; do with it what you will."

Then Gawain, who was overjoyed and delighted at this, thanked him for it.

"Sir," said he, "I am well rewarded with the girl alone; I have no desire for your gold or for your silver, nor for this castle."

Then both Gawain and the girl got up, as was fitting.

All through the region went the news that a knight was come who wished to have the girl – a Knight on whom the sword had been twice drawn, but without doing any harm to him. And they all vied with each other to be the first to come. There was very great joy in the castle among the ladies and the knights, and very rich was the feast that the father had prepared. But I do not want to stop to tell what the dishes were, for they ate and drank a great deal. When they had eaten their fill and the cloths were removed, the entertainers, of whom there were many, each showed what he could do. One tuned his viol, another fluted, another played the reed-pipes, and the others sang part-songs and played either on the harp or on the rote; some read tales and some told stories. Some knights played backgammon, or on the other hand, chess; or dice or games of chance. They spent their time thus all the day until nightfall and then they supped with great delight; there were birds in plenty and fruit, and a great deal of good wine. When they had happily finished their supper, they very soon went to bed. They immediately conducted the girl and Sir Gawain to the room where they had lain the night before, and the host went with them, and married them with good will, and joined together the girl and the knight without further obstacle. He then came out and shut the door. What more would you have me tell you? That night he had his desire, and no sword was unsheathed there. If he returned again to the attack on the courteous damsel, it does not distress me, and she was not upset.

So Gawain remained a long time in the castle with great joy and delight. Then he thought to himself that he had stayed there a long time, so that his relations and friends would certainly think that he had been killed. He went to the host to ask for leave to go:

"Sir," he said, "I have stayed a very long time in this land, so that my friends and family must think that I am lost. And so I ask for leave to go away, of your grace, and that you will see that this lady is adorned in such a way that I may have honour in taking her, and you in giving her to me; and so that when I come into my own country it may be said that I have a beautiful beloved and that she is come from a good family."

The host gave him leave and Gawain went back to his own country and the girl too. The palfrey on which the girl was mounted was richly adorned at bridle and saddle; Gawain was mounted on his horse. Why should I make you a longer tale of it? He took the arms that he had brought and with the leave of the host he went away, happy and rejoicing in the adventure ...

[**Source**: Elisabeth Brewer, *Sir Gawain and the Green Knight: Sources and Analogues*, (Cambridge and Rochester, N.Y. 1992), pages 109-121. Reprinted with permission.]